How to Get Murdered in Devon

By Stephanie Austin

Dead in Devon
Dead on Dartmoor
From Devon with Death
The Dartmoor Murders
A Devon Night's Death
Death Comes to Dartmoor
A Devon Midwinter Murder
Death on Dartmoor Edge
How to Get Murdered in Devon

How to Get Murdered in Devon
STEPHANIE AUSTIN

Allison & Busby Limited
11 Wardour Mews
London W1F 8AN
allisonandbusby.com

First published in Great Britain by Allison & Busby in 2025.

Copyright © 2025 by STEPHANIE AUSTIN

The moral right of the author is hereby asserted in accordance with the Copyright, Designs and Patents Act 1988.

*All characters and events in this publication,
other than those clearly in the public domain,
are fictitious and any resemblance to actual persons,
living or dead, is purely coincidental.*

All rights reserved. No part of this publication may be reproduced, stored in a retrieval system, or transmitted, in any form or by any means without the prior written permission of the publisher, nor be otherwise circulated in any form of binding or cover other than that in which it is published and without a similar condition being imposed on the subsequent buyer.

A CIP catalogue record for this book is available from the British Library.

First Edition

ISBN 978-0-7490-3133-6

Typeset in 11.5/16 pt Sabon LT Pro by Allison & Busby Ltd.

By choosing this product, you help take care of the world's forests. Learn more: www.fsc.org.

Printed and bound in Great Britain by Clays Ltd. Elcograf S.p.A.

EU GPSR Authorised Representative
LOGOS EUROPE, 9 rue Nicolas Poussin, 17000, LA ROCHELLE, France
Email: Contact@logoseurope.eu

For Sue Tingey

CHAPTER ONE

'There's a body in the boot of my car.'

I considered this joke in very poor taste. Just because I've discovered the odd corpse myself. 'That's not remotely funny,' I said.

There was a pause at the end of the line. Daniel sounded breathless. He repeated his words deliberately, weighing each one with care. 'There is a body in the boot of my car.'

I realised he wasn't joking. 'When you say body, you mean . . . ?'

'A dead one, yes.'

I struggled to make sense of what he was saying. I'd dropped him off at his car barely fifteen minutes before, outside Moorview Farm. I'd only just got back through the door of *Old Nick's*. 'Have you phoned the police?'

'Of course. They're on their way. Now I'm phoning you.'

'Where are you?' I knew there was no phone signal at the farmhouse. 'You must have run down the hill.'

'I didn't fancy driving, obviously.'

The sarcasm didn't fool me. I know the man I love,

and I could hear how shaken he was. 'Daniel, are you sure this person is dead?'

'Oh yes,' he answered softly.

'I'm coming straight back.'

'If you could, Miss B. The police will want to talk to you anyway.'

'I'll be there in a few minutes,' I promised him.

'I'm going to have to go,' he told me. 'I can see a police car coming. I'd better get back to the farmhouse. Meet them there.'

The line went dead. I shoved my phone back into my bag and swept up my keys from the counter, where I had dropped them a minute before. 'I've got to go.'

Sophie looked up reproachfully from the painting she was working on. 'It's Friday, Juno. You haven't forgotten I'll be going in a little while?' She'd be off to catch her bus to Cardiff soon, to spend the weekend with her boyfriend who was at university in St Davids. She'd come in early to open up the shop as a favour to me. I was supposed to be in charge today. Pat, busy at the animal sanctuary she helps to run, couldn't do Fridays.

'It's okay, Soph. Just put the CLOSED sign on the door if I'm not back before you go.'

She arched her dark brows quizzically, as if finally taking in the fact something was wrong. 'Are you alright?'

'I've got to go back to the farmhouse. There's a problem with Daniel's car.'

She frowned. 'The one you just bought him?'

'Yes, that's the one,' I called back as I headed for the door. The car I'd just bought him.

* * *

We weren't even due to pick the dratted vehicle up until later in the day, but our plans began to go awry before Daniel had even arrived for the weekend. He was booked on a flight direct from Donegal to Exeter. Not the friendliest way for an environmentalist to travel, I admit, but the train–ferry–train journey just took too long for a weekend trip. By the time he made it to Ashburton, it would be time for him to turn around and go back again. I was supposed to have collected him at the airport at five yesterday afternoon. We had tickets for a concert in the evening. But an accident on the road from Inishowen meant he missed his flight from Donegal and there wasn't another direct one that day. The best alternative was for him to board a flight to Bristol and then take the train down to Devon. In the end, I picked him up at Newton Abbot railway station at close on midnight. We'd both missed the concert. I didn't fancy going on my own.

I raced back up the hill to Halsanger Common, making Van Blanc take the twisting narrow lanes as fast as I dared. One day soon I must do something about Van Blanc. Trying to run two businesses and having a plain white van was a waste of advertising space. But which one should I advertise? Or should I have *Old Nick's Antiques and Collectibles* painted on one side of it, and *Juno Browne, Domestic Goddess* on the other? I couldn't make up my mind. But right now, I had more important things to think about.

The glowing green leaves of summer, the flickering sunlight and lush, frothy hedgerows, which had delighted me on my leisurely drive down the hill, whizzed by unnoticed now. I was worried about Daniel. It must have been a shock opening up that boot and discovering, well, whoever it was. He had never found a dead body before, whereas I had a nasty reputation for finding them. Could this all be an elaborate hoax, I wondered as I hammered up the hill, someone's idea of a not-at-all-amusing joke?

The common opened up around me, and I brought Van Blanc to a jerky halt at the end of the track leading to Moorview Farm. I could see two police cars parked outside the farmhouse. The old stone building had been almost derelict when Daniel inherited it, most of the farmland sold off. Now it stood caged in scaffolding while seemingly endless renovation work went on, and the day when it might be ready for him to live in slipped further and further away. Nearby was the caravan he had bought to stay in while the work went on; but that was before a shortage of funds forced him to take a job in Ireland to pay for it all.

The car I had bought him a few days before, a dark grey Volkswagen Bora – old, reliable and cheap – was being guarded by a nervous-looking constable in uniform. The boot, I noticed, was tightly shut. It would remain shut, I imagined, until the divisional surgeon arrived to examine its grisly contents. A second officer was busy unreeling tape with DO NOT CROSS printed on it, one end tied to the gatepost. As I climbed out of the van he strode towards me, about to give me the *I'm-sorry-madam-you-can't-come-in-here* routine, when a voice hailed me from the door of the caravan. Detective Constable Dean Collins waved as he jogged down

10

the path. 'It's alright, Charlie, let her in,' he told his uniformed colleague. 'Hello, Juno. Daniel said you'd be on your way.'

'Where is he? Is he alright?'

'He's a bit shaken up, but he's okay.' He grinned suddenly. 'He's not like you, always discovering dead bodies.'

'Not *always*,' I responded indignantly. 'I've only found the odd one, occasionally.'

'It's not catching, is it?' he asked, his grin fading. 'Your lover boy's not going to turn into a sleuth as well?'

I decided to ignore this. An amateur detective was the last thing Daniel would want to turn into. We've broken up before because of my investigating activities. He's always hated my tendency to poke my nose in where it wasn't wanted, begged me to stick to safer behaviour like dog-walking and selling antiques. 'So, where is he?'

'In the caravan there, telling the boss all about it.'

'He'll want to see me after?'

'The boss will, yeah. Meantime,' he said as opened the door of a police car, 'why don't we sit inside and you tell me what happened. Off the record.'

Off the record perhaps. Dean and I might be friends – in fact, I was godmother to his daughter Alice – but that didn't mean he wouldn't be comparing what I said to him now with whatever I told Inspector Ford later. I slid into the back seat, and he sat in the front and turned around to look at me. 'So, first off, tell me about this car.'

'Okay. Well, Daniel's been coming backwards and forwards between here and his job in Ireland for the last few months, as you know, whenever he can take the time off. He usually grabs a quick flight and leaves his car behind in Inishowen. But he decided it would be useful to have his own set of wheels to drive when he's here. It would save him borrowing my van. If he's here on weekdays, I need it myself for getting about between clients.'

Dean nodded patiently, waiting for me to get to the relevant bit.

'He didn't want to spend a lot. We thought we'd look for something this weekend at the car auction in Exeter. Then one day last week, I saw this car parked in Ashburton with a FOR SALE sign in the window.'

'This car over here?' He pointed to the Bora.

I nodded. 'The price was right and it had recently passed its MOT, so I called the phone number and arranged to see the owner.'

'When was this?'

'Monday. She had moved it by then, had the car at her house. So, after I'd finished work for the day, I drove up to see it.'

'Where?'

'Not far from here, a big place on the road to Bag Tor. Langworthy Hall, it's called.'

'And who was the owner?'

'It was Julian Horrell.'

'Hang on,' he stopped me, frowning. 'Where do I know that name from? Antiques dealer, isn't he?'

'Antiques and fine art. He had a shop in Buckfastleigh, part of a family firm. He specialised in country house sales.'

Dean grinned. 'You mean he sells proper antiques, not like the rubbish you sell.'

I ignored this slur on *Old Nick's*. 'He did. If you remember, Julian Horrell died last year.'

He nodded. 'Accident, wasn't it? Turned over his quad bike. Broke his neck. So, who does the place belong to now?'

'His daughter, Amber. The estate's just been through probate. She didn't want to keep his car.'

'Right. So, when you went to see it, you looked in the boot, did you?'

'Of course I did!' I answered indignantly. 'And under the bonnet and underneath the car. And I took it for a test drive.' Honestly, what did he take me for?

Dean held up his hands in surrender. 'Alright, keep your hair on! And this was on Monday?'

'Yes, and there was no dead body in the boot then.' A horrible thought occurred to me. 'It's not Amber in there, is it?'

He shook his head. 'No. It's a male.'

'Thank God! Sorry,' I corrected myself, 'whoever it is, it's horrible, but I'm glad it's not her.' I'd only met Amber briefly. She seemed a complete nutcase but I'd liked her. 'How did he die?'

'I can't tell you that.' I gave him a cynical look and he added, 'We don't know yet. Not until the doctor arrives. Any road . . .' He cleared his throat as he changed the subject. 'What happened then?'

'I took some photos of the car and phoned the details through to Daniel. He said if I was happy with its condition, we should grab it. He paid for it straight away by bank transfer. Amber and I sorted out the paperwork. The plan was for me to drive Daniel up to her house later today so he could pick it up. But then . . .'

Dean frowned at my hesitation. 'What?'

'I thought this was odd at the time,' I admitted. 'I got a text on my phone yesterday, from Amber. She said the car had been delivered here at the farmhouse and the keys were under the wheel arch. That was all. I thought the message was a bit abrupt, but I assumed she must have had to go away unexpectedly.' I shrugged. 'She could've just left the car at Langworthy Hall and we could have picked it up from there. She needn't have bothered to deliver it.'

'You didn't see her again?'

I shook my head. 'I tried calling her as soon as I got her text, but her phone was off. I drove up here to rescue the car keys. I checked the handbook and the paperwork were in the glove compartment. I didn't bother to look in the boot again.'

'No.' Dean puffed out his cheeks. 'Pity, really.'

Langworthy Hall was a rambling Devon longhouse with low white walls, a golden thatch and mullioned windows. I'd tried to stifle a groan of envy as I drew Van Blanc to a halt outside the gate on that Monday evening. The garden full of foxgloves, and the roses hanging in clusters of apricot blooms over the roof of the tiny thatched porch, didn't help much either. Amber Horrell had inherited this. All I'd inherited was a run-down antique shop with a grotty flat above it, and I was lucky to get that. But any inclination I might have had to hate her guts evaporated when she opened the door and greeted me with a warm and radiant smile.

Hers was a lively face set beneath a fringe of short blondish hair. She had the straight nose, wide cheekbones, fine jawline and long, smooth neck that the gods don't give out very often, and large, speaking brown eyes. She was a bit younger than me, late twenties at most. She wore leggings and a silk waistcoat, and, hanging from one ear, a complicated earring composed of what looked like metal clock parts. 'The famous Juno Browne!' she cried, as she flung back the door. 'I've read about you in the *Dartmoor Gazette*.'

There are times when I could cheerfully murder the *Dartmoor Gazette* and all who sail in her. 'Don't believe all you read,' I warned her.

'But I want to,' she insisted with a gurgle of laughter. 'And I love your hair!' Everyone does, except me. 'Is that red natural?' she asked.

'I'm afraid so,' I replied – as was its unruly nature. I decided the sooner we turned our attention to the car, the better. 'Can I take a look?' I could see the Bora parked across the lane. I could also see what looked like another acre or two of garden, just to ramp up the envy stakes. And there was a quaint cottage in that garden, not much bigger than a summerhouse. 'That's sweet,' I said. 'Looks like a gingerbread house.'

'My granny used to live there,' she told me, leading the way to the car. 'But it's been empty for years now.'

After I'd given the vehicle a thorough once-over, Amber let me take it for a test drive. I told her she could keep Van Blanc as a hostage till my return. The Bora was old but behaved perfectly, and I phoned Daniel as soon as I arrived back at Langworthy Hall. He decided we should go ahead with the deal. I was pleased, and a bit surprised, that he trusted my judgement. Men can be fussy about cars.

Amber invited me in for coffee while we sorted out the paperwork. I didn't refuse the offer. I was longing for a look inside that longhouse and I wasn't disappointed. The walls were crooked and plastered white, faded rugs covered its ancient flagstones. Above my head, the ceiling sloped and sagged with age. Some of the supporting beams had come from a wrecked galleon, Amber told me, which meant the building must have been at least five hundred years old. The evening sun, slanting through mullioned windows, cast fingers of light on the oak wainscot and glowed on copper pans hanging by the inglenook fireplace, an old bread oven built into its wall. In the hall, a grandfather clock ticked away the centuries, giving the whole place an atmosphere of measured calm.

The room Amber showed me into was cheerfully untidy, two bulging carrier bags dumped against a wall spilling quantities of fabric onto the floor, a nearby table scattered with sheaves of paper. She pointed to an elderly drop-end sofa, inviting me to sit, which eventually I did. But first I enjoyed the moments when she was busy in the kitchen to look around.

This had been Julian Horrell's home and he had been an antiques dealer – so I had to assume the heavy silver candlesticks on either end of the mantlepiece were genuinely William III, and the Delftware plate in the middle of the shelf dated back to the seventeenth century and was worth a lot of money. Thank God I didn't have the responsibility of dusting it. A lacquered Chinese cabinet stood in one corner, its doors inlaid with mother-of-pearl and folded back to show me rows of ingenious little drawers just begging to be teased open and pried into; but I kept my itching fingers to myself.

On the wall above the cabinet, an eighteenth-century lady stared down at me from a heavy gilt frame. She was dressed fashionably in a silk gown with a low-necked bodice and bunches of foaming lace at her elbows, a large ruby glinting at her throat. But the interesting thing about her was that she was obviously not European. Brown-skinned and black-eyed, she stared out from her frame with a kind of wary defiance. Curious, I went for a closer look. It was then I noticed a marble bust sitting in a deep windowsill, the head of a Roman emperor sporting a leather flying-helmet and goggles. I decided this must be Amber's touch.

An elderly brown spaniel appeared in the kitchen doorway, his tail waving slowly, his claws clicking as he plodded across the stone-flagged floor towards me. I was forced to turn away from the emperor to make his acquaintance. He gazed up at me questioningly, his brown eyes ringed with grey-flecked fur. I sat down and smoothed his noble head.

'That's Ben.' Amber came in carrying two coffee mugs and placed them on an iron-bound chest that looked as if it was made for pirate treasure. It was currently doing duty as a table, sheets of paper slewed across the top of it, covered in drawings of people in Victorian costume.

Some had snippets of fabric pinned to one corner.

'Are you a costume designer?' I asked as she gathered them up.

'Fashion is my passion,' she responded with a self-mocking smile. She gathered up her designs and laid them carefully on a side table. 'But not my job,' she carried on cheerfully. 'I am trapped in the family firm.' She plumped down beside me on the sofa, kicked off an expensive-looking pair of spike-heeled ankle boots and curled her legs underneath her. Ben collapsed beside her on the rug.

'I was sorry to hear about your father,' I said.

She just shrugged her shoulders. I didn't know what to say then, how to respond to her display of indifference. I sipped coffee. 'Does Mrs Horrell live here too?' I asked. I couldn't believe she lived in this rambling place by herself.

She gave a crack of laughter. 'No, thank God! Anita ran off with her yoga instructor when I was fourteen. Left us to get on with it.' She paused suddenly, her thoughts turned inward. 'Poor Dad, he was devastated. I haven't spoken to her since. She didn't even turn up for his funeral. Anyway,' she announced, brightening, 'I want to know about you. You took over that old junk shop in Shadow Lane, didn't you? It used to belong to some foreign man.' She clicked her fingers, searching for his name.

'Mr Nikolai,' I supplied for her. 'Everyone called him Old Nick.'

She nodded. 'It was a really creepy, run-down old place. When we were kids, we were frightened to walk past there. It looks lovely now,' she added hastily.

'It ought to, after what I've spent on it.'

'Dad said he was a crook,' Amber ventured.

'Dad was right.'

She hugged her knees. 'Is it true he was murdered? I was working in London at the time and I missed all the gory details.'

I could have told her she was lucky to have missed them. But then, I'd found his body. He might have been a crook, but I'd been fond of Old Nick. I'd taken him on as a client of Domestic Goddess, my home-help business. When he was killed, I was astonished to discover he'd left the shop to me. Why he'd done so, I've never really worked out. 'Yes, he was murdered.'

'And is that what started you off on all your sleuthing?' she asked enthusiastically.

This kind of conversation makes me uncomfortable. 'It wasn't intentional.'

'Sorry!' she said, picking up on my discomfort. 'I'm being a pain. Of course, it's not just antiques any more, is it?' she went on, going back to the shop. 'You sell all sorts, arts and crafts and stuff.'

'Sophie sells her artwork,' I explained. 'And Pat makes crafts to raise money for Honeysuckle Farm – you know, the animal sanctuary? She runs it with her sister and brother-in-law. I sell antiques, well, mostly junk,' I admitted, 'from the storeroom at the back. I shouldn't describe it as junk really. I do sell some quality items, when I can buy them cheap enough.'

Amber's mobile phone, which up until now had been lying on the chest, began to buzz and vibrate. She glanced at the display and grimaced in distaste. 'He can wait,' she pronounced, refusing the call.

'And talking of antiques,' I said, patting the iron-bound chest, 'this is an amazing thing. It must take two men to lift it.'

'Actually, it takes four,' she told me laughing. 'It's been in our family for centuries.' The phone rang again and she rolled her eyes. 'Sorry. I'm going to have to take this.' She got up and wandered into the kitchen. 'For God's sake, Peter!' I heard her complain as I sipped my coffee. 'I've told you the answer is no! I don't care. I don't want anybody here . . .' There was a long pause while she listened. 'I'm not selling! I don't care. How many more times do I have to say it? And you don't have to keep checking up on me every five minutes. I'll be there in the morning, okay? First thing . . . no, I haven't . . . Yes, I promise. Look, I've got someone here about Dad's car . . . Tomorrow. Yes. For God's sake . . . Goodbye.'

She wandered back into the room and threw her phone down on the lid of the chest with more force than was probably good for it. 'Treats me like a child,' she muttered. 'Sorry about that.' She smiled bitterly. 'My Uncle Peter is a royal pain in the arse. He's just checking to see I'm going to turn up at work tomorrow.'

'You work for him at *Horrell's Antiques*?'

'For my sins.' She came to sit, running a hand through her short, spiky hair. 'Where were we?'

'You were telling me about this chest.'

'It's quite a story . . .' she began, but stopped suddenly. A noise came from above our heads, a muffled thump and the creak of floorboards. I looked up in surprise and she followed the direction of my gaze. 'There's no one up there,' she told me, a little too hastily. 'Except for the ghost.'

I laughed. 'Really?'

'No, not really. This house is full of creaks and groans.' She hesitated, and then a moment later, turned our conversation back to the chest. 'It's got four locks,' she pointed out.

There were certainly four chunky lock-plates, but only two of the keyholes had keys in them. 'Why four?' I asked. But before she could reply, the grandfather clock delicately chimed the half hour, and she looked at her watch. This was obviously my cue to depart. The warmth had gone out of our conversation anyway, the mood ruined by the call from Uncle Peter. I left shortly after, promising to return with Daniel on Friday and pick up the car.

As I opened the door of Van Blanc, I turned back to look at Langworthy Hall.

I almost expected to see a ghostly face at an upstairs window, peering at me through the mullioned glass. Amber might have insisted we were alone in the house, but I wasn't sure I believed her. Because when I had looked up at that noise from above, Ben the spaniel had raised his head from the rug and had waved his plumy tail, in recognition.

CHAPTER TWO

I told all this to Inspector Ford when I was eventually summoned to the caravan, a few minutes after Daniel had been escorted out of it into a waiting police car. It was obvious we weren't going to be given a chance to talk to each other until the police had taken our separate statements. I saw the car drive off as if they were taking him away.

'Where is he going?' I demanded, as soon as I got inside the caravan.

'My officer is giving him a lift into Ashburton.' Inspector Ford smiled as he gestured for me to sit. 'I'm sure you'll catch up with each other later.' The inspector is unfailingly polite, even if, like Daniel, he disapproves of my sleuthing activities. But then, I have helped him catch a few criminals.

The caravan was snug inside. He and I sat on opposing banquettes with the put-up table between us, trying not to nudge each other's knees. He listened to me in thoughtful silence, arms folded across his broad chest, as if he was trying to make himself as small as possible. Detective Sergeant Christine deVille, a.k.a.

Cruella, sat beside him and scratched away on her notepad. Dean Collins and one of the uniforms had already been despatched to Langworthy Hall in search of Amber. She wasn't answering her phone.

'This text you received about the car being moved,' the inspector asked, 'you're sure it came from Miss Horrell?'

I pulled my phone from my bag, found the message and showed it to him. He studied it for a moment. 'Thank you. Now, as far as you could tell, when you talked to her on Monday evening, she seemed happy enough? She didn't strike you as at all worried or upset?'

'Quite the opposite. She seemed happy and eager to chat, at least until the phone rang. She took a call from her Uncle Peter . . .'

'Peter Horrell?' the inspector cut in. 'He's related to Julian Horrell, a cousin I believe,' he explained to Cruella, 'carries on the family firm.'

'Well, she accused him of checking up on her,' I went on.

The inspector grunted. 'Probably with good reason.'

'Oh?'

'Shall we just say Miss Horrell is not unknown to us.'

I waited, hoping he was going to explain further, but he just said, 'Carry on, Miss Browne,' so I did.

'The conversation on the phone seemed to be about selling something. It was really more of an argument.'

'You didn't find out what was for sale?'

'No. Except whatever it was, Amber seemed adamant she didn't want to sell it. Then, soon afterwards, we heard the noise from upstairs.'

'Which you're convinced was caused by someone up there?'

'I don't believe it was a ghost,' I told him frankly.

Cruella took the opportunity to look up from her notepad, flicking back her bob of dark hair and favouring me with one of her killer glares. I smiled sweetly.

'Tell me, once she had delivered the car here yesterday,' the inspector went on, oblivious of our silent exchange of mutual loathing, 'would it have been possible for her to walk back to Langworthy Hall?'

I nodded. 'It can't be more than a couple of miles.'

'She wouldn't have needed a lift then, someone to drive her back there?'

'Not unless she was in a hurry.' I hesitated for a moment. 'You're wondering if there was someone else with her when she delivered the car?' I thought for a moment. 'What you're really asking is whether she could have put that body in the boot on her own, aren't you? Or whether she would have needed an accomplice.'

The inspector gave me one of those long, searching stares which I try not to find intimidating. 'Is that what I'm asking you, Miss Browne?'

'Well, if that *is* what you are asking . . .' I'd started digging a hole, so I thought I might as well keep going. 'Then the answer is no. I wouldn't have thought her big and strong enough to heave the weight of a dead body into the boot on her own.' The truth was, I was having difficulty imagining Amber murdering anyone, let alone driving a car two miles with a dead person in the back.

The alternative was that she might be a victim too. I was having difficulty with that as well.

Inspector Ford cleared his throat. 'Thank you for your observations, Miss Browne. And when you arrived here yesterday morning and saw the car parked outside, there was nothing about it to arouse your suspicions?'

'No. There was no one else around. And the car looked just as it had when I'd seen it on Monday evening. Of course, if I'd looked in the boot . . .'

Cruella's voice cut in sharply. 'Why did Mr Thorncroft phone you this morning, immediately after he'd phoned us?'

'Well, obviously, to tell me what he'd found,' I said, puzzled by this change of direction. 'And because I was the one who purchased the car. He knew you'd want to speak to me about it.'

Her little mouth twisted. 'It wasn't so you could get your stories straight?'

I bit back a laugh. Cruella and I detest each other and she loves to make insinuations. I think she fantasises about seeing me in handcuffs. It seems her resentment also extends itself to Daniel because he and I are lovers. 'Are you accusing him of something? Or just me?'

'It's alright, Miss Browne, you don't have to answer that question,' the inspector assured me with a weary sigh. 'Sergeant deVille was just indulging in a flight of fancy, weren't you, Sergeant?' He directed a glance at her from beneath his heavy brows and her tiny mouth shut like a trap. His phone rang at that moment and he pulled it from his pocket.

'Collins,' he informed Cruella. 'Any joy?' He listened

in silence for a moment. 'No sign of her? Right, well get yourself inside there, Collins. We have to assume Miss Horrell could be in some danger. Break in, if you have to.'

He disconnected and shot a glance at me. 'Thank you, Miss Browne. That's all the information we need from you for the moment. You can go. Apologise to Mr Thorncroft once again, for his having to cancel his meeting with his builder.' He nodded through the caravan window in the direction of the Bora and the blue tent the forensic team were constructing around it. 'I'm afraid an inspection of the renovation work on his farmhouse won't be possible just now.'

I had to find Daniel. He wasn't answering his phone. I drove Van Blanc back from Halsanger Common, down the hill and past Belford Mill, an odd, wedge-shaped building local people call 'the coffin house', and back into Ashburton. At Great Bridge I crossed the little river Ashburn and turned right, passing a row of old weavers' cottages and *The Victoria Inn*, now sadly defunct, and on into North Street. The pavements were busy with shoppers, knots of small children and dogs on leads.

Daniel didn't have a key to get into my flat, so it was unlikely he would be waiting for me back there. I took a detour into *Sunflowers*, the café owned by my landlords, to see if he'd turned up there, but neither Kate nor Adam had seen him, so I drove around to Shadow Lane.

He wasn't waiting outside *Old Nick's* either. Unfortunately, Ricky and Morris were. My old friends kept a clothes rail in my part of the shop, and had come to replenish their display of vintage clothing, bits and pieces from their vast stock of costumes they could no longer hire out for theatrical purposes. They were also the last people you wanted to bump into when you had information you should keep to yourself. As I parked Van Blanc, Ricky's tall, rangy figure unfolded itself from their old Saab. It was almost an antique itself. 'What sort of time do you call this to open a shop?' he demanded, grinning.

I didn't answer, just headed for the shop door with the keys in my hand. It was locked. Sophie must have set off for Cardiff already. Ricky began pulling garment bags from the back seat of the car. 'You been lying about in bed with that bloke of yours?' he called out, just loud enough for the whole of Ashburton to hear. 'I suppose we're lucky you're opening at all.'

I love Ricky, but there are times I could kill him and this was one. 'You are lucky, as a matter of fact.'

Morris came puffing after him, his short arms clutching bags trailing scarves and feather boas. 'Take no notice of him, Juno,' he recommended, shaking his bald head.

'Sorry, I got delayed.' I unlocked the door and flipped on the lights. 'There's a problem with Daniel's car.'

'What, his new one?' He dropped a boa and stooped to pick it up. 'Won't it go?'

'I'm pretty sure it's not going anywhere for the moment.'

I was worried about Amber. I couldn't stop thinking about her. Was she in danger? Where had she gone?

Had she really not known there was a dead body in the boot when she'd driven that car the short distance from her place to Moorview Farm? Had whoever killed the man in the boot also killed her? And when Dean Collins broke into Langworthy Hall, what would he find?

It was gloomy in the back room where I sold my antiques. There was only one small window, high up in the wall, and even in the daytime it needed lights on if customers were to stand any chance of seeing what they were buying. I went around flipping switches on a variety of old table lamps. Lamplight was more atmospheric, more suitable to antiques, I always felt, and it didn't show the dust. The vintage clothes rail was certainly in need of a refill. Someone's costumed birthday party last week had more or less cleared it out, and empty wire hangers hung from it in a row of forlorn triangles.

'Mavis could do with a new outfit an' all,' Ricky commented, lingering in the hallway. 'She's been wearing this green frock for ages.' Mavis was a mannequin he and Morris had brought into the shop. She stood in the hallway with a sign around her neck pointing the way to *Antiques and Vintage Clothes*, and taking up a lot of room in the narrow passage, forcing everyone who wanted to go that way to squeeze past her or get poked by her outstretched fingers.

'The red polka-dot suit should fit her,' Morris called out to him, dumping all his various bags on a nearby table, and brushing a boa feather from his lips.

Ricky lifted her wig and whispered in her ear. 'You haven't put on any weight, have you, Mavis?'

I used the shop phone to try Daniel's mobile again, but there was still no answer. 'I'll make some coffee,' I called out, mounting the stairs to Nick's old kitchen.

'About time,' Ricky responded.

'I've brought cake,' Morris yelled from the back room. Then I could hear him muttering. 'It's in one of these bags here somewhere, I know it is.'

The truth was I wanted to be alone for a moment. I wasn't in the mood for idiocy or banter. I needed time to think. Where had Daniel got to? He hated it when I got involved in murder investigations, hated the thought of me putting myself in danger. Finding that corpse must have been a shock to his system. I just hoped the discovery wasn't going to lead to arguments, opening up old wounds. At least this time I couldn't be blamed for finding the body myself. Just for buying the car the damn thing was hidden in. I filled up the kettle. *Damn thing*, I repeated, chiding myself. The dead body wasn't a *damn thing*. It was a someone.

There were voices down in the shop, quick footsteps on the stairs, then Daniel burst into the kitchen. For a moment we stared. Then we fell on one another, clinging together like survivors from a shipwreck. He breathed softly into my hair. 'That was God-awful, Miss B.'

In spite of myself, I smiled. Miss B. It used to annoy me when he called me that. It's short for *Miss Browne with an e* and is a result of his reading about my exploits in the *Dartmoor Gazette*. Now I recognise it as his most tender term of endearment. If he just calls me Juno, I'm usually in trouble. He pulled back to stare at me, frowning, his dark brows drawn together, searching my face. He looked pale, strained, as if the experience of the morning had drained the life out of him. 'Are you alright?' he asked.

'I am now you're here. Where have you been?'

'I needed a walk to clear my head.' He managed a smile. 'I didn't remember I'd switched my phone to silent until just now. Sorry.'

'Where did you go?'

'Around the lanes towards Cuddyford, more or less where we took the Tribe earlier.' He'd got up early that morning and accompanied me on my daily dog-walking duties. We'd taken five dogs out to chase about in the sunshine, tails wagging and carefree. It seemed a lifetime ago now.

We were both silent. Neither of us wanted to be the first to mention the corpse in the car. I remembered, with an inward cringe, that one of the reasons we'd liked the Bora was because of its capacious boot. 'This body . . .' I began.

He sat down heavily at the kitchen table, rubbing his face with one hand. 'I just opened the boot and there he was,' he said helplessly, 'staring at me. Just his face. His body was wrapped in some kind of plastic.' He hesitated a moment, his grey eyes bleak as he remembered. 'I couldn't see any obvious sign of injury, but then I didn't . . .' He paused a moment and swallowed. 'I didn't want to touch him.'

'No, of course not. Inspector Ford didn't give you a hard time, did he?'

'No, he was very kind.' For a moment a look of bitter amusement crept into his eyes. 'But Cruella seems to think we're involved in a criminal conspiracy.'

'She'll be loving this! We'll be her prime suspects.' I thought for a moment. 'Are we really suspects, d'you think?'

'Of course not.'

'But the circumstances are incriminating. I bought the car. You found the body.'

'I'm sure they can eliminate us from their enquiries as soon they talk to Amber Horrell.'

'If they can find her. I'm worried something awful has happened to her.'

There was a knock on the kitchen door. I knew it must be Morris. Ricky would have breezed straight in.

'Sorry to interrupt you two,' he said as he entered, carrying a brick-sized object wrapped in tinfoil, 'but I thought it would be easier to cut the cake up in here. It's only lemon drizzle,' he added, almost in apology.

'Sounds delicious,' Daniel said manfully. I didn't suppose he had much appetite for cake right now. I didn't either, but refusing Morris's homemade offerings would be like kicking a puppy.

'I haven't made the coffee yet,' I realised.

'Don't worry, Juno love, I'll do it,' Morris volunteered. 'You're needed down in the shop. There's a lady down there who wants to know the price of a tea caddy and you haven't got a price label on it.'

'It must have fallen off,' I protested. 'I'm obsessive about labelling. I label everything.'

'Well, she needs rescuing. Ricky's trying to talk her into buying a tea set as well and I can see she doesn't want it. You'd better get down there before she runs away.'

I cast an apologetic glance at Daniel and headed for the door. As I passed, Morris laid a hand on my arm. 'Is everything alright?' he whispered, his blue eyes blinking anxiously over his little round specs.

'Of course.' I patted his arm comfortingly and fled downstairs.

I managed to rescue my customer from Ricky. She got off lightly, escaping out of the door with only the tea caddy and not a twenty-four-piece, bone-china tea set to go with it.

Ricky shook his head sadly. 'You're a hopeless saleswoman, Princess.'

'I know,' I agreed. 'But I don't like the hard sell, and anyway I'm not much good at it.'

Morris and Daniel came down into the shop then, bearing coffee and plates of cake. 'It's a shame you being stuck in the shop while Daniel's here,' Morris said as he handed me my mug.

'Well, someone's got to be here,' I told him. 'Sophie's gone away for the weekend to see Seth, and Pat can't do Fridays, she's too busy with the animals. Elizabeth has offered to come in tomorrow and I didn't like to ask her to come in today as well. In any case, she's seeing her sister in the care home.'

I'd been quite happy to be on duty on Friday morning, because Daniel had arranged to see his project manager up at the farmhouse. In fact, a chance to talk to the builder face to face was the main reason for his coming back from Ireland for a long weekend, apart from seeing me of course. But that plan had been thwarted by the turn of events.

'Ricky and I could look after the place for a few hours, couldn't we?' Morris volunteered. 'If you two want to go off together. It's a lovely day. You should be up on the moor.' He looked around him as if he'd suddenly noticed something missing. 'Where's your dear little whippet, then?' he asked Daniel. 'Didn't you bring her with you?'

He shook his head. 'Lottie gets terrified on planes. I decided I wouldn't bring her again unless I'm coming over on the ferry.' He grinned. 'She'll be alright. My landlady back in Inishowen has just got a Labrador pup. He and Lottie are great friends. Anyway,' he added, 'it's easier at Juno's place if I don't bring her, because of the cat.'

'He's not my cat,' I objected. Bill belonged downstairs with Kate and Adam. But he decided long ago he owned me as well as the flat I live in, and hasn't quite adjusted to the idea of sharing me with Lottie when she visits. Which is a shame, because, although I love Bill dearly, I also love Lottie and I miss her when Daniel leaves her behind.

Ricky wasn't interested in pet-talk. 'Yeah, take the day off.' He swept a disparaging arm around the objects in the room. 'Give us a chance to shift some of this old tat.'

'That's a very kind offer.' Daniel raised his brows at me in a querying glance. 'Why not?'

Much as I would have loved the opportunity to flee up onto the moor with Daniel, I had my reservations. I'd left Ricky and Morris in charge of the shop before and they couldn't resist rearranging things. I didn't care about my own stuff, they could mess about with it as much as they liked, but Sophie and Pat weren't too keen on their stock being interfered with. Admittedly, the men's flair for design meant everything looked more professionally arranged after their interventions, and they always managed to sell more in a day than we did. But that was usually because they couldn't resist buying things for themselves. 'Well,' I began weakly. I was saved from going further by the bell on the shop door, which jangled annoyingly.

The door did not open to admit a likely customer, but Detective Sergeant Cruella deVille, accompanied by an officer in uniform. 'I'd like a few words with you, Mr Thorncroft,' she told Daniel, not bothering with subtle niceties like *hello* or *how are you feeling after your terrible experience?* She swept a scorching violet glare around the rest of us. 'Perhaps somewhere less crowded.'

'Kitchen?' Daniel suggested, looking at me. I nodded, but by then Cruella was already leading the way up the stairs. He followed her, and after a moment we heard the door shut firmly behind them.

Ricky leant forward in his chair. 'Right, Princess,' he asked softly. 'What's up? Bog Man looks as if he's seen a ghost.'

I opened my mouth to tell him not to refer to Daniel as Bog Man, but shut it again because I knew that would only make him do it all the time. 'There's some trouble with his car,' I said weakly.

His eyes narrowed in suspicion. 'Cruella wouldn't be here because of a parking ticket.'

'There's been an accident.' I tried to avoid his eye, and that of Morris whom I could feel gazing at me over his specs.

'Blimey! He hasn't had it five minutes.' He shook his head. 'You can't fool us, Princess. Tell us what's really going on.'

CHAPTER THREE

'You didn't tell them anything, did you?' Daniel had been released by Cruella and we'd taken Ricky and Morris up on their offer to mind the shop, but had only escaped as far as the nearest wine bar. It was early in the day to start drinking but we reckoned we needed alcohol. We sat at a table in the tiny, sunny courtyard at the back of *No.14*, calming our nerves with glasses of Sauvignon Blanc.

'I couldn't tell them anything, could I?' I responded.

'I can't imagine Ricky and Morris being satisfied with that.'

'Well, they had to be, at least for the present. I told them, it's a police matter.'

'It is, Miss B, and let's make sure it stays that way,' he said sternly.

'What do you mean?' I asked, although I knew perfectly well what he was getting at.

'It's their job to find out what happened to the dead man, not yours.'

'I'm far more worried about what's happened to Amber.'

'I know.' He took my hand, idly caressing my fingers. 'But I want to go back to Ireland on Monday night and not be worrying about you . . .' He frowned as he groped for the right words, 'getting into trouble,' he finished lamely. *Trouble*, of course, was a euphemism for something much worse. 'This is assuming I'm allowed to leave on Monday at all,' he added with a bitter smile. 'That was Cruella's parting shot. "Don't leave town without informing us, Mr Thorncroft. We may want to question you again." This was after she'd told me I can't go back to the farmhouse until they've finished poking around. The car is being taken away for forensic investigation and I might not get it back for weeks.' He pulled a face. 'To be honest, Miss B, I'm not too keen on getting it back at all.'

I felt the same. The Bora would be forever tainted by the memory of the poor murdered man in the boot. 'What did she want, anyway?'

He shrugged. 'Just to run through my statement again. She wanted to be sure I hadn't touched the body.'

'You didn't. Did you?'

He shook his head. 'You know what it's like when you get a new car. I sat in the driver's seat, played around with the controls for a minute or two. I got the handbook from the glove compartment, and the only other thing I remember touching was the catch to open the boot. And to close it again,' he added, his eyes troubled by the memory. 'I couldn't leave it open while I ran down the hill to pick up a phone signal. I felt bad enough leaving the poor man at all.' He returned his eyes to my face. 'But going back to what I was saying just now.'

'I won't interfere in the police investigation,' I assured him.

'Promise?'

'I promise, but . . .'

'But?'

'I can't really believe Amber is involved in this man's death,' I told him. 'But if she isn't, where is she? What's happened to her?'

'You think she might not have known about the body in the boot?' Daniel frowned. 'But then, why the change of plan, the sudden unexplained departure?'

'I don't know,' I admitted. 'But why put the body in the boot in the first place? Suppose she did kill this person and decided to run away. Why put his dead body in a place where she knows it'll soon be discovered? Why not just roll it in a ditch? It would have been far easier for a start.'

He was quiet for a moment, staring pensively at the table. 'Do you think she could have lifted that body into the boot? Could she have managed it by herself?'

'No. I don't think I could do it on my own, and I'm bigger than she is, as I told the inspector. Not that he asked,' I remembered, feeling faintly foolish at having blurted it out. 'But if Amber did put him in the car, she'd have needed someone to help her lift him. Unless,' I added after a moment, 'she was being forced to help someone else.'

He looked puzzled. 'Why would you think she was being forced to help someone?'

'Because the idea of Amber killing a man, stuffing him in the boot, then driving the car to your place doesn't make sense,' I huffed impatiently. 'But perhaps she didn't drive it. Perhaps she knew nothing about it.'

Daniel looked sceptical. 'Could someone have put the body in the boot without her knowledge?'

'While it was parked outside Langworthy Hall?' I shrugged. 'It was there for a couple of days. I suppose they could have done it while she was away at work. But it's a bit random.'

Daniel smiled suddenly, and leant forward, reaching out to touch my hair. 'Keep still.'

'What is it?'

'Just an insect,' he said, his fingers moving gently. 'It's dropped out of this jasmine here.' That's the problem with hair like mine. It traps wildlife. It was a tiny beetle, and he let it run over his fingers before he gently blew it away.

'I wonder what Dean found when he broke in there,' I pondered aloud. 'I could phone him later, try to pump him for info.'

Daniel shook his head. 'No, you don't, Miss Browne with an e,' he said, catching my arm. 'This is a police matter. If there's anything they want us to know, they'll tell us soon enough. Till then, stay out of it. You promised, remember? Not five minutes ago.'

'Sorry. Let's talk about something else.'

For about a minute there was complete silence. 'I hope I'm going to get a chance to speak to Howard about the house over the weekend,' Daniel said eventually, 'although there's not much point if we're not allowed to go in there. I need to see the state of this staircase he's been telling me about. If the dry rot has got to it, it's going to need replacing.' He frowned and sipped his wine. 'That'll cost me another few thousand.'

He'd already spent a fortune on the place. I reached out a hand to him. The farmhouse had suffered from years of neglect, but it was a fine old building with wide and sweeping views of the moor, the kind of place I'd always dreamt of living in. 'It'll be worth it in the end.'

He checked his watch. 'I wonder how long the police are going to be.'

'They'll be a while. They'll need to search the ground around the car for traces of whoever has been there.'

He raised an ironic eyebrow. 'A footprint from a handmade shoe? A carelessly thrown cigarette butt? Monogrammed, of course.'

'I expect they're searching for the murder weapon. I don't suppose you've any idea how he was . . . ?'

'No, I haven't. And you're doing it again.'

'What?'

'Speculating. Talking about it.'

'You're the one going on about monogrammed cigarette butts!' I retaliated. 'It's a pity you don't have any neighbours, someone who might have seen something.' A house next door with CCTV would have been useful right then. As it was, Moorview Farm was in a secluded spot, the nearest habitation a good mile down the hill. And even that was a holiday let and might have been empty.

'You're right of course,' he admitted. 'It's impossible not to think about it.' He ran a hand through his hair. 'I can't stop wondering who the poor man is. Or was. And how long he'd been in there.'

'Well, he wasn't there on Monday evening,' I said practically. 'Amber said she was going to get the car valeted next morning. If she did, then Tuesday afternoon is the earliest he could have been put in there.'

Daniel shook his head. 'Today's Friday. I don't think he could have been in there long. Not that I know much about these things, but the weather's been warm and the body. . .' He paused for a moment, then added with a grimace of distaste, 'I mean, it hadn't started to um . . .'

There was no need for him to go into detail. 'The police won't know until they've done the post-mortem.' My phone buzzed then and I rooted for it in my bag. The display told me it was DC Dean Collins. 'Any sign of Amber?' I asked, before he could speak.

'No sign of her at Langworthy Hall,' he answered. 'Nor of the dog you mentioned,' he added quickly as if forestalling my next question. 'Where are you at the moment?'

'The wine bar in North Street.'

'Can you meet me back at your place? I need to go over your statement.'

'I'll be there in a few minutes,' I told him, and disconnected. 'Dean Collins,' I said to Daniel. 'He wants to see me back at the flat. Go through my statement again.'

Daniel nodded and heaved a sigh. 'This isn't just going to go away, is it?'

CHAPTER FOUR

It was four in the morning. Despite our valiant efforts, doing the sort of activities that usually lead to deep and blissful sleep afterwards, we were both still wide awake. The visit from Dean Collins hadn't helped. His breaking into Langworthy Hall had revealed no sign of any violent struggle having taken place, or of anyone having left in a hurry: and no sign of Amber or her dog. So far, there was no trace of any murder weapon, either at Langworthy Hall or at Moorview Farm, and absolutely no identification on the dead man: no wallet, driving licence, photos, credit cards or passport. There were no car keys in his pocket, or house keys, and no mobile phone.

'He must have been robbed,' Daniel had said.

'Or whoever killed him removed anything that might identify him.'

'How do you identify someone in a case like this?' he had asked.

Dean had puffed out his cheeks. 'Well, if he hasn't got a criminal record and the fingerprints don't give us anything, we just have to hope someone of his description has been reported missing.' He added with a sniff, 'I didn't tell you any of that.'

We both nodded. This went without saying.

'You've no idea how he died?' I asked.

He shook his head. 'Not yet. Now,' he went on, 'just to go back to your statement a minute, Juno. You said when you visited Langworthy Hall you thought there might have been someone else in the building, someone upstairs, something which Miss Horrell denied, is that right?'

'Yes, it is.'

'And what made you think there might be someone up there?'

'Because I heard a noise from the room above which sounded like a footfall. And the dog reacted to it. Amber was very quick to tell me there was no one there, which I also thought was odd. After all, why shouldn't there have been anyone upstairs? There might have been someone staying with her for all I knew, or even living there. I'd have taken less notice if she'd said nothing.'

'And there was no sign of anyone? No other cars, for instance, apart from the one you were buying?'

'There was a gold-coloured Mini Clubman parked on the drive, which Amber told me was hers.' I shook my head. 'That was all.'

'And you didn't notice anything else unusual?'

'No. But I didn't go anywhere except the sitting room.' Much as I would have loved a grand tour of the property, I hadn't been offered one. No chance to count the unwashed dishes in the sink or notice the extra toothbrush in the mug in the bathroom. The very least I should have done is asked to use the loo so I could snoop about. But at the time I hadn't known any snooping would be necessary.

'You see,' Dean went on, clearing his throat, 'there is some evidence that someone else has been staying there, as well as Amber Horrell. But she didn't mention anyone?'

'No. What evidence?' I asked, interested.

'More than one bed has been slept in.' Dean tugged thoughtfully on the lobe of one ear. 'Now, when you originally phoned her about the car being for sale, was it the same number she later texted you from?'

'No. The telephone number on the sale notice in the car window was the landline for Langworthy Hall, not a mobile number.'

He looked disappointed. 'Ah!' was all he said.

'Why?'

'Well, this number that she, or someone, texted you from about the car being left at the farmhouse, the same one you then tried to call her back on . . . am I right?'

I nodded, impatient for him to get to the point.

'It's a burner,' he said at last. 'Not registered in her name.'

'So, you can't use it to track her whereabouts?' Daniel asked.

'No, we can't. We sent an officer over to *Horrell's Antiques* earlier today to see if she'd turned up for work but the proprietor, Mr Peter Horrell, told us she wasn't expected. Apparently, she'd left a message with a colleague to say she'd decided to go away for the weekend and wouldn't be coming in.'

'That must have been around the same time she sent me the message about the car,' I said.

Dean pulled a face. 'We won't know about the sequence of events until we can talk to her. So, we just have to hope she returns after the weekend.'

'Didn't she tell this colleague where she was going?'

'No,' he said, closing his notebook, 'so until then, there's not much point in speculating about what may or may not have been her involvement in all of this. She's certainly a person of interest and we want to speak to her, but as she's informed her colleague she was going away, we can't count her as officially missing until she fails to come back.'

'Tell me something,' I replied. 'The inspector said Amber was not unknown to the police. What did he mean?'

Dean hesitated for a moment and then shrugged. 'Nothing much. She was a bit of a wild child, that's all. We hauled her over for drink-driving when she was a teenager, and being under the influence of drugs. I think she spent a couple of spells in rehab. But nothing recent.'

I sensed he was holding out on us, and thought a little bribery and corruption might help. 'Tea?' I offered. 'Biscuits? I've got flapjacks in the kitchen. Kate baked them this morning.'

'No thanks, Juno,' he said, standing up. 'I've got to get on. Besides,' he added, tapping his tummy, 'I'm watching my weight.'

It was true he had taken to jogging recently, but I was still flabbergasted at his refusal. 'Well!' I declared after he'd gone. 'Fancy that.'

'He's lost a few pounds.' Daniel nodded approvingly. 'It looks good on him.'

I didn't care how good it looked. The contents of my biscuit tin have always been an essential tool in getting Dean to open up about what was going on at the police station. I hoped I wasn't about to lose a valuable asset.

Daniel stood up and stretched his long arms. 'Let's get out of here. I need some air.'

'Where do you want to go?' I asked, grabbing my car keys from the table.

'Anywhere away from here.' He shrugged. 'I don't care. Just drive.'

We'd headed west, away from the confines of Ashburton and the horrors at Halsanger Common, and made for Dartmeet, where the rivers of the East and West Dart come together. We parked just off the road, and from there we walked, following the grassy tracks between clumps of bracken fern and golden-flowering gorse towards the top of Sharp Tor. We picked our way up the slope to reach the summit, stepping around scattered stones and piles of pony droppings, until we reached the foot of the outcrop. The rocks were deeply grooved by wind and weather and we clambered to the top, the wide blue sky opening up around us.

The wind stole our breath, blowing through us, cleansing, sweeping away the horrors of the morning. I breathed in deep. From here we could look down to the Dart valley, a deep fold in the wooded hills hiding the secret gleam of the river. Beyond, fields and open moorland faded to merge with the blue smudge of the horizon. To the west we could see Princetown, and to the south, a sheet of water shining in the sun, Venford Reservoir.

The rocks were flat enough to lie on and warmed by the afternoon sun. We lay back and closed our eyes, but the blasting wind made it too chilly for sunbathing. After a few minutes, I sat up. 'We could walk across to Mel Tor,' I suggested. 'It's not far.'

Daniel rolled up onto one elbow. 'Or we could head back to the car and drive on to Dartmeet for a spot of wild swimming.'

I didn't fancy swimming much. 'I didn't bring my costume.'

He crooked an eyebrow. 'You don't fancy skinny-dipping?'

'Too many tourists about. I don't want to ruin anyone's picnic.'

It was good to hear him laugh. He took my hand and kissed it. 'We'd better settle for a cream tea then.'

I smiled. 'A far more civilised suggestion.'

But in the quiet darkness of the early hours, it wasn't so easy to smile. 'I can't stop opening the boot of the car,' Daniel whispered, 'and seeing that poor man's face.' I rolled my body against his, snuggling into his shoulder, and he nestled his chin in my hair. After a moment he asked, 'Don't they haunt you, Miss B, the dead faces?'

It was something I'd never talked about, the faces of the dead appearing in my dreams. Poor Sandy Thomas, her lifeless blue eyes staring up at me; young Gavin Hall dead on the forest floor, a leaf clinging to the childlike smoothness of his pale cheek; or Luke Rowlands, his body dropping straight as an arrow into the cold lake of Foggintor, never to surface again. But right now, it was someone living I couldn't stop thinking about. At least, I hoped she was still living. 'What if Amber left the car at your place *because* she knew the body would be discovered?'

'I don't follow.'

'What if it was a cry for help?'

'Then why not park it outside the police station? Better still, crash it in their drive?'

'What if she couldn't? What if this other person who was at the Hall is someone she's afraid of? What if he's abducted her? What if he's the killer?'

'That's a lot of what ifs, Miss B.' Daniel sucked in his breath and cursed softly as Bill leapt on the bed and landed on his chest. 'Where did you come from, you fiend?' Bill ignored the question, purring with pleasure and treading his paws up and down on his solar plexus. 'Will you kindly keep your claws to yourself,' he added through gritted teeth.

'He'll settle down in a minute,' I told him.

'Perfect.'

'But what if . . .'

'What if, Miss B, we try to get some sleep?'

I closed my eyes, and waited. Sleep did not come. I heard the St Andrew's church clock strike five. I could tell by his breathing that Daniel wasn't sleeping either. The only one sleeping was Bill. We could hear sheep bleating to their lambs on the hill above the town. Daniel groaned. 'I never realised sheep could be so noisy.'

'Don't be fooled by all that silent grass-chomping they do in the daytime,' I told him. 'They gossip in the dark.'

There followed a few more minutes of frustrating silence. 'What if I got up and made us a cup of tea?' I suggested.

'Perfect,' he said again.

Several hours later, fortified by an early breakfast at *Sunflowers*, we were standing in the sunshine outside a premises in the small neighbouring town of Buckfastleigh. The town has much to recommend it. As well as the Benedictine abbey at nearby Buckfast, world-famous for its 'Bucky' wine, it boasts an otter sanctuary, a butterfly farm and a steam railway whose delightful station has been much used in films and on TV. Its main street is lined with houses in sugar-almond colours and there's an old stone bridge over the river.

I was surprised to learn Daniel had never been there. I tend to forget that like me, he is not a home-grown Devonian, but what locals refer to witheringly as a 'blow-in'. He is only in this part of the world because a distant aunt, whom he can vaguely remember meeting once when he was seven years old, left her estate to him. Which just proves, I suppose, that even at seven years old he must have been impressive. Or she didn't have anyone else to leave it to.

'An interesting fact about Buckfastleigh,' I told him, airing my guidebook knowledge, 'is that the name contains thirteen of the twenty-six letters of the alphabet – exactly half – and not one of them is repeated.'

He frowned as he mentally checked the accuracy of my statement. I could see him spelling it out in his brain. 'So it does,' he agreed. 'But what are we doing here, precisely?'

I'd brought him to see one of the town's little jewels, *The Valiant Soldier*, a pub which closed its doors back in the 1960s and has remained preserved exactly as it was ever since. Everything from the adverts and price lists on its walls to the condiments on its kitchen shelves are as they were on the night last orders were called for the final time. 'Didn't you like it? I asked.

'I liked it very much,' he assured me. 'I particularly enjoy a museum where they encourage you to peer into cupboards. But we have since walked on, Miss B,' he said in that old-fashioned English professorial tone he often adopts, 'and I can't help observing that the house we are now standing outside has a sign with the words *Horrell's Antiques* above the door.'

'It's their shop,' I told him. *Horrell's* didn't stoop to anything as ordinary as shop windows. They displayed their wares in the rooms of an impressive Georgian house, which meant if you wanted to view them, you had to go inside. And the polished front door with its heavy brass knocker was invitingly open.

'I don't care if they run it as a brothel,' Daniel retorted. 'I repeat my question. What are we doing here?'

I felt like stamping my foot. 'Aren't you the least bit curious? About the man in the car, I mean? About Amber?'

'I'm extremely curious, but I don't see how snooping about in Peter Horrell's shop is going to help.'

Neither did I, to be honest, but you never know. Besides, I was curious about Peter Horrell. I wanted to get a look at him, the man who had quarrelled with his cousin's daughter on the phone.

'We already know Amber isn't here today,' he insisted.

'But we might as well take a look inside,' I wheedled. 'After all, I do have a professional interest in antiques.'

He scowled. 'You promised you wouldn't interfere.'

'How can it be interfering in a police investigation when the police aren't even here to investigate?' I pointed out reasonably.

'We'll go inside,' he conceded grudgingly. 'But the first sign of a copper and we're off. Agreed?'

'Agreed,' I said sunnily, and took him by the arm.

There is a certain quiet that pervades in the presence of expensive artefacts. No one talks too much or laughs too loud; it's a kind of reverence for wealth, for the past, like being in a museum. So it was when we opened the half-glass inner door that led into the tranquil hush of Peter Horrell's establishment; it was quiet. We stood for a moment in the marble-floored hallway, feeling lost. There was a small console table to our right with a visitors' book on it. I wondered briefly if we'd accidentally blundered into a hotel. But presently, a slim young woman in a white blouse and dark skirt walked down the elegant curving staircase. 'Would you mind signing in?' she asked pleasantly, crooking her head on one side.

'No, of course not,' I responded, slightly taken aback. Security in this place was obviously tight. I couldn't help noticing the CCTV camera mounted high on the plaster cornice. Meanwhile, Daniel had already leant forward and was entering our names in his bold, black scrawl. *Mr and Mrs Smith.*

'Is Amber in today?' I asked, taking advantage of the fact he was occupied for a moment.

'No, she's away for the weekend,' the young woman responded. She was a remarkably pretty girl, blinking from long-lashed blue eyes beneath a straight fringe of fine brown hair that almost hid her eyebrows. 'I'm Kirsten. Can I help?'

I shook my head. 'No, thank you, it's alright.'

'Did you need to speak to Mr Horrell?'

'Mr Horrell?'

'Mr *Peter* Horrell,' she explained. 'The late Julian's business partner.'

Daniel had straightened up and, remarkably quickly, got with the programme. 'Brothers?' he asked.

Kirsten seemed suddenly to be taking him in, all six foot four and a half of him. She smiled delightfully, a brace across her teeth making her look ridiculously young. 'No, cousins actually.'

He smiled back, just as charmingly, the bastard, and crooked a dark, satanic eyebrow. 'Is it alright if we look around, Kirsten?' he asked politely.

'Please.' She pointed at the doorway on our right. 'If you'd like to start in this room and then just follow your nose.' She blinked again beneath that fringe, a slow sweep of soft lashes. 'Let me know if I can help with anything.'

'Thank you,' I said firmly, giving Daniel a discreet shove into the room.

'Mr and Mrs Smith?' I hissed at him as soon as we were out of earshot.

'What if the police come back here?' he whispered back. 'Do you want them to know we've been snooping?'

'Good thinking, Sherlock,' I muttered from the corner of my mouth, 'but I think the CCTV might just give us away.'

He glanced up at a camera mounted in the corner and groaned in embarrassment. We were standing next to something I'd have described as a rather ugly sideboard. The price card placed upon it described it as '*a French* bombe commode *with curved front. £1,500.*'

'Bit fancy for my taste,' Daniel commented, touching its decorative gilt mountings, and we moved on. A long oak refectory table took up the centre of the room with antique items displayed tastefully upon it. There was none of the clutter I was used to in antique shops. Everything was carefully arranged, allowed to breathe, given space on the table's gleaming surface. Daniel was testing the hinge of a brass letter-clip shaped like a hand, ending in a frilled cuff.

'How much?' I asked.

He consulted the price-card. 'Seventy-five.'

I tutted. 'I sold an identical one last week for thirty.'

'I'm sure that's nearer what it's worth.'

'In this game a thing is worth what you can get for it.'

He had turned his attention to a glass dome containing an arrangement of stuffed hummingbirds, caught in flight. 'Except for these, of course,' he added sadly, gazing at their jewelled feathers, 'which were priceless.'

Despite the quiet atmosphere, we weren't the only

customers in *Horrell's*. Soft voices drifted from above and after inspecting another room full of French furniture heavy with ornate gilding, we climbed the stairs, pausing on the way to lament the cost of a plain oak library chair. It would have looked perfect in Daniel's farmhouse, and was priced at three times what he could afford. 'Have you noticed that every sideboard is described as a *commode*?' he whispered.

'And every wardrobe is an *armoire*,' I added.

We stopped at a table bearing a very fine bronze sculpture of a horse. '£7,500,' Daniel read out and whistled softly.

We reached the landing, where other rooms full of antiques opened up to our left, and a staircase to our right led to an upper floor. These stairs had plush carpeting, and the door at the top was marked PRIVATE in elegantly curling letters. Did Peter Horrell live in a flat up there, I wondered? It looked as if it might be rather more opulent than the flat above *Old Nick's*.

In the nearest room we found a man talking to a couple about a set of dining chairs. He was silver-haired and deeply tanned, wearing a striped shirt open at his neck and gold cufflinks. Peter Horrell, I assumed. He was probably in his sixties. Some women would have described him as a silver fox; I sensed he had more of the wolf about him. And looking at the smoothness of his skin, a certain tautness around the eyes and mouth, I wouldn't have been surprised if he'd had *work* done, which was definitely a turn-off in my book. We didn't stay to listen to him extolling the virtues of cabriole legs and ball-and-claw feet, but drifted into the next room.

On the wall, hanging in a heavy gilt frame, was a painting I'd seen before.

I'd just clutched Daniel's arm to draw his attention to it when I heard Peter Horrell's voice raised in farewell. 'Just pop downstairs and Kirsten will sort out your payment.' He'd closed the deal on the set of dining chairs, obviously, and sounded pleased with himself. A moment later he wandered in to greet us. 'Can I help you at all?' He smiled, showing perfect dentistry.

'Yes.' I returned his smile. 'I've seen this portrait before.'

His gaze swept over me and he raised his eyebrows. 'I doubt it. It's a copy; the original is hanging in Langworthy Hall.'

I determined to keep smiling. 'I know. I was there the other evening, with Amber.'

For a moment his blue gaze hardened. 'You know Amber?'

I held out my hand. 'Juno Browne,' I introduced myself. 'I own an antiques shop in Ashburton, *Old Nick's*.'

For a moment he seemed dumbfounded. '*You're* her? I heard he left it to his cleaning woman, some old biddy who thinks she's Miss Marple.'

From the corner of my eye, I could see Daniel putting up a hand to hide a smile. 'That would be me,' I admitted, although I wasn't too keen on the *old*. 'And I was more of a home-help really.'

'Sounds like the right business to be in.' He said it pleasantly enough but I didn't laugh. I wasn't sure it was a joke. 'So, you took over old Nikolai's place?' He gave a smug little smile. 'Forgive me, but hardly *antiques*.'

I decided to ignore the man's rudeness, and pressed on. 'The portrait?' I asked.

'Ah yes. That dark-eyed beauty is India Horrell.'

We all stared up at her. 'India?' I repeated.

'That wasn't her real name, but it's what everyone called her. It's a rather sad reflection of the attitudes of the day towards foreigners, I'm afraid. My great-grandfather several times over made his fortune with the East India Company. He married a prince's daughter and brought her back home to Devon, along with her considerable dowry.'

'Was the ruby part of it?' Daniel nodded at the glowing jewel around her neck.

Peter Horrell seemed happy to show off his superior knowledge. 'That's not a ruby. It's something far rarer, a red diamond.'

I hadn't known diamonds could be red. For a moment I studied India's expression, the wary defiance in her eyes. Was it loneliness lurking at the back of them, or fear? 'Was she happy here?' I asked. 'So far away from home?'

'Not for long,' he told us wryly. 'She was found dead at the foot of the stairs a few months after she arrived. Neck broken.'

Daniel raised an eyebrow. 'Sounds suspicious.'

Horrell laughed. 'Oh, I doubt it was an accident. But of course, in those days, no one could prove anything.'

'Was this at Langworthy Hall?' I couldn't remember seeing a staircase.

'No, no.' He shook his head. 'This was back in the

day when the Horrell family owned a much grander pile, Gadd House. Sadly, it's no longer standing. Pulled down after the war, like a lot of great houses. Death duties and all that. The estate was broken up and sold off. Anyway,' he carried on, 'my ancestor married again shortly after the death of the Indian bride. An English lady,' he added with a smile, 'far more suitable.'

He seemed to find this part of the tale amusing. I decided I really didn't like him. Poor India, married for her wealth and brought back to England, murdered and not even mourned. 'And the red diamond?' I asked.

He spread his hands in a helpless gesture. 'Sadly, nobody knows. Lost without trace. But you didn't come here to talk to me about India Horrell.' He adopted a brisker tone. 'Was there something I can help you with?'

'No, no,' I assured him. 'I just came in out of professional curiosity.' I gestured at the surrounding *objets d'art*. 'And I did wonder if Amber might be here.'

He still smiled but there was a definite dimming in the wattage. 'She's not, I'm afraid.'

I waited to see if he might say more, but I suppose he wasn't likely to tell a complete stranger that the police had been asking for her. 'Ah well,' I smiled. 'I'll catch her another time.'

'Now, if you'll excuse me,' he added, clearly having had enough of my company, 'I must get on. Let Kirsten know if there's anything else you need help with.' And with that he turned, climbed the stairs and disappeared through the door marked *Private*. We made a pretence of looking around for a bit longer, then went downstairs to ground level.

I was greeted by the sudden appearance of Ben the spaniel, waving his plumy tail like a flag. 'Hello, where did you spring from?' I bent to pat him, then straightened up to see Kirsten watching me from a doorway. 'This is Amber's dog,' I said.

'She asked me to look after him.' She smiled nervously. Her voice dropped to an anxious whisper. 'Is she in some kind of trouble?'

Daniel and I glanced at each other. 'Why would you think she's in trouble?'

'Well,' she began hesitantly, 'the police were here yesterday. I didn't speak to them but Peter said they were looking for her. She rang me on Thursday and told me she was taking a long weekend, asked me if I would look after Ben. She dropped him off at my house. She didn't tell Peter she was planning to go. We've got a really big sale coming up next week and she knew he'd be furious with her for taking the time off.'

'Do you know where she went?'

She blinked her long lashes. 'I think so. She told me she wanted to go to a festival, but she couldn't get a ticket. Then she managed to get one at the last minute, so decided she'd go after all.'

'Festival?' Daniel asked. 'What kind of festival?'

CHAPTER FIVE

'Steampunk?' Inspector Ford repeated incredulously. 'What exactly is a steampunk festival when it's at home?'

'I'm not exactly sure what goes on,' I admitted. 'There's a big festival every year in Whitby, but this one is being held in Bristol.' I glanced at Daniel sitting beside me in the interview room. 'We just thought you ought to know where she's gone. At least, that's what Kirsten thinks. She says Amber was desperate to go.' It made sense to me now: the flying-helmet and goggles I'd seen at her place, the earring she'd been wearing made of cogs and wheels. I didn't know much about the subject, but I knew these were accessories of steampunk fashion.

The inspector frowned. 'And you obtained this information from Miss Kirsten Blake?'

'We just happened to bump into her,' I lied hastily. 'In Buckfastleigh.'

The inspector gave me a penetrating stare but decided to let it go without comment. 'Well, if she knew where Miss Horrell had gone, why didn't she tell my officers when they were there yesterday?'

'She probably didn't want to mention it in front of her boss. She said she didn't want to get Amber into trouble. And besides, I think Kirsten's a bit . . .'

I'd been about to say *dim*, which wasn't fair on a first impression. 'Timid,' I finished lamely.

'Well, thank you, Miss Browne. We'll contact the Bristol force and see if they can locate her. You don't know how long this steampunk shindig goes on for, I suppose?'

'Just the weekend, I think.'

'Well, that's half over.' He turned to look at Daniel. 'By the way, Mr Thorncroft, I'm happy to tell you, you can have your house back. Forensics are packing up. They'll be clear by this evening.' I was bursting to ask if they'd found anything, but was quelled by a glance from the inspector and forced to bite my lip. 'I can't say when you're likely to get your car back, I'm afraid,' he added as he showed us out.

Daniel took my arm as we walked away from the police station. 'I suppose I should be grateful you're not trying to drag us both to Bristol to that steampunk festival.'

'I would if I thought you'd go,' I told him frankly.

'Well, I won't. That's not why I'm here. I'm going to phone Howard in a minute and see if I can make an appointment to meet him at the farmhouse tomorrow. And then I'm taking you to lunch.'

'I should call in at the shop,' I warned him. I knew I could safely leave Elizabeth to look after *Old Nick's* for the day, but I'd no idea what Ricky and Morris had got up to yesterday and thought I'd better check things out.

'We can do it on our way to *Rust and the Wolf*,' he said.

I laughed. 'I can tell you've not been around Ashburton for a while. *Rust and the Wolf* closed ages ago. It's been *Rafikis* for some time now.'

'I'm sadly out of touch,' he confessed. 'Never mind, it's always nice to discover new eating places.'

'Oh, I agree.' There was a new Italian restaurant in the old bank building he didn't know about either. I wondered whether we could make time in the weekend for him to discover that too.

'You know, Miss B,' he said, frowning, 'I'm not sure I really understand what steampunk is.'

'Neither do I, if I'm honest,' I told him. 'But I know someone who will.'

Olly was only too pleased to share with us his latest purchase from *Gnash! Comics*. He walked into *Old Nick's* carrying it under his arm about ten minutes after we'd arrived. Elizabeth was behind the counter, looking impeccably groomed as usual, with a book in one hand and a cup of coffee by her elbow. 'I've swept and mopped the floor,' she told me without looking up, 'just in case you think I'm slacking.'

'Slack away,' I told her, 'I'm just grateful you're here.'

She stood up and shimmied from behind the counter to allow Daniel to enfold her in a hug. 'Good to see you,' she told him fondly. Of all my friends, Elizabeth has always been the most sympathetic to Daniel and to what he's been through since he lost his wife, Claire, to cancer, a few years ago. She's a widow herself and knows about loss.

I left the two of them to their canoodling, and wandered into the back room to see what havoc Ricky and Morris had wrought in my antiques empire. Mavis was now wearing the red polka-dot suit, I noticed, with a floppy yellow hat, but had suffered no alteration to her wig. The vintage clothes rail was full to bursting, with stiff net petticoats and feather boas in abundance. And there was a collection of gentlemen's tailcoats in an assortment of odd sizes which could have suited up a male voice choir. A small mahogany table had been taken over by a basket of long gloves, genuine articles from the Edwardian era, which fastened with tiny pearl buttons at the wrist. I held one up. The hand was narrow and the arm too thin to fit any normal, healthy woman. We ladies must have been more finely boned and delicate in the days when long gloves were an essential item of evening wear. Perhaps a shrimp like Sophie might wriggle her arm into one. I stood no chance. Their only value now was to collectors of bygone fashions. Fortunately, there are plenty of those about. There were also two pairs of glove stretchers, which proved that even Edwardian ladies must have struggled to get their dainty digits into these things. A basket of bead necklaces stood there too, with a note from Morris. *These might be of use to Pat for making earrings. Tell her to help herself.* Oh, she will, I assured him silently.

I looked around me carefully for evidence of sales. There seemed to be gaps on the shelves of a pine dresser but for the life of me, I couldn't remember what had stood there before. I peered into the locked glass cabinet where I kept items that were small and nickable, but they seemed to be just as I remembered. I wandered back to the front of the shop to consult the ledger where the sales from yesterday should have been recorded.

'I've counted the float,' Elizabeth told me as she pushed the ledger in my direction. 'And there's an extra £396 in the cash box. The boys had a busy day.'

As it turned out, they had sold a painting of geese for Sophie, which accounted for half of the money; several of her greeting cards; and five pairs of earrings and a toy hedgehog for Pat. I was richer by the price of a jelly mould, two salt-glaze storage jars and one white enamel bread bin – all to the same customer by the look of it, someone who collected vintage kitchenalia. I'd also been relieved of a pretty Carlton Ware teapot in the form of an apple which, I was willing to bet, was currently residing in the breakfast room at Druid Lodge, where it would fit in nicely with the rest of Morris's teapot collection. He wouldn't worry about the little chip on the spout.

The jangling of the shop doorbell announced Olly's arrival. He was munching an Eccles cake from the local artisan baker's and carrying a slightly greasy paper bag, his newly purchased comic tucked under his arm.

'I swear that boy's got worms,' Elizabeth muttered, watching him come in. 'He never stops eating.'

'I'm a growing lad,' he responded cheerfully. 'Least that's what your Tom says. 'Lo Juno, 'lo Daniel,' he added, brushing flakes of pastry from his sweatshirt onto the newly mopped floor. He certainly was growing, no longer the smallest boy in his class but one of the tallest, and stringy as a bean.

'Tom Carter has a lot to answer for,' Elizabeth said severely.

'Well, you should know, he's your boyfriend.' Olly grinned at her and held up the brown paper bag. 'I bought an Eccles cake for you too.'

'Thank you, but I'd hate to deprive you of it,' she responded. 'We don't want you fainting from hunger.'

'How did the GCSEs go?' Daniel asked him.

Olly shrugged. 'Dead easy. But that's cos I'm a genius.'

Elizabeth raised an eyebrow. 'Let's hope the results bear out your estimation.'

'Yeah. Don't get them till August anyway.' Suddenly, his eyes lit up and he pointed a skinny finger. 'I've got an idea. You'd be brilliant!'

'I would?' Daniel looked mildly surprised.

'Yeah. I mean, you'd think they'd let us stay home now all the exams are over, but we've still got to keep going to school until the end of term. They keep giving us these rubbish projects to do.' His face puckered in distaste. 'I've got to do this one interviewing someone about their job. I wanted to interview Juno about finding dead bodies, but our teacher says that's not a proper job, so I didn't know else who to ask.' He grinned at Daniel. 'But you'd be brilliant! I could ask you about peatbogs.'

'Certainly. I'd be honoured.'

'Can we do it now?'

'Perhaps later?' Elizabeth suggested. 'Don't you have to record it?'

'Yeah, but I can do it on my phone.'

'You need to think up some questions.'

Olly nodded sagely. 'Good ones.'

'I've got a question for you,' I told him, as he began tucking into his second Eccles cake. 'Tell us what steampunk is.'

Chewing, he jabbed a skinny finger at his magazine.

'Don't speak with your mouth full,' Elizabeth warned him as he was about to start.

He swallowed. 'Sorry.' He neatly smoothed out his comic on the counter and pointed at the illustration of the girl on the cover. 'This is Lady Vengeance.' She was wearing a demure Victorian hat and bodice but also toting a very strange firearm that looked as if it was made from clock parts. From the expression on her face, she meant business with it. 'Like, it's science fiction, but all Victorian.' He flipped a page. 'See this spaceship? It's steam-powered. But it's a proper spaceship, it'll go to Mars, but all the machines are steam-powered or they're clockwork. Like this one.'

'It looks like an illustration from something by H. G. Wells,' Daniel observed, 'or Jules Verne.'

Olly frowned. 'Who's she?'

'He wrote *Twenty Thousand Leagues Under the Sea*.'

Olly clicked his fingers. 'I saw the film. Captain Nemo.' He nodded enthusiastically. 'That's just what it's like.' He leafed through pages and stopped to point at an illustration of a gentleman in a waistcoat and top hat. 'See?'

'So, steampunk is basically science fiction, but with Victorian technology and costumes?' I asked.

'Retro-futuristic,' Daniel murmured. For a moment we looked impressed, until we realised he was reading the blurb on the back of the magazine.

'Yeh,' Olly agreed uncertainly. 'But it can be set in the Wild West too,' he added. 'Or it can be pirates.'

'Brown leather seems to be popular.' Daniel was leafing through the comic. 'So do goggles and pocket watches.' He traced a drawing of a machine with his finger. 'I love this steam-powered whatever-it-is.'

'So, what goes on at a steampunk festival?' I asked.

Olly shrugged. 'People just dress up, I suppose. Show off. Have fun and that.' He turned his attention back to Daniel. 'So, we can do this interview later?'

'If Daniel has the time,' Elizabeth reminded him. 'He's only here for the weekend and he's here to see Juno, not you.'

'It's fine,' Daniel assured her. 'Our plans for the weekend have been scuppered anyway. I'm sure we can find the time.'

Before she could ask what might have done the scuppering, three people came through the shop door one after another: Ricky, Morris and Tom Carter, who was weighed down by something heavy in a canvas bag. Tom had once been a client of mine, barely able to walk. Following a hip operation he no longer needed my services, and it was good to see him walking upright and without crutches, even if it meant I had lost him as a client. Seventy-something, with a deep voice and a twinkle in his eye, he is currently courting the lovely Elizabeth and has become a regular visitor to the shop, at least on days when she's here.

'What on earth have you got in there?' she asked, nodding in the direction of his bag.

'A clock I'm trying to mend,' he told her. 'I'm taking it to the Despair Café for further investigation.'

'Despair Café?' Daniel frowned.

'He means the Repair Café,' Elizabeth said, flicking a glance heavenward. 'He volunteers there, mending things for people.'

'I know what I mean,' Tom said solemnly. 'We try to keep stuff out of landfill,' he added, 'although I seem to spend most of my time repairing kettles and toasters, and un-bunging hoovers. Most of the things people bring in just need a damn good clean.'

'Is it really a café?' Daniel asked.

'No, it's a shed, but I can make you a diabolical cup of coffee if you fancy turning up there.'

He smiled. 'I think I'll pass, thanks.'

Tom turned to Olly. 'I came here to see if you wanted to come with me. You like taking things apart.'

Olly glanced up from his magazine. 'Okay.'

'We've got to be able to put 'em back together, mind, afterwards,' he warned him.

''Course,' he responded indignantly. 'I'm ace at that stuff.'

Elizabeth smiled. 'His modesty is so endearing.'

'Never mind all that.' Ricky flicked an arm in impatience and pointed at Daniel and me. 'Have you managed to find out what these two have been up to?'

'Up to?' She raised her eyebrows at us. 'Have you been up to something?'

'The police were here yesterday,' Morris put in. 'At

67

least, Cruella was, asking questions.'

'Something to do with a car,' Ricky added, his eyes narrowing.

Daniel and I glanced at each other. As yet, no news of the dead man had been made public, and we were still sworn to secrecy. As if on cue, the door opened again. This time, DC Dean Collins' stocky form stood blocking the doorway.

'I wanted a word.' He stopped when, as one, the entire shop turned to look at him. For a moment he surveyed the faces of the assembled audience. 'Perhaps outside, Mr Thorncroft,' he added and Daniel followed him out into Shadow Lane.

'Mr Thorncroft – that's formal,' Ricky muttered. 'Official police business, obviously.' Outside, Dean and Daniel were engaged in a hushed conversation, watched through the windows by a shop full of people regretting that they'd never learnt to lip-read.

'What's going on, Juno?' Ricky hissed at me.

'I don't know.' Truthfully, at that moment I didn't. I couldn't contain myself. I darted outside, carefully closing the shop door behind me. After all, I was in on this secret. 'What's up?'

'Nothing,' Dean told me. 'I was just telling Daniel we'd like to go over his statement one more time before he heads back to Ireland on Monday.'

'Have you found Amber?' I asked.

He shook his head. 'The local force couldn't trace her at this festival in Bristol. *If* that's where she went,' he added significantly.

'You think she might have lied to Kirsten?'

'It's possible. To put us all off the scent. For all we know, she might have skipped the country by now. Anyway,' he went on to Daniel, 'if you could come to the station on Monday.'

'Yes, of course.'

'Any news on the dead man?' I asked.

'Not yet. Enjoy the rest of your weekend,' he said. 'Some of us will be working.'

Daniel smiled. 'A policeman's lot.'

He rolled a jaundiced eye. 'Try not to find anything else.'

CHAPTER SIX

The news about the dead man in the boot of the Bora didn't break until the Monday evening, by which time Daniel was already on his way back to Ireland. It was announced on the local television news, with a plea for anyone who thought they might know the man's identity to get in touch with the police. There was no photograph of his face, as the only one available would have been taken in the morgue and probably didn't show him at his best. There was a sketch by a police artist of a dark-haired man with a receding hairline and unremarkable features. There was also a photograph of a rather pallid forearm bearing a tattoo of a dagger surrounded by a circle of laurel leaves, his only identifying feature. There was no mention of Amber Horrell. I still wasn't convinced something nasty hadn't happened to her.

About two minutes after the television appeal ended, my phone began to ring. I didn't need to look at the display to know it was Ricky and Morris, eager for details. Since Dean's departure from the shop on Saturday, Daniel and I had been fielding questions about what was going on. We'd decided our best course was to avoid everyone for the rest of the weekend. This hadn't worked. Our trip up to Moorview Farm to meet Daniel's project manager was complicated by the broken ribbon of police tape left hanging from the gatepost. The words POLICE, DO NOT CROSS had aroused Howard's curiosity and he'd taken a little persuading that the tape must have been left by kids as a joke. Fortunately, he was easily distracted by talk of dry rot in the staircase and what it was going to cost to put right. It was going to take time too, he warned us. Buildings within the national park were subject to strict regulations from the Dartmoor National Park Authority. Any renovations had to be inspected and signed off before further work could proceed, often delaying things by weeks if not longer. Daniel wasn't worried about these delays, he told me in private. They gave him more time to earn the money for whatever had to be paid for next.

Then there was his promise to give Olly an interview about his job. We needn't have worried about this, as it turned out. As she opened the door to us, Elizabeth held up her palms in a gesture of surrender. 'I promise I won't ask about what's going on,' she assured us. 'What's more,' she added, pointing to where Olly was sitting at the kitchen table, 'neither will he.' Olly opened his mouth, about to protest. 'Will you?' she insisted and he shook his head.

He had a long list of questions on the table, and Daniel sat down next to him and began drawing a diagram of how tiny sphagnum mosses build into peatbogs and their place in the carbon cycle. Elizabeth and I watched on, coffee cups in hand.

'Peatlands hold more carbon than tropical rainforests,' he explained. 'It's important to keep them wet. Once they dry out, they release their carbon into the atmosphere and become a fire risk.'

He paused while Olly scribbled this down. 'Is that what you do in your job, then?' he asked. 'Keep bogs wet?'

'My job's about trying to reverse damage, giving bogland plants a chance to re-establish themselves. They can hold up to twenty times their own weight in water, so this helps prevent flooding as well.' He grinned suddenly. 'Have you ever heard of a bog burst?'

Elizabeth laughed. 'It sounds distinctly unpleasant.'

'I can show you one as it's happening.' Daniel tapped the lid of Olly's laptop. 'Open this thing up and search for "Donegal Landslide". Someone happened to be taking a film of it on their phone.'

He angled the screen so we could all see. We were looking at a dismal stretch of brown bog under a sodden grey sky. In the distance was a line of fir trees. 'There had been torrential rain over a period of several weeks, more than the bog could hold,' he told us. 'Watch those trees on the right.'

As if they were on a conveyor belt, the trees began to move, sliding slowly from the right to the left of the screen, the sound of roots cracking like gunfire.

Olly watched, open-mouthed. 'That's awesome!'

'When bog becomes liquid, it flows like lava,' Daniel explained, 'which is what's happening here.'

We watched as the trees tipped and a horrible river of black sludge swept them down the hillside, smothering everything in its path in a glistening slick.

'I'm gonna show this film when I present my project in front of the class,' Olly cried excitedly. He turned to look at Daniel. 'So, which bit do you do, then?'

'I apply for grants and funding, talk to businesses and government bodies, try to persuade them about the importance of our work.'

Olly looked disappointed. 'Don't you go out on the bog?'

'Very much so. Getting out there and training volunteers is part of what I do.'

'Do they smell?'

Daniel crooked an eyebrow. 'The bogs or the volunteers?'

Olly laughed. 'I mean, do bogs pong horrible?'

'No, they pong fantastic!' He grinned enthusiastically. 'They've got a really rich smell, lush and earthy like a forest after rain.'

I realised I was wasting my limited supply of expensive perfume. If I wanted to turn Mr Thorncroft on, all I needed behind each ear was a discreet dab of bog water.

'This is great!' Olly declared. 'This interview's gonna be the best in the class. All the rest will be rubbish.' He sniggered. 'Marcus is interviewing his dad about being an accountant.'

'Well, if there's nothing else you want to know,' Elizabeth began, glancing at her watch.

But Olly hadn't finished. 'Have you ever found a body in a bog?'

For just a moment, Daniel's gaze flickered. 'Not personally.'

'But don't people drown in bogs? Like, on Dartmoor there's all these stories. Like that bloke who went missing and they only found his top hat . . .'

'Olly, I think you have enough material for your project now,' Elizabeth interrupted, 'and you've certainly taken enough of Daniel's time.'

'My pleasure,' Daniel assured her. He and Olly fist-bumped and I felt a silly tug of fondness in my heart. It's always good when people you love get on together.

I dropped Daniel off at Exeter airport late that afternoon for his flight back to Inishowen. I'd rearranged all my clients so I could take the day off. He'd been to the police station in the morning to go over his statement for a final time. Then after we'd grabbed some lunch, we had to set off for the airport.

'It's that time again,' he said as we stood together in the concourse.

I wrapped my arms around him and hugged him hard. 'We always seem to be saying goodbye.' It could be weeks before I saw him again.

He drew back to look at me, taking my face between his hands and staring into my eyes. 'You will keep out of this police business, won't you, Miss B?' he asked, frowning.

'Of course.'

'I wish I could take you with me to Ireland.'

'I'm not so sure I'd like those peatbogs. I didn't realise they could move about.'

'It doesn't happen often. And,' he went on, narrowing his eyes in mock suspicion, 'if you were in Inishowen, I could keep an eye on you.'

'I don't need keeping an eye on,' I said indignantly. 'There's nothing I can do.' And until they either identified the man in the boot or found Amber, there was nothing the police could do either.

'Hmm,' he muttered doubtfully, then kissed me. 'Just be careful,' he whispered. 'Keep safe.'

'You too,' I whispered, pressing my lips against his warm neck. Then he picked up his bag and strode off towards the departure lounge, turning to smile at me lovingly before he disappeared through its doors and was lost to sight.

A wave of longing swept through me and a big sigh escaped my chest. For a moment I waited, foolishly hoping I might catch another glimpse of him. Then I turned away. Now, I thought, with a twinge of guilt as I headed towards the exit, now I can get started.

I picked up the phone in answer to Ricky's call. 'I don't know anything,' I told him before he could ask.

He plunged on as if I hadn't spoken. 'It said on the TV the body had been found in the boot of a car on Halsanger Common. It was Daniel's car, wasn't it?'

'It was,' I acknowledged. 'And no, the body wasn't in it when I bought it.'

'You said the same thing when we found that bloke in the wardrobe.'

'Thank you, I don't need reminding.' It had been a particularly unpleasant experience.

'It's getting to be a habit.'

'It wasn't me who found the body in the car. It was Daniel.'

'Poor bugger.'

I wasn't sure if he meant Daniel or the man in the boot. 'Was there something you wanted?' I demanded tartly. 'Because if there isn't, I am putting the phone down.'

'Hold your horses, Princess! The police say they don't know who he is.'

'They don't. Or if they do, they're not telling anyone.'

'You want to get onto your friend Collins,' he recommended. 'Get him to give you all the low-down.'

'I intend to.'

'Good, then you can tell us.'

'Tell her to come to supper tomorrow night,' Morris's voice called from somewhere in the background.

I knew I should resist the invitation, but Morris is a wonderful cook. 'Well, thank you, that will be lovely. But I can't promise I'll know any more then than I know now.'

Ricky chuckled down the phone. 'Don't be silly, Princess. Course you will.'

I lay in bed, missing the warmth of Daniel's body and worrying about Amber. 'It doesn't make sense,' I told Bill, who had curled up in the crook of my knees. 'If you'd just murdered someone, you wouldn't go off and enjoy yourself at a steampunk festival, would you?' I supposed you might if you were a psychopath and just didn't care, or perhaps if you felt safer hiding in a crowd. But why leave the body in the car? Why not throw it into a peatbog? There were enough of them up on Dartmoor. But then, unless you had an off-road vehicle, driving there would not be an option. Neither would carrying the body. Even two people working together would struggle to lug a dead weight across open moorland, even on a stretcher. I came back to my original opinion. Amber could not have known about the dead man in the boot. Someone must have put him in there without her knowledge.

I knew I should have dragged Daniel up to Bristol. I'd looked up the steampunk festival on the internet when I got home from the airport. We could have enjoyed a *Corsets and Top Hat Dinner with Music, Magic and a Mystery Cabaret*. He'd look good in Victorian gear. It would go with that antiquated English professor air he adopts so much. I suspect he's been born in the wrong century. But I sometimes think the same thing about myself. I wouldn't look bad in a corset either. But steampunk wasn't just about fashion, I'd found out, or literature. Steampunk followers stood for sustainability and against the throw-away society. Good for them, I thought lazily as I drifted off to sleep.

I dreamt of the man in the boot of the car. I saw his receding dark hair, his pale, plain face, his eyes wide open. Only, in my dream, he wasn't in the boot of the car – he was sinking slowly into a peatbog, one arm raised above his head in defiance, or desperation. I watched the black ooze fill his mouth and nostrils as he sank, his dead, expressionless eyes. Then the top of his head disappeared beneath the surface. His upraised arm with its tattoo of a dagger encircled by leaves was the last thing to sink, his dead fingers stiff, frozen in a wave of farewell.

CHAPTER SEVEN

'How's your mum?'

I turned to stare at Maisie in surprise. 'Sorry?'

'Your mum. I haven't seen her for a week or two. How's she doing?'

Maisie, about to celebrate birthday number ninety-eight, was my most elderly client and one of the most long-standing. For a moment, on my knees in her tiny kitchen, unloading her washing machine while she sat watching me from her armchair, I was tempted to say *she's fine*. But Maisie knew I was an orphan. 'I haven't got a mum. She died when I was three, remember?'

'Did she? You poor little bugger.' She was smiling at me, the sunlight streaming through the kitchen window lighting her ridiculous apricot curls. A wig plonked on the grinning head of a skeleton would have looked as convincing. 'What did she die of, then? Cancer, was it?'

Drugs, she'd died from taking drugs, I could have told her, drawing her last agonised breath in a damp subway with graffiti-scribbled walls, while I screamed my head off next to her, a tiny prisoner strapped in my

buggy. 'She died of a heart attack.' This was almost true –
a heart attack induced by whatever toxic substance her
stash had been cut with. She was twenty-three.

'What about your dad?'

Unknown. 'I don't have one of those either, Maisie.
Just my Uncle Brian. Remember?'

'Oh yeah!' Maisie nodded her head as if the light
was gradually dawning. 'He works abroad, don't he?
Got some posh job.'

Uncle Brian, my only surviving relative, was really
a cousin. He had rescued me from the clutches of the
social services after my mother died, and had sent me
to boarding school. 'He's a diplomat. He's in Paris at
the moment.'

Maisie held up a knotty finger. 'And there was some
woman, fortune-teller or something.'

'That's right. My cousin, Cordelia.' I'd spent my
school holidays with her, a few miles away in Totnes.
She'd been an astrologer and had owned a New Age
shop. She'd been like a mother to me. And like my
mother, she was dead now too.

Jacko came waddling across the kitchen to stick
his bristly terrier snout in the basket of wet washing.
I shoved his head aside. 'There's nothing in there for
you,' I told him as I stood up, hefting the basket on
my hip. I decided it was time to steer Maisie's thoughts
away from my uncertain heritage. 'Are you looking
forward to your birthday party?'

She didn't answer at first, just frowned. 'Why
weren't you here yesterday?'

'I took the day off. Daniel was here.'

'Oh, I see.' She sniffed disparagingly. 'If he's here, I don't get a look in!'

I laughed. 'Oh, come on, Maisie!' I was paid to visit her three times every week. In fact, I usually popped in more often, just to check on her welfare, although agency carers came in to look after her every morning and evening. We all reported to Our Janet, Maisie's daughter who lived up north. I'd also asked Maisie's neighbour, Bev, to pop in yesterday and to walk the horrible Jacko.

'Who is he, anyway?' she demanded.

'Daniel? He's my boyfriend.'

She scowled. 'Have I met him?'

'No.'

She tapped her gnarled finger on the arm of her chair. 'Well, you bring him here! I want to get a good look at him.'

'Next time he's here,' I said, biting back a smile. 'He's gone back to Ireland.'

'Ireland!' she repeated, scandalised. 'What's he doing over there? He's not Catholic, is he?'

'Do you know, Maisie, I've never asked him.' For a variety of reasons, my relationship with Daniel has been sporadic and full of gaps, not to mention misunderstandings. I didn't like him when I first met him. I thought he was weird. I even thought he might be a murderer.

I'd only discovered yesterday that he played the piano. After his interview with Olly, the two of them had disappeared into the living room so Olly could show off the bassoon piece he was trying to master, when a sudden burst of Scott Joplin brought Elizabeth and me hurrying into the room. Daniel had looked up from the keyboard with a grin. 'I'm a bit out of practice,' he told us, his long fingers moving over the keys. Which made me realise there was much about the man I loved I had yet to discover. 'I'm going to hang this washing out now,' I told Maisie, and headed for the garden door.

'Yeh, get on with it,' she tutted. 'I'm gasping for a cup of tea.'

In the garden, pegging out Maisie's nighties, knickers, pillowcases and tea-towels, I pondered whether her lapses of memory were anything more serious than extreme old age. Forgetful one minute, she was sharp as a tack the next. I decided not to mention it to Our Janet next time she phoned, not to make an issue of it. But it was one more thing I needed to be aware of.

I made her tea and, armed with her shopping list and Jacko on the lead, made ready to go into town – making sure before I left that she was wearing her pendant alarm. We'd had a lot of argument over this in the past. She held it up for me to see, as proudly if it were an Olympic medal. I gave her the thumbs up. 'I shan't be long.'

'Take your time,' she called back graciously. Then added, 'Your dad's alright, is he?'

There was still no sign of Amber Horrell. I phoned Dean Collins on Tuesday evening. It had been a full-on day, filling in any gaps in my schedule with some of the clients I hadn't seen on Monday. I hadn't made it back to *Old Nick's* until closing time, when I'd dashed in to check the takings. By this time, I was hot and sweaty and looking forward to a shower, followed by supper cooked by Ricky and Morris.

'No, she has not come back yet,' Dean informed me. 'She was supposed to be back at *Horrell's Antiques* this morning but failed to show up. Peter Horrell says it's typical of her to take off without a word and turn up again when she feels like it. He described her as selfish and irresponsible.' He chuckled down the phone. 'I don't think they get on.'

'But isn't he worried? Doesn't he realise something terrible could have happened to her?' I couldn't understand his attitude. I'd only met Amber once, and it seemed I was far more worried about her than he was. I was afraid she might be lying in a ditch somewhere.

'I asked him if he'd seen the report about the man found murdered in the boot of a car on TV. When I told him the car was a dark grey Bora, he caught on, turned as white as a sheet. He's promised to contact us the moment Amber turns up, or if she communicates with him in the meantime.'

'So, what happens now?'

'We redouble our efforts to find her.'

'What's that supposed to mean?' It sounded like police-speak to me. I didn't think they were taking her disappearance seriously enough either.

'It means we get a warrant to force her bank to give us her details. That way, we can track her through her credit cards. If she's paid by card or used an ATM machine anywhere in the last three days, we'll find out. And we'll be publishing her photograph in the media, asking her to get in touch.'

'Well, that's something, I suppose,' I conceded grudgingly.

'We have made a bit of progress on the identification of the dead man,' he went on. 'After the TV appeal, someone phoned the station to say they recognised the tattoo. The commando knife in a laurel wreath is a symbol of the South African Special Forces.'

'Really?'

'Of course, his time in South Africa might be ancient history. But it gives us another lead to go on.'

'Any idea how long he'd been dead when Daniel found him?' I asked.

'Pathologist reckons about thirty-six hours.'

Well, at least that let Daniel out as a suspect. He'd only been in the country twelve hours when he found the body. 'And do you know how he died?'

There was a pause at the end of the line. 'You didn't get this from me, right?' Dean lowered his voice, although I doubt if the two infant daughters I could hear fighting in the background were interested.

''Course not.'

'He was run through.'

I wasn't sure I'd heard him right. 'Sorry?'

'Single stab through the body with a long blade like a rapier.'

'You mean a *sword*?' I asked, incredulous. 'Had he been in a duel?'

'Got him through the heart. Death would have been instantaneous.'

I whistled softly. 'Doesn't it take a fair amount of force to thrust a sword through a body?'

He grunted. 'Not if the blade is sharp enough. The trouble is, if you stab someone with a sword, or any long blade, you don't have to get up close and personal like you do if you use a knife. There's not as much contact with the victim. Doesn't help when you're looking for evidence.' He sounded despondent. 'That's the problem with our mystery friend. Very little evidence on the body and nothing we can match. Anyway,' he went on, 'the boss has called forensics in at Langworthy Hall now. Looking for blood this time and a murder weapon.'

'And if you find either, what does that mean for Amber?'

'It means she'll have a lot more questions to answer when she gets home.'

'Unless it's her blood, of course.'

A sudden shrill scream in the background cut off whatever answer Dean was about to give. 'Oh, bloody hell!' he muttered. 'Alice!' he called out to the elder of his two girls. 'Put that down!' Little Hannah was well away in the crying department by now, so I gathered that whatever *that* was, my god-daughter had whacked her younger sister with it. I had to stifle an impulse to feel proud. 'I'll have to go, Juno,' he sighed.

'Poor Daddy,' I purred sweetly, and he put the phone down.

CHAPTER EIGHT

In the old days, Maisie will tell you, trains used to stop at Ashburton. Cattle sold at market in the centre of town were herded straight down St Lawrence Lane, past the chapel and *The Railway Inn*, on to the waiting cattle wagons. Not anymore. The stationmaster's house and the station buildings are still there, the engine shed now a café. The old line is a muddy track through the trees where people walk their dogs. It runs straight for about half a mile or so until it stops abruptly, hits invisible buffers at the edge of town, the rest of the line buried beneath the tarmac of the A38. Trains can never run there again; the railway cannot be restored. The old route is lost and *The Railway Inn*, now named *The Silent Whistle*, mourns its passing.

I take Jacko there sometimes, just for a change. And it's walking there I've noticed a lovely but deadly invasion – pale pink blossoms among the greens and browns, the spreading of Himalayan balsam. Over the last few summers, the first delicate plants have turned into a great drift, a field of pink, spreading through the nettles between the old railway and the stream. Their profusion is a bad sign. The plants are not poisonous, but they are highly invasive. Each one can grow to over six feet high and when its seedpods ripen they explode, sending seeds with the force of a missile up to twenty feet away, spreading down paths and animal tracks and along riverbanks where they fall in the water and float downstream. Bees are so intoxicated by their perfume they forsake our native plants, leaving them unpollinated. If Himalayan balsam gets a hold, it will crowd out our plants and flowers, destroying the delicate ecosystem. This is why wherever it is found, it has to be eradicated. Like the purple rhododendrons that have escaped from private gardens onto the moor, we owe its presence to those pioneering botanists who travelled the Empire, bringing home the flowers they found enchanting when they discovered them in their native habitat. Which just goes to show how beautiful things can turn out to be deadly. Something I should have been wise to remember, as it happened.

Showered and refreshed, my hair still damp and smelling of coconut conditioner, I drove Van Blanc up the hill towards Druid Lodge, the lovely Georgian house belonging to Ricky and Morris, and the base of operations for their theatrical costume hire business. I arrived to be greeted by supper served on the terrace, the table set beneath the dappled shade of the pergola overlooking the garden. There was a summer vegetable tart with a watercress salad and minted new potatoes, accompanied by a crisp white Burgundy and followed by raspberries and cream. Conversation, Morris insisted, would be limited to trivialities while we ate. Which meant we weren't allowed to discuss murder. Then the cheese board came out.

'So, what's new, Princess?' Ricky asked as he loaded crumbly white Stilton onto a cracker. 'Have you found out anything?'

'Not a lot,' I admitted. 'It seems the murdered man may have come from South Africa. The tattoo on his arm is from the South African Special Forces, although this was probably done years ago.' I paused over the cheese board, hesitating between Sharpham Rustic or a small round cheese wrapped in shredded flower petals that looked too pretty to break into.

'And how was he murdered?' Ricky asked, munching. 'Do we know?'

'According to Dean . . . no, *not* according to Dean,' I corrected myself. 'He's not told me anything, obviously.'

'Obviously,' Morris repeated, blinking. Ricky, still munching, just mumbled.

'He was run through with a sword,' I went on. 'A single stab wound probably from a rapier.'

Ricky nodded sagely. 'A rapier would be right. It's a thrusting weapon. Whereas a sabre is more for slicing and slashing.' He'd done a lot of stage fighting in his younger days.

Morris suppressed a shudder. 'You are going to try some of this, aren't you, Juno love?' he asked, pointing to the floral-wrapped cheese. 'I bought it for you.'

'Well, if you insist.' I sliced through the petals into its creamy centre. 'The police are searching for the murder weapon.'

'And what about Amber? Have they talked to her yet?'

I shook my head. 'She hasn't come back and they haven't found her.'

'I hope she's alright.'

'So do I.'

Morris began to pour coffee from a cafetière. 'A very talented young lady.'

'You know her?' I asked, surprised.

'Do you remember the day she came here?' he asked Ricky.

'She brought a load of costume designs with her,' he answered, reaching for more cheese. 'She wanted us to work with her, make her designs up.'

'What happened?'

'We were making costumes for a touring production of some Dickens thing . . .'

'*A Tale of Two Cities*,' Morris reminded him.

'That's it. Cast of thousands.'

'We'd have been very happy to work with her,' Morris went on, 'she had lovely designs.'

Ricky chuckled. 'But we were up to our eyes in it. We told her we couldn't start work for several weeks. She expected us to drop everything and start straight away.'

'But we couldn't,' Morris added sadly. 'So, she went elsewhere.'

'She had some designs at Langworthy Hall,' I remembered, 'but I didn't really get a chance to look at them properly. What were these costumes for?'

'Oh, they weren't really theatrical costumes,' Morris said as he passed me a coffee. 'They were um, what d'you call it?'

'Steampunk?' I suggested.

'That's it!' he said, nodding. 'Steampunk. She wanted to start her own company.'

Ricky grinned. 'She was having a go about her dad, d'you remember? 'Cos he wouldn't put any of the firm's money into her business.'

'Do you know anything about the Horrells?' I asked. 'The family, I mean.'

Morris shook his head. 'Not really.'

'Amber says her mother ran off with her yoga instructor when she was fourteen.'

Ricky produced his cigarettes from his pocket and pressed one between his lips. He lit up and leant back thoughtfully, his eyes narrowed against the smoke, one long leg crossed over the other knee. 'There was something about a boy,' he said after a moment.

'That's right, there was,' Morris agreed. 'Amber had a brother. There was some tragedy at his school. Oh, this was years ago now.' He frowned, struggling to remember.

'He went to one of those posh fee-paying schools,' Ricky grinned, 'a bit like you, Princess.' My expensive education always seemed to amuse him. I poked my tongue out. 'Wiltshire or Somerset somewhere,' he added. 'There was an incident.'

I began to suspect a skeleton in the Horrells' armoire. 'What kind of incident?'

'There was a lot about it in the news at the time,' Morris remembered. 'A boy was killed.'

'That's right.' Ricky exhaled smoke as he nodded. 'There was a stabbing. The school tried to hush it up, pretended it was an accident. And because the killer was a minor, his name was never released. He was sent away to some sort of institution, locked up.'

'And was it Amber's brother who was killed?' I asked, horrified.

'Oh no.' Morris laid a conspiratorial hand on my arm. 'It was the Horrell boy who was believed to be the killer. Well, that was the rumour.'

'Why did people think it was him?'

'Because he was known to have *problems*.' Ricky laid a heavy emphasis on the last word. 'And he was never seen again afterwards. Julian claimed the boy had gone to live with his mother.'

'But the rumours still went on.' Morris shook his head. 'I wish I could remember the boy's name.'

'Oh, bloody hell, *Maurice*,' Ricky moaned, flicking ash into a flowerbed. 'I was relying on you to remember.'

I laughed, but their joint memory lapse was frustrating. I hoped they weren't going to get like Maisie. They weren't that ancient for a start.

'Well, I'm not sure that it was ever made public.' Morris pushed his gold-rimmed specs up the bridge of his nose. 'I tell you who might know more about it,' he added, 'your friends who run the antique shop.'

'Which antique shop?' I asked. Ashburton probably has more shops dealing in antiques than any town of its size in England.

'The one in St Lawrence Lane.'

'You mean *Keepsakes*. Ron and Sheila.'

'They're the ones. If I remember rightly, they were living in Buckfastleigh at around the time this was all happening. In fact, I believe they had a shop there. They'll know more about it. You should talk to them.'

'Oh, I will.' I drank more wine and watched the sinking sun melt like butter into the clouds. The light began to grow dim, a bat swooping across the lawn on its evening hunt for moths. I most certainly will, I thought.

The little town of Ashburton, which in its old commercial heart is just a rough cross of four streets, contains one butcher, one greengrocer, one baker, two pubs and twelve antique shops, not counting mine. Some of these rival *Horrell's* in the high value of their sale items and the loveliness of their displays. Some are more designer-orientated: a single piece of furniture, carefully distressed, or an ancient garden bench speckled with rust will be the sole attraction in their window. Others are Aladdin's caves, where genuine treasures can be discovered if you don't mind rooting among a glorious hotchpotch of tat. And some are, like mine, mostly cluttered with junk. Occasionally I get my clutches on valuable items, but most of my decent stock lately has come from my friend, Lady Margaret Westershall, who is allowing me to gradually clear out the unwanted contents of her loft.

At the lovelier and more expensive end of this range of antiques businesses is the gallery belonging to Reuben Lenkiewicz. Son of famous artist Robert Lenkiewicz, he has recently opened a gallery celebrating his father's work. As well as his dad's paintings, he sells fine portraiture, antiques and jewellery. Frankly, his place makes even *Horrell's* look shabby.

I passed his gallery the next morning, on my way to Ron and Sheila's. Reuben was arranging rings in his window, something he had to do at the start of every day, as they were too valuable to be left on display at night and had to be returned to the safe. He gave me a brief wave. 'Morning, Juno.'

'Isn't it a nuisance?' I asked, stopping. 'Having to put all this stuff out every morning?

'It is. But it's more of a nuisance being the victim of a nocturnal smash-and-grab raid.'

He had a point. I pointed lustfully to a large emerald, surrounded by diamonds. 'That one's lovely.' I suspected the entire stock of my shop wouldn't buy it. I smiled at Reuben and moved on.

Keepsakes, the shop owned by Ron and Sheila, falls into the glorious hotchpotch category. Getting into it is quite a dangerous endeavour for someone as tall as I am. For a start, they pile so much junk out on the pavement that it's difficult for anyone to squeeze their way through the shop door. I had to negotiate an iron plant stand complete with aspidistra and a precarious stack of brass trays. They were great round things, originally the tops of tables, and I was terrified that if I nudged them, they'd go rolling off down St Lawrence Lane like wagon wheels and I'd have to go running after them.

Once inside, there were further hazards from all the stuff hanging from the ceiling. I have tangled my hair in a chandelier and brained myself on pots and pans before. As a result, I have developed a special posture for going into Ron and Sheila's: knees bent, head lowered and shoulders hunched, until I find a spot where it's safe to straighten up.

'Alright there, Juno?' Sheila asked, watching me come in. 'Have you hurt your neck?'

'No, that's what I'm trying not to do.' Seeing that the space above my head was hazard-free, I relaxed my shoulders, although I found myself dangerously near the snarling snout of a stuffed boar.

'I've told Ron, don't buy any more taxidermy,' Sheila said firmly.

'Do you sell much of it?'

She folded her arms. 'Now and again. But these boars' heads are ten a penny. They come from the EU, most of them, from all the hunting they do at weekends in Germany and France.'

'They're not old, then?'

'Not very, no. Anyway, how's your shop doing?'

'Up and down,' I admitted. 'Mostly down. We have the odd good day. I just wish I could get those two upstairs rooms rented out. You'd think someone would want them.' The rooms had used to be *Old Nick's* sitting room and bedroom before I'd emptied and redecorated them. So far, I'd rented one room out to a silk-painter, whom I'd almost managed to get murdered, and who had removed herself to her own gallery in North Street; and another to a bookbinder who turned out to be a criminal and had removed himself to the Dominican Republic. As far as I know, he's still there.

'Why don't you take them over yourself?' Sheila suggested. 'Extend your antiques empire. You've let

Sophie and Pat have the best spaces at the front of the shop and stuck yourself in that back room.'

'I have thought about it.' But extending my antiques empire into Nick's old rooms would mean buying a lot more stock, and I struggled to keep the back room filled as it was.

Sheila perched half of her rather ample backside onto the corner of a dressing table. 'So, what are you after?'

I thought I might as well come straight out with it. 'I hear you used to have a shop in Buckfastleigh. I wondered how well you knew the Horrells.'

So far, Amber's name had yet to appear on the evening news, so Sheila's face showed only mild interest. 'Oh, yes? We never had much to do with them, business-wise. For one thing, we always reckoned Julian and Peter were a bit dodgy.'

'In what way?' I asked.

'Well.' Sheila looked slightly uncomfortable. 'Let's just say they weren't very thorough in checking out where things came from.'

'You're talking about stolen goods?'

She shrugged in a way that didn't confirm it, or deny it either. 'Matter of fact,' she went on, 'rumour had it they used to do business in your shop back in the old days, you know, with Old Nick.'

'Did they indeed?' Old Nick had been well known for his back-door trading, and had even served time for it. Ultimately, it was what had got him killed. And the Horrells had done business with him? Interesting.

'I'll tell you who did have business with them,' she

went on, 'Reuben Lenkiewicz. He can tell you about their dirty dealings.'

'Reuben?' Drat, I'd only just been talking to him.

'And I don't want to speak ill of the dead,' Sheila continued, obviously about to do just that, 'but we never liked Julian. He was a terrible snob. Anita Horrell was a lovely woman. I got to know her quite well. I'm not surprised she left him. She was much too nice for that family.'

'Ran off with her yoga instructor, according to her daughter.'

Sheila looked uncertain. 'Ooh, I couldn't say about that, I'm sure.'

'But she didn't take her children with her?'

She nodded sadly. 'Julian fought Anita for custody and of course, once she'd left him, she didn't have his kind of money to keep going through the courts.' She hesitated. 'And that girl Amber was running wild. I think Anita thought she would be better off if she stayed with her father. She told me Julian had ruined her, spoiling her the way he did.'

'Wasn't there also a son?'

'Oh, him!' Sheila's hand fluttered nervously to the base of her throat. 'The less said about him, the better.'

No, don't stop at the interesting bit, I begged inwardly. 'What was his name?'

She frowned. 'Now, what was it?'

'Tristan,' boomed a voice from somewhere, and it was only then that I realised Ron was in the shop, well hidden. I peered around the corner of an oak hallstand and found him sitting on an overstuffed sofa, painstakingly polishing the lid of a wooden cigar box with yellow beeswax. I could smell it from where I stood. I waved my fingers at him; he nodded and carried on polishing.

'That's right,' Sheila confirmed. 'Tristan.'

'I heard he was in some trouble at school.'

'He was accused of killing another boy,' she confided, lowering her voice. 'Because he was a minor, he wasn't named, but everyone in Buckfastleigh knew it was him.'

'If he was never named, why was everyone so sure it was Tristan?'

'He had mental health problems, you see, everyone knew that. But he was a junior champion. He represented his school. Everyone thought in a couple more years he'd be heading for the Olympics.'

'Doing what?' I asked.

'Fencing,' she said. 'He was a fencing champion.' She lowered her voice. 'And this other boy, he was killed with a sword.'

I thought I'd better pass this information on to the police. I tried Dean's phone but he wasn't taking calls, so I dropped in at the police station. He was out and so was Inspector Ford. I should have kept my mouth shut, but I told the desk sergeant I had information and he passed me on to the one person I was hoping to avoid: Cruella.

'All this is pure speculation,' she told me after listening to what I had to say, her little foot tapping impatiently under the desk all the while I was speaking. If my information about Tristan Horrell was of any importance, she seemed determined to hide it well.

'It's pure gossip, if you don't want to put too fine a point on it,' I admitted honestly. 'But I thought I should tell you what I'd learnt. The coincidence is interesting at least,' I went on, 'with the sword.'

'Thank you for being such a model of good citizenship.' She paused, staring at me from those strange violet eyes, an implicit *you may go* hanging in the air between us. But I wasn't ready to leave. Dean and I have an understanding. Any information is on a strictly *quid pro quo* basis, and has been since I saved his life a while ago. At least, that's the way he thinks of it. To be honest, I was trying to save us both.

Unfortunately, no such understanding existed between me and Cruella. 'Thank you, Miss Browne, that's all.' She had obviously decided I was too thick to realise my exit was required.

I sat back in my seat as if it were a comfy armchair, and had the satisfaction of seeing her little mouth twist in annoyance. 'So will you start looking for Tristan?' I asked.

'*If* Tristan Horrell was responsible for the death of his school friend, and *if* he has been released from whatever institution he was sent to – and it is an *if* at the moment,' she went on with the strained patience of a teacher explaining something to a backward pupil, 'he will almost certainly have been given a new identity by now.'

'But the police can still find him?'

She puffed out her breath like a little dragon, reluctant to tell me more. But unless she tried to throw me out physically, she could see I wasn't going anywhere.

'Accessing his records would not be without difficulty,' she explained. 'It may involve a court order, an application to Public Protection . . .'

'But that's a formality, surely,' I objected, 'if we're talking about murder.'

'You know I can't discuss this with you.' She stood up, her impatience fizzing like a lit fuse. 'Now, you really must excuse me.' She strode to the door and held it open. 'Thank you for coming in,' she said stiffly.

I stood up slowly and sauntered to the door. 'My pleasure,' I told her as I passed, hiding my frustration with a sunny smile. 'My pleasure.'

'So, what's up, Soph?' I asked, when I got back to the shop. Pat had just gone home to Honeysuckle Farm and we were alone in the shop. She had been working on a painting when I arrived back at *Old Nick's*, and she'd been too quiet for too long. In fact, she'd not been herself since she'd returned, unexpectedly early, from her last trip to Cardiff. I watched her now, her red-framed spectacles halfway down her tiny nose, her long dark lashes downcast, her hand making tiny strokes on the paper with a very fine brush. Sophie cannot help but project her feelings. Gloom hung over her bowed head like a cloud.

'She's been like this all day,' Pat had whispered to me fiercely on her way out. She rolled her eyes heavenward. 'She won't tell me what's the matter. Sorry I can't stay till closing time,' she apologised, 'but we've got three rescue ponies arriving this afternoon.'

'Don't worry about it, Pat. You look after those

ponies.' I would try and deal with whatever was ailing Sophie. I hadn't seen much of her for the last few days.

'Have you had a row with Seth?' I asked.

'Not a row exactly,' she mumbled, her paintbrush pausing.

'Do you want to talk about it?'

She finally looked up and gazed at me, her dark eyes tragic. 'It's Imogen.'

I hadn't heard her name before. 'Who's Imogen?'

'She's one of the PhD students, in the same department as Seth. She's obviously really keen on him, always hanging around. The thing is,' she sighed heavily, 'she's very attractive, you see. I've wondered whether . . . well, whether something might be going on between the two of them when I'm not there.'

Only seeing Seth on weekend visits did leave opportunities for him to have another relationship on the side. But he didn't strike me as the type. I liked Seth. 'Have you asked him about it?'

'He says he went out with Imogen a few times before he met me, but it was never serious.'

'But you think she's still keen?'

'I know she is. She doesn't bother to hide it.' She put down her paintbrush, dripping watery blue paint across her desk like a trail of tears, and took off her specs. 'Last Friday, I'd only just got there when we heard her knocking on Seth's door. It was almost as if she'd been lying in wait for me to arrive. She came in and asked him if he'd seen her necklace. She wears this stupid gold chain all the time,' she explained, 'with the letters of her name hanging off it. She's always fiddling with it. She said she'd lost it, and must have dropped it somewhere. She thought perhaps it might be in his bedroom.'

'His bedroom?'

Sophie nodded. 'There had been some gathering at his place the night before and everyone had thrown their coats down on the bed. Imogen thought she might have dropped it then and not realised it. Seth told her to go and look for it. And after a minute she came out and said she couldn't find it. It wasn't there.' Sophie's dark eyes were huge and shiny with tears. 'Except it *was* there. I found it later, *in* the bed. Well, there's only one way it could have got there, isn't it?'

'What did Seth say?' I asked.

She gave a helpless shrug. 'He denied there was anything going on, said it wasn't in the bed before. He claimed she must have planted it there herself when she pretended to go and look for it, just to make me think there was something going on between them.'

'Don't you believe him?'

She wiped a tear from her cheek. 'I don't know,' she confessed miserably. 'I *want* to, but I'm not sure . . . I mean, Seth's angry with me now because he says I ought to trust him. And I know he's right. But Imogen is blonde and slim, and well, clever. She's sort of sophisticated, and I'm not, and I feel . . .' She began groping in her pocket for a tissue.

Poor Soph. Small and asthmatic, she looked so young for her age that despite being in her late twenties, she still had to produce her ID sometimes in pubs. There was a vulnerability about her that was endearing, and just the kind of weakness a savvy woman like Imogen would home in on. 'Don't be silly!' I told her gently. 'You are beautiful and you are clever.' I pointed at the painting she was working on. 'And amazingly talented.'

'But not like she is . . .'

'No, you're not like she is. She sounds like a conniving bitch to me.'

Sophie just sobbed. 'Did you and Seth quarrel?' I asked, digging in my pocket for a tissue. I found one, crumpled but clean, and held it out to her.

She took it and sniffed miserably. 'I told him to fuck off and then I came home.'

'Didn't he try to stop you?'

She nodded and sobbed a bit more. 'Yes. But I felt like everything was ruined and I just wanted to get away.'

'And since you've been back, hasn't he tried to contact you?'

She shook her head. 'No,' she sniffed. 'I keep hoping he'll phone.'

'I'm sure he will.' It would be sad if she and Seth broke up. I'd introduced them, and their first meeting was the nearest thing to love at first sight I'd seen. Not that it had taken me long to fall in love with Daniel. But it had taken me a lot longer to realise I had.

'But I walked out on him, shouldn't I be the one to apologise?' she asked.

'If you're sure he was telling the truth. Or if you can't be sure nothing happened, Soph, then be sure you think he's worth another chance.'

She stayed silent, miserably biting her lip. 'If you want to know what I think,' I went on after a moment, 'I think you've let this Imogen woman get inside your head, which is exactly what she was hoping you would do.'

'You think Seth was telling the truth?'

'I'd believe him rather than her. And the only reason I think you're not doing so is because you've let yourself believe that this Imogen is better than you, more attractive. Which I'm sure isn't true. If Seth values you as much as he ought to, he'll be in touch.'

'You don't think I should ring him then?'

'I can't say, Soph, it's up to you.' I shrugged. 'Perhaps it wouldn't hurt to let a bit more time go by.'

She gave a decisive nod and managed a tremulous smile. 'I won't ring him tonight then.'

I decided it was time to take refuge in alcohol. 'Let's go for a drink.' Sophie needed cheering up. What worried me was that she might abandon the painting project she was working on. It was Seth's uncle who had commissioned her to illustrate a book about hedgerows he was publishing. She'd been working on the illustrations for over six months now and the project was very near completion. But if she didn't finish, she wouldn't get paid. The shop doorbell announced the late arrival of two customers, looking to find a birthday present. Now wasn't the time to talk.

CHAPTER NINE

I walked the Tribe early on Thursday morning, before it got too hot, taking them along up the riverbank towards Waterleat, through fields thankfully empty of sheep or cattle where it was safe to let them off the lead to race around unhindered. Then I took them back along the lanes to Cuddyford, emerging at the western end of town. After I'd delivered them to their various homes, I visited Buckfastleigh again and *Horrell's Antiques*, in search of Kirsten.

There didn't seem to be any sign of Peter Horrell when I entered the hallway, which I was relieved about, but Kirsten was busy talking to customers. I signalled to her that I needed a word, and she excused herself to come over to me. 'I can't talk to you now,' she whispered, glancing furtively up the stairs in a manner that indicated Peter might be lurking in his flat. 'You know the park by the old bridge? Meet me there at one o'clock.'

I checked my watch. I had an hour and a half to kill. After a coffee and a brownie in the nearest café, I took myself to the local library and browsed my way through the reference section, in the hope of finding information on the Horrell family. I didn't learn much, except that back in the eighteenth century, about the time India had met her unhappy end at the foot of the stairs, they had owned a lordly pile called Gadd House. This must be the place Peter had mentioned. After the house was demolished, the estate had been broken up, with just two or three properties remaining in the family's hands. Langworthy Hall was one, and the house in Buckfastleigh, now the antiques shop, was another.

Another building that had burnt down in suspicious circumstances, and which the library was full of information about, was Holy Trinity Church. Now a ruin, it stands on a hill above Buckfastleigh, reached by a long, steep flight of stone steps which I didn't feel inclined to labour up on such a warm summer morning. But I was sufficiently fascinated by its story to read a newspaper report about the fire, which took place on a July night in 1992. '*The stone walls became so hot in the blaze that the stones burnt red, reducing some of the church's stone shell to flakes.*' Only the outer walls and spire were left standing.

It was one of a spate of fires in Devon churches around the time, and satanists were suspected. Holy Trinity was reported as having been the scene '*of satanic rituals and wanton vandalism*', both before and after the fire.

There was another reason for these suspicions. If you wander around the ruined church's graveyard, you can't fail to notice one monument so large and substantial that at first sight it might be mistaken for a bus shelter or a public convenience. This is the grave of Richard Cabell, said to have been the inspiration for the wicked squire in Conan Doyle's *The Hound of the Baskervilles*. Or one of them. There are more places around this part of Devon claiming to have inspired that story than the poor old hound has teeth.

Anyway, the coffin of wicked Richard Cabell was buried beneath a massive slab of granite and then enclosed behind stout iron bars topped with an overhanging roof, in order, legend has it, to prevent the bastard from getting out. The reason that locals were so fearful of him rising up and walking the night was because he was said to have murdered his wife, and got away with it by making a pact with the Devil. Had Peter Horrell's ancestor made a similar pact, I wondered, and sold his soul to get away with pushing his wife down the stairs?

Remembering India Horrell turned my thoughts in another direction. I asked the librarian for a book on eighteenth-century portraiture and she produced a tome which, while it wasn't restricted to reference only, was far too heavy for me to want to lug home.

The portraits of eighteenth-century ladies of fashion were depressingly similar. All pale-skinned and long-necked, their heads turned at a three-quarters angle towards the artist, it was as if they were painted according to some fashionable template. Sometimes a ringlet of hair was allowed to fall over one shoulder, but despite the glowing satin dresses they wore, which so often slipped from those delicate white shoulders, there was a noticeable absence of jewellery. Their shoulders and low necklines were almost always bare. So perhaps the portrait of India in her necklace was less about rendering her likeness, and more about showing off the priceless jewel she wore, the disappearing red diamond.

A quick glance at my watch showed me that if I wanted to meet Kirsten, I had about five minutes to get to the park – so I slammed the volume shut, thanked the librarian and hurried out.

The old stone bridge, at the spot where the little river Mardle joins the river Dart, leads to a park, and here I found Kirsten, sitting in the leafy shade of some trees, with a plastic lunchbox placed on the bench beside her. I suspected daintily cut sandwiches, but a quick peek into the open box showed she was more of a salad girl. She picked the box up as I sat next to her, and placed it on her lap. I hoped this was to make room for me to sit down, and not because she thought I was going to steal her tomato. Ben, dozing on the ground by her feet, had no interest in salad. Possibly the heat was too much for him, but he just raised his head and thumped his tail lazily as I sat down.

'Any news of Amber?' I asked.

She shook her head. 'The police came into the shop again on Tuesday,' she told me a little breathily. 'They said the car the dead man had been found in was the one that belonged to Amber, before she sold it to you.'

'It was actually bought by my boyfriend. He found the body when he opened the boot.'

'That's awful!' she pronounced, her blue eyes wide.

'But they can't suspect Amber of having anything to do with it, surely?'

'Well, she's disappeared. She hasn't come back when she said she would. Which suggests either something has happened to her . . .'

'Oh no!' She blinked in horror and a sprig of watercress dropped from her little wooden fork.

'Or,' I went on, 'she's hiding from something.'

Kirsten frowned. 'She has gone off before,' she admitted reluctantly, 'not bothered to tell anyone where she was going or when she was coming back. It used to drive Julian mad. And Peter gets furious. But he doesn't get on with Amber, anyway.'

Dean Collins had formed the same impression. 'Why not?'

'Amber's not really into antiques. I mean, she's been brought up in the business and of course she's very knowledgeable. But what she really wants to do is run a clothes business selling the steampunk fashions she designs. She does anyway, in a small way. She buys and sells stuff online and she sometimes has stalls selling clothes at festivals. But she wants to expand, put the firm's money into it, but Julian wouldn't hear of it and Peter won't either.'

'Then you think she really went to this festival?'

She nodded earnestly. 'That's what she told me. She was going to Bristol for the festival, and she was going to be staying with her friend Tasha. She's got a flat in Clifton.'

Clifton was a very expensive district near the famous suspension bridge. It was probably full of girls called

Tasha. 'You see, one of the things that puzzles me,' I went on, 'is why she decided to deliver the car and park it outside Daniel's place, rather than just leaving it for us to pick up at Langworthy Hall.'

'Well, that does sound like Amber.' Kirsten dabbed at her lips delicately with a paper napkin. 'She'd think if she did that, then she had no more responsibility for it. It wouldn't be her fault if it got nicked or something.'

'Well, it wouldn't have been anyway. By then, the car was legally Daniel's. It would have been his tough luck.' I wished someone had stolen it. The thief could have found that body then. Serve him right.

Kirsten wagged her head thoughtfully as she chewed on the wayward watercress. 'Hmm. Even so.'

'So, you've no idea where she is now?'

She turned to gaze at me with anxious eyes. 'I wish I did. I wouldn't normally worry about her staying away, but now, with this murdered man in the car, of course I'm worried. And poor Ben misses her.' She leant down to ruffle his ears. 'I know he does.'

'She wouldn't abandon him, would she?' I watched him half sit up, lazily scratch his flank and flop down again with a sigh. 'Do you always take care of him when Amber goes off?'

She shook her head. 'It used to be her dad who looked after him.'

'Of course.'

We were quiet for a moment. We could hear water splashing and kids screaming in the open-air pool across the park. The local primary school must have been having their swimming lesson.

'When I was with Amber on the Monday evening, there was a phone call from Peter. They seemed to be having an argument about something. I couldn't help overhearing,' I added, not adding that my ears had been on stalks. 'It sounded as if Peter was trying to persuade Amber to sell something.'

Kirsten nodded slowly. 'That would be the cottage.'

'The little cottage in the garden?'

'It's on Amber's land. Her Granny Horrell used to live in it.'

'And Peter wants her to sell it?'

Kirsten looked uncomfortable. 'I'm not sure if I should talk about this, really.' In my experience people usually say this when they're just about to spill the beans. I waited. 'Well, you see,' she went on, turning her face towards me, 'Amber's inheritance is tied up in a trust fund until she's thirty. She was always in trouble when she was younger, and her father decided it would be better if she didn't have access to her money until she could prove she was more responsible.' She bit her lip, looking anxious. 'You won't tell Amber I told you this, will you?'

'Of course not.'

'Thank you. You see, the only money she has is what Peter gives her as a monthly allowance.'

'He's the trustee?'

She nodded. 'Amber always says Peter doesn't give her enough.' She smiled. 'I think he's quite generous actually, but she seems to get through it very quickly. Peter told her he can't do anything about altering the terms of the trust and she'll just have to wait. Amber won't accept that. They're always quarrelling.'

'So why does he want Amber to sell the cottage?'

'Because it's hundreds of years old and it needs an awful lot doing to it. Peter says it's nearly falling down. He says it will cost Amber at least a hundred thousand to get it done up and she can't afford it. She would be better off if she sold it, then she could have the money, eventually. Even in the state it's in, it would fetch a good price. It's a lovely old building and it is in a gorgeous spot, but it needs someone who's prepared to take it on as a project. Peter says he knows someone who wants it, who'd be willing to do the work, a friend of his.'

'But Amber doesn't want to sell?'

'She hates the idea. She's always loved her granny's cottage and can't bear the thought of strangers living in it.'

'I see.' I could understand Amber's feelings. It sounded to me as if she didn't trust Peter. If I'd been in her situation, I didn't think I would trust him either. I couldn't help wondering if he stood to make a profit on the deal.

'You won't tell Amber I told you, will you?' Kirsten repeated, staring at me with huge, fearful eyes. 'Only, she does have a terrible temper and if she thought I was gossiping about her behind her back . . .'

'I won't tell her, I promise.'

'Thank you.' Kirsten snapped the lid on her lunchbox and began to make obvious preparations to return to work.

'Do you know if she ever hears from her brother at all?' I asked, before she could escape.

'You mean *Tristan*?' She shook her head. 'Oh no. I

don't think so! At least, she's never mentioned that she has.'

'Were they close?'

'I don't know really. It all happened long before I came to work at *Horrell's*. Amber told me her brother had been locked up for killing this boy. She said it was an open secret, but because of a court order or something, the papers weren't allowed to report his name.' She shook her head. 'But she's never really talked much about him. And as I said, it was a long time ago.'

'Well, wherever he was sent, I expect he's out by now.'

She turned to give me one of her long, slow blinks. 'You don't think he's *back*?' she breathed in horror.

'I don't know what to think,' I said. But someone had stabbed the man in the boot of the car with a sword, and I couldn't help wondering if that footstep I'd heard above my head in Langworthy Hall, belonging to someone whose presence Amber had been so quick to deny, might have belonged to Tristan Horrell.

On the way home I called in on Maisie. In this hot weather I have to be sure she drinks enough. If she gets dehydrated, she can end up in hospital. The trouble is, she's only interested in cups of tea, of which she only drinks half, and getting her to drink her way through a glass of squash can involve cunning if not subterfuge. I put the glass down on the table next to her, negotiating my way around Jacko who was snoring on the cool lino of her kitchen floor.

'I don't want that,' she told me.

'You need to drink it, all of it.'

She wrinkled up her face in distaste. 'It's orange. I want lemon barley.'

I stifled a groan. She'd preferred orange on Tuesday. 'I'll go and buy you some,' I told her, heading for her kitchen door, 'as soon as I've filled up the birdbath.'

'You did that last time you were here.'

'The water evaporates quickly in this heat. Like you,' I told her, nodding at the glass on the table beside her. 'You'll evaporate if you don't get some of that inside you.'

She gave a dramatic tut as she reached for the glass. I went into the garden and filled up her little stone birdbath from a watering can. I could see her plants could do with a watering as well. But now was not the right time; the sun was too high in the sky, and there was too much risk of scorching the leaves. Early morning or evening would be better.

'I've drunk some,' she told me proudly as I walked back into the kitchen.

I surveyed the level of orange liquid in the glass. 'At least a teaspoonful,' I agreed, and went out to buy her lemon barley and a box of choc-ices for her freezer. I didn't disturb Jacko. The sun was fierce at this time of day and I reckoned the pavements were too hot for doggy paws.

Sophie was alone when I got back to *Old Nick's*, her neat dark head bent studiously over her latest painting. I was glad to see she was still working. She looked up and stretched wearily as I walked in. I stood behind her and massaged her shoulders.

113

Her painting showed a summer hedgerow in almost forensic detail. Laid down centuries ago, it was a tangle of brambles, thorn, hazel and oak, a sanctuary against circling predators and the grab of giant agricultural machines. Wriggling stems of bindweed writhed through nettles and the deserted nests of tiny creatures, their pointed white buds like parasols about to unfurl. In the air above hung lacewings, tiny hoverflies and one solitary brown butterfly. None of it was pretty or picturesque, but all of it looked real.

'It's amazing, Soph,' I breathed.

'It's the last one.' She groaned in ecstasy as I rubbed her shoulders. 'Can you go left a bit?'

I obliged. 'You mean it's the final illustration?'

'Yes. When I've finished this one, I will actually be done with the whole project.'

'That must be a great relief.'

She hesitated a moment. 'The end of a chapter,' she said sadly.

I stopped rubbing, pulled up a chair and sat down opposite her. 'I take it you haven't heard from Seth?' I ventured.

She looked at me then, her little chin raised in defiance. 'If he wants to talk to me, he knows where I am.'

'Good for you!' I took the paintbrush from her grasp and rinsed it out in the pot on her desk. 'Pub or wine bar? The choice is yours.'

She shook her head. 'Thanks Juno, but I can't. I've got a waitressing shift at the Dartmoor Lodge later.'

'Okay. Let's do something tomorrow night. Or Sunday.'

'I can't Sunday.' She gave a tremulous smile. 'I've signed up to go balsam bashing.'

I blinked. 'To do what?'

'There's a group of us going to get rid of that Himalayan balsam down by the Ashburn,' she explained.

'Where the old railway used to go?'

She nodded. 'They've been asking for volunteers and I've signed up for it.'

That was better than moping about all day, hoping Seth would ring. 'Well done, Soph,' I said.

CHAPTER TEN

It turned out my conversation with Cruella at the police station hadn't been wasted after all. She might not have wanted to, but she was duty-bound to pass on any information about the case to her boss, and Inspector Ford, bless him, had got Dean to look into it. He had requested the original police file on Tristan Horrell from the local force near his school in Wiltshire. It seemed that, contrary to what Cruella had told me, following his incarceration he had not been assigned a new identity.

'They don't usually do that with minors,' Dean told me between sips of tea. We were sitting together in *Old Nick's* kitchen where, despite his diet, he was unable to resist the allure of a chocolate Hobnob. 'Just don't tell the wife,' he grinned.

'So that should make him easier to find,' I said.

He shook his head, popping an escaped crumb into his mouth with the tip of his tongue. ''Fraid not. Because as soon as he was legally able, Horrell changed his name himself, by deed poll.'

'But the authorities must know what he changed it to.'

He reached out for a second biscuit. 'Like I said, he changed his name as soon as he could, as soon as he'd finished his sentence. At the time, he was still under licence to his probation officer.'

'Then there is someone who'll know his new name.'

'Yes, there is. And the fact I've requested his original file will certainly have been flagged up to them. But that doesn't mean they're going to hand over the name just for the asking. If they're anything like all the other probation officers I've had experience of,' he went on, brandishing the biscuit, 'they'll make me go through all sorts of malarkey before they decide whether they'll give up his name.'

'But haven't they got to, if it's a murder inquiry?'

Dean gave a twisted smile. 'You'd think that would be enough, wouldn't you? The victim was found in his sister's car, a few miles from his old home, killed in the same manner as Horrell's original victim.' He shrugged his shoulders. 'They'll say it's all circumstantial. It's not proof of his involvement.'

'Well, what do they want,' I demanded, 'more bodies run through with swords? What if he's a homicidal maniac?'

Dean, who had been eating his second biscuit while listening to this, took another sip of tea and reached out for a third. He'd fallen off the biscuit wagon completely. He'd yielded to temptation and now the damage was done. And I was the one who'd tempted him. What a wicked woman I was, I thought smugly.

'The thing is,' he confided, 'Horrell denied he'd killed that boy. See, it didn't happen during the fencing match.'

He sat back in his chair. 'Fencing is a very safe sport, as it happens. I've been looking it up,' he added proudly. 'Apart from one accident at the Russian Olympics when a blade broke, there hasn't been a serious fencing accident in years.' He grinned. 'Do you know the most common injury a fencer is likely to suffer from? Ankle strain from lunging forward. Not what you'd call life-threatening, is it?'

'Then what happened in Tristan Horrell's case?'

'He'd been involved in some kind of inter-school contest. The lad he killed wasn't a schoolmate, he came from a visiting school, a school near here as it happens. Horrell had lost the match on points and made no bones about the fact he wasn't happy about it. Any road, the lad was found dead in the gym two hours later, run through. The safety button of the foil had been snapped off.'

'Tristan's foil?'

'Well, it had no fingerprints on it, but as was pointed out in court, if it had been a premeditated act then he would have worn a fencing glove.'

'How old was he at the time?'

'Fifteen. Seems to me he argued with this lad and had a sudden rush of blood to the head, snapped the button off his foil and . . .' Dean shrugged and sipped more tea.

'But he denied it?'

'He did. And he stuck to that all through the investigation, despite being offered a way out, like it being an accident and he didn't mean to kill. He swore he hadn't seen this lad again once the match was over. But,' Dean wagged a finger, 'he had no alibi. He couldn't account for what he'd been up to for the two hours between the end of the match and the discovery of the boy's body. Claimed he couldn't remember anything. He'd woken up in his dormitory, knowing nothing – the previous two hours were just a blank. Thing is, Tristan was known to have a temper and was also prone to blackouts. He'd been tested for epilepsy but that wasn't the cause. According to the medical reports, his blackouts were psychogenic.'

'Meaning?'

'Caused by extreme stress or anxiety.'

'You might feel a bit anxious if you'd just murdered someone,' I pointed out.

'The psychiatrist at the time said he'd probably blotted out the memory because he couldn't face up to what he'd done,' Dean went on. 'He was sent to a young offenders' institution. Eventually, after a lot of psychotherapy, he admitted he did remember killing the boy. He showed genuine remorse, and after a couple more years, they judged it was safe to let him out, provided he stayed on his medication. But what he calls himself now, or where he's currently living, we've got no way of telling unless his probation officer decides to play ball.'

I frowned. 'Frustrating.'

He gave a grim chuckle. 'Welcome to Devon CID.'

For a moment we were both silent, sipping tea. 'What about the man in the boot,' I asked. 'Any news on him?'

Dean shook his head. 'We've made enquiries at local hotels and the like. He must have been staying somewhere around here. But so far, no joy. We're just hoping he's going to turn up as a misper. And forensics have drawn a blank so far. There is no evidence of any crime having taken place inside Langworthy Hall. He must have been murdered elsewhere. Judging from the pollen the pathologist found in his airways, somewhere in the open air.'

'What kind of pollen?' I asked.

'Himalayan balsam. The pathologist says it usually grows near water.'

'Well, it's growing all over the place this year,' I told him ruefully, 'so that's not really much help, is it?'

'No.' Dean looked dejected. 'We're putting out a national appeal on TV tonight for Amber to get in contact. The friend she was staying with in Bristol, um . . .'

'Tasha,' I supplied.

'Aye, that's it, Tasha,' Dean acknowledged, 'swears Amber left her place on Monday after the steampunk festival was over. She says she didn't tell her where she was going, so she assumed she was heading straight home.'

'But she *was* there over the weekend, in Bristol?'

He nodded. 'At least we know she hadn't come to any harm there. Not before Monday, anyhow.'

'Well, that's something, I suppose.' But it was already Friday, which meant there were four days unaccounted for. Plenty of time for something to have happened to Amber. I couldn't say I felt reassured.

I communicated this feeling of unease to Daniel when I spoke to him on the phone that evening. He greeted me with, 'Oh, there you are, Miss Browne with an e!' as if he'd been the one trying to call me and getting no response, instead of the other way around.

'Yes, here I am. Where have you been for the last four days?'

'Sorry. Work. I got a bit bogged down.'

'Ha! Ha!'

He ignored my sarcastic laughter. 'I've just come back from a walk with Lottie. We're both missing you, Miss B. You should be here with us, cuddling up.'

I had to admire the way in which he'd sidestepped the issue of not attempting to call me and managed to make me feel I was the one choosing to be miles away. But then if he wasn't such a clever bastard, I wouldn't love him so much. 'Bill feels the same,' I countered. This was a feeling of which, judging by the way in which he was sleeping blissfully on the sofa on his back with all four paws in the air, Bill was currently unaware.

'What have you been doing with yourself, Miss B, apart from keeping the dogs and old folk of Ashburton in good order. Sold any antiques?'

'Not many,' I admitted, although I had sold a desk set and inkwell that afternoon, and a pair of silver knife-rests, my most expensive sales for weeks. I told him about Sophie and Seth's break-up and he made the right sympathetic noises. So far, neither of us had mentioned the dead man in the boot of the car. Possibly Daniel was avoiding the subject, but we both knew we'd have to come to it in the end. 'Any news?' he asked at last.

I told him how long the man had been dead, the South African origin of the tattoo, and about Amber's failure to return after the steampunk festival in Bristol, information I'd obtained innocently enough from Dean. Then I made a fatal error. I was telling him that our mystery dead man had been run through with a sword, and mentioned Tristan Horrell. I came out with the words *Kirsten said*.

'Kirsten?' His voice cut sharply through my words. 'You've been talking to Kirsten?'

'Just chatting,' I said, trying to sound nonchalant.

'You've been at it again,' he accused me. 'Sleuthing.'

He made it sound as if I'd been up to something filthy. 'Noooo.' I stretched the vowel like chewing gum.

'I suppose you just happened to bump into her?' he asked sarcastically. 'You promised me, Juno.'

'I just asked her a few questions,' I said evasively. 'It was only about something that happened a long time ago.'

There was a moment's irritated silence. 'Go on, then. Tell me what you found out.' I relayed what I'd learnt about Tristan Horrell and the murder at his school, and what I had found out about him since. Daniel listened in ominous silence. I also told him about the quarrel between Amber and Peter about selling the cottage.

'I suspect the whole family is bonkers,' he said at last. 'Think of that poor woman found dead at the foot of the stairs. They've been murdering each other for generations.'

A slight exaggeration, perhaps. 'We don't know Amber is involved in any of this.'

'I don't care. You stay well away from the Horrells, Miss B. Let the police do their job.' I muttered something that sounded sufficiently like agreement, just to mollify him. 'And when Amber comes back, if she ever comes back,' he carried on, 'stay away from her as well.'

I knew he was upset because I'd broken my promise by asking Kirsten questions, but this sounded dangerously like ordering me about. Something I didn't take to as a rule. Almost as if he'd read my mind, he added, 'Not that my asking you not to do something is going to make any difference.'

It wasn't the asking, I thought to myself, it was the telling. 'Look Daniel, until Amber shows up – one way or another – or the dead man can be identified, there's nothing anyone can do.'

He made a sceptical snorting noise, suggesting he wasn't impressed by my argument.

'It's true,' I assured him.

'Just be careful, my love,' he pleaded in a soft voice, and for the first time I felt guilty.

'I will,' I promised. 'Besides, there's nothing to worry about.'

He laughed sadly. 'Now I *am* worried.'

'I love you,' I told him simply.

'Ditto, Miss B, but don't change the subject.'

'I don't know what you want me to say,' I told him, frustrated. 'I won't take any unnecessary risks, okay?'

'I believe you. But it's the risks you seem to consider necessary that bother me.'

'Oh. For God's sake!' I was tempted to slam the phone down; instead, I took in a deep breath and counted. 'I promise,' I said dutifully.

Our conversation turned lovey-dovey then, and more

than a little indecent, and we ended it in a peaceful warm glow that vanished like mist the moment I put the receiver down. I fumed for a moment and then phoned Sophie. She was just going to bed.

'Can I come balsam bashing with you on Sunday?' I asked.

'Of course you can,' she yawned. 'The more the merrier.'

'Good,' I told her. For some reason I couldn't quite put into words, I felt like bashing something.

CHAPTER ELEVEN

There was a problem with Maisie's birthday cake. For a start, the woman who was making and icing it, and who rang me up, referred to it as 'Mary's cake'.

'I'm a bit concerned about the green,' she told me, speaking in the loud voice of someone who is a more than a little deaf.

'What green?' As far as I was concerned, there was no green on Maisie's cake.

'I don't think it's going to look very good with the raspberry pink,' she informed me.

'Peachy pink,' I insisted. It was Maisie's favourite colour and the shade she dyed her hair.

'Sorry?' she asked loudly. 'Could you say that again?'

I decided the best thing I could do was to go and see her. The original order had been taken over the phone, and this was obviously not the best means of communication where this lady was concerned. Our Janet had phoned it through and given my number, as she always does, as a local contact in case anything went wrong; not imagining that anything could, obviously.

As *Angel Cakes* had their premises in Buckfastleigh,

this would also allow me to pop into *Horrell's* and see if there had been any more news on Amber. She still hadn't turned up and hope of her safe return was fading every day.

I drew up outside a house painted icing-sugar white, with a little angel bearing cake on a notice by the door. I rang the bell, twice, the second time pressing harder and backing it up with knocking. Angela appeared after a few moments, fiddling with a hearing aid making shrill whining noises, and led me into her immaculate kitchen. Here two completed cakes were awaiting collection. One was covered in a grass-green icing and decorated all around its edge with little footballs. Tommy, whose name appeared in large red letters, was represented by the iced figure of a footballer standing in the middle.

The second was a wedding cake, a white masterpiece in three tiers, a delicate veil of lacy icing sweeping down from the top tier to the bottom, ending in a knot of iced roses and lily-of-the-valley, like a wedding bouquet.

'This is astonishing,' I told her, thanking God I didn't have to transport such a fragile item in my van.

Angela blushed a delicate shade of fondant pink as she finally fixed her hearing aid. 'Thank you. I'm quite proud of the veil, took me ages. Now, about this cake for Mary—'

'Maisie,' I corrected.

She drew out the order she had written out from her phone conversation with Our Janet and we went through it together. It was to be peachy pink and cream, not raspberry pink and green, with Maisie's name, not Mary's, and her age iced onto its surface. 'There won't be room for ninety-eight candles,' Angela warned me with a smile. We agreed that she should edge the cake with cream- and peach-coloured flowers, leaving space for a candle-holder between each one.

'She'll be lucky if she can blow out any at her age,' I pointed out.

Angela assured me she'd already received a deposit from Our Janet. We arranged a collection date and I said goodbye, telling her, quite genuinely, that I was looking forward to seeing the result.

From her place, it was only a short walk to *Horrell's Antiques*. Was it because I'd promised Daniel I'd stay away that I felt drawn to the place like a magnet? I had a legitimate excuse to go there. Amber was still missing. Had there been any word of her? I decided it couldn't do any harm to ask.

It was quite busy when I got there, several people mooching among the furniture and fine ceramics. I followed a couple in through the door, managing to avoid signing myself in at the desk. I had no real reason to avoid doing it, but childishly it made me feel I had scored a point over Peter Horrell. There was an auction coming up and there seemed to be a greater quantity of stock than when I had visited the place with Daniel.

One of the new items was a trifold Japanese lacquer screen – although it would doubtless be listed in the auction catalogue as a *byōbu* – showing two dancing cranes and some pine trees on a background of gold. I knew that sixfold screens painted by known artists had sold for hundreds of thousands at auction. This was modest by comparison, but it was still a fine piece of workmanship, and I wondered what it would fetch.

Curious, I went round to survey it from the back. And it was from this position, more or less hidden by the screen in front of me, that I got a view of something I wouldn't otherwise have seen. I was looking at the back of the sales counter. Kirsten was standing behind it, in her pale blouse and dark pencil skirt, her back to me, dealing with a customer. Peter Horrell suddenly slid into the small space beside her, also talking to a customer. What the customers couldn't see, but I could, was what he did with his left hand, which was to place it in the small of Kirsten's back and slide it, slowly and deliberately, to rest on the curve of her backside. A tiny tremor went through her. I realised as she raised her hand towards her face that this was not a shudder, but a stifled giggle. The hand stayed exactly where it was, and went on to give a squeeze.

This amounted to sexual harassment, or at the very least, inappropriate behaviour by an employer towards an employee. Or so I thought. A moment later I changed my mind because Kirsten's free hand, far from attempting to remove his offending one, slid over the top of it, enclosing it with her own and encouraging him to squeeze all the harder.

I froze for a moment and then, under the cover of the customers' chatter, backed out from behind the screen on tiptoe, the dread of banging into it, and sending it crashing to the floor to reveal me lurking there, making me grit my teeth until I'd successfully negotiated the hazard. I slid, unobserved, around the corner into the next room. I couldn't believe what I'd just seen. Could I dismiss it as a physical form of friendly banter between colleagues? Peter Horrell was years older than Kirsten. They couldn't be engaged in a sexual relationship, could they? I decided I'd rather not think about it.

Unfortunately, I had no way of making an exit from the building unobserved. My only way out was to go back into the room I'd just come from, past the customer sales desk, and from there back into the hall. I decided I might as well brazen it out. In any case, I'd come to find if there was any news about Amber and if there was, I wanted to know about it.

I heard the front door shut behind the recent customers and walked back into the room I'd come from. Imagining themselves alone, Peter and Kirsten had progressed from buttock-fondling, their lips locked together in a kiss. Peter's hands were now exploring the curves of Kirsten's blouse. I cleared my throat and they leapt apart as if I'd thrown a bucket of cold water over them; which I would have done if I'd had one to hand.

'Oh, I didn't realise . . .' Kirsten began, a nervous hand fluttering at her throat.

I pretended not to notice. 'Hello,' I said artlessly, looking from one to the other. She had blushed a deep shade of pink while Peter had turned grimly pale. I should think so. Such behaviour. It was barely coffee time. 'I just popped by to see if you'd heard any news of Amber?'

Peter cleared his throat. 'I'm afraid not.'

'You must be desperately worried.'

He shrugged. 'Not really. She'll turn up when she feels like it.'

Whatever might, or might not, be going on between him and Kirsten, I still found it difficult to believe he could be so indifferent to Amber's fate. She could have been murdered by now.

'I'll call you, Juno,' Kirsten said hurriedly, sliding out from behind the counter, 'as soon as we hear anything. I promise.' She grabbed my arm. Her intention was obviously to hurry me out of the building. But just for a moment I lingered. 'Lovely *byōbu*.' I smiled at Peter. 'It's almost as beautiful from the back.'

'You won't say anything, will you?' Kirsten whispered as she bundled me down the hall.

'It's none of my business,' I assured her, 'as long as you're a willing participant.'

'Oh yes, of course,' she responded indignantly. 'I mean, it's nothing like *that*!'

'Does Amber know?' I asked.

Her eyes widened in terror. 'No! Please don't tell her! She'd be furious! She hates Peter and if she thought he and I . . . you won't tell her, will you?'

'Like I said, it's none of my business.'

'Promise?' she implored childishly.

'Promise,' I said. Although as time went by it seemed increasingly unlikely anyone was going to be able to tell poor Amber anything.

My visit to *Horrell's* gave me a lot to think about. I was pondering it all day. Could Kirsten and Peter Horrell really be involved? He was Amber's father's cousin and so much older than Kirsten that he could be her father. The idea made me shudder. But a lot of young women are attracted to older men, especially rich ones. Perhaps Kirsten was one of those. Perhaps she was into father figures. I could understand her not wanting Amber to find out. If she really hated Peter as much as Kirsten said, discovering her trusted friend was conducting a secret and passionate affair with him was not likely to go down well.

The other thing that puzzled me was Peter's apparent indifference to the danger Amber might be in. For a couple more years at least, he had control of all her money. Perhaps he didn't like the idea of losing control. Perhaps he stood to gain from Amber's disappearance. Which led me to a rather nasty thought. Perhaps he, and possibly even Kirsten, were responsible for it.

It can't be considered *sleuthing*, can it, just to find out a few things? Especially if you look them up on the internet and don't actually ask a real person. I needed to know more about the Horrell family. Daniel was right, they were an odd lot. Peter Horrell's attitude towards his cousin's missing daughter was taking on a more sinister implication. A bit of research, I decided, was what was needed.

The historical stuff was easy to find. The story of India Horrell, her priceless dowry and her tragic fall down the stairs was well documented, as was anything that had taken place at Gadd House, including its demolition.

One of the objects that had escaped destruction was the Horrell Chest, an iron-bound box with four locks and four separate keys. It seemed at one time there had been three Horrell brothers who distrusted each other completely, each believing the other two were conspiring to cut him out of his inheritance. Their father didn't trust his offspring either. After a duel between two of them nearly ended in tragedy, the father had the chest made, built of solid oak and strapped and studded in iron. All the family wills, deeds and papers of importance were locked inside and each brother was given a key. It took all four keys to turn the locks, so it couldn't be opened without the father and all three of his sons being present. This way, he hoped, the brothers couldn't do the dirty on one another.

Whether it worked or not, the records didn't say, but this must have been the same chest I had seen at Langworthy Hall, doing duty as a coffee table. It was certainly an indestructible-looking lump of furniture and boasted four locks. Amber had started to tell me it had an interesting history before the footstep from the floor above had brought an end to our conversation.

As I moved forward through the centuries, information about the Horrell family became more scattered and more difficult to find. The four keys had been passed on down the generations. The last time the chest was known to have been opened was at the end of the First World War, when Peter and Julian Horrell's great-grandfather died and his will was read. His key had been inherited by his eldest son, Julian's grandfather, who had two brothers, Richard

132

and Neville, and a sister, Deidre. She hadn't married and had died without issue, leaving her key to Julian. Her younger brother, Neville, went off to fight in the Second World War, taking his key with him. He never returned and the key was lost forever. The chest has never been opened since.

This meant, and I gave myself a headache working this out, that Julian had inherited his grandfather's key as well as his Great-Aunt Deidre's. Then on his death, these would have been bequeathed to Amber. Or to Tristan. Peter would have inherited his grandfather Richard's key, and presumably still had it. Which left Neville's key, now missing. When I'd seen the chest, there had been two keys in the locks. These must have been Amber's two keys. Peter must keep his key in his possession. But it really didn't matter. Even three keys wouldn't open the chest. It was the missing one, the one Neville had taken to war with him, which was important. And that was lost forever. Although if all the chest contained was a few dusty historic documents, that didn't really matter either.

I found little information about the Horrell family from then on. An old issue of a society magazine showed me a wedding photo of a young Julian Horrell with his stunning bride, Anita – she who had later fled the marriage with her yoga instructor. It was from her that Amber had inherited her stunning looks, the same fine bone structure and dark eyes.

She had also inherited Langworthy Hall on Julian's death, while Peter had inherited the Buckfastleigh property from his own father, the place where he now lived and sold antiques. I realised I didn't know whether Peter had ever married or had children. My search on the laptop brought me only a few photographs of him dressed in a dinner jacket at Rotary events. In these photos he seemed to be accompanied by a succession of well-dressed females, all different, and always younger than him.

I got Sophie to take a video of me on my phone, standing welly-deep in water, pulling long stems of Himalayan balsam from the river's edge, roots and all. I folded and crushed the stems in my gloved hands, casting them up onto the bank where they would be taken away in a wheelbarrow. If left on the ground, they would simply re-root.

There were ten of us in the water. We'd started the day with a lecture from Dave, the organiser, on the damage done by these pretty pink assassins to the local flora and fauna and why they had to be rooted out at all costs. We worked for hours, determined to clear our stretch of riverbank. This was a job that would go on every weekend until September, in the hope of eliminating the plants before they set seed. Then it would start again in the spring when any remaining seedlings germinated. A couple of years of balsam bashing, we were assured, would be highly effective in ridding this section of the river Ashburn of the invasive species.

It was fun, working in the dappled sunshine of the wooded bank, with cheerful company and regular breaks for refreshments; but I didn't intend to make this a regular thing, despite the fact I had enjoyed myself. Just for today, I was engaged in a worthwhile, environmentally important task that would certainly win Daniel's approval. More importantly, I wasn't sleuthing, and I had the film to prove it.

CHAPTER TWELVE

As soon as I'd walked the Tribe the next morning, I called in on Maisie. It promised to be another sunny day and I wanted to walk Jacko before it got too hot. I couldn't take him with the other dogs; he was too badly behaved. Anything with four paws or wheels was a target for attack in Jacko's universe. He was only a stubby-legged terrier, but he wasn't put off by the size of anything he deemed a foe, so taking him out into the fields where he might encounter sheep or cattle was unwise. This meant he stayed on the lead all the time, briskly trotting beside me as I did Maisie's shopping in Ashburton. This seemed to satisfy him. Distance was not important; he was only interested in the chance to sniff lamp posts, bark insults at cats, and prove he was boss with any canines whose owners hadn't had the sense to cross the street when they saw him coming.

Before I took him out, I watered the flowers in Maisie's back garden. Her few scrubby roses were beginning to hang their heads after the long spell of dry weather, and her lupins were droopy. I didn't want them to shrivel in the sun. Her ancient lavender bushes, tough as old boots and unaffected by drought, were humming with bees as I splashed the hose about. It was peaceful, Maisie safe inside watching her breakfast TV, Jacko snuffling in the flowerbeds, snorting water from the dripping leaves. Sometime soon, I realised, I would have to mow the lawn. But not today – today there was too much to do already, no time even for a lawn as small as Maisie's.

Her shopping was accomplished with almost no bother, Jacko disgracing himself only once, when I was forced to leave him tied up outside the Co-op. Whilst I was queueing to pay for Maisie's sliced loaf and frozen peas, he almost throttled himself trying to launch an attack on a cyclist who had the effrontery to park his bike outside the wine merchant's. He also growled foul language at the lady selling the *Big Issue*, causing her to sidle nervously further along the kerb. Apart from that, his behaviour was perfect.

Shopping and Jacko safely delivered, I went back to Buckfastleigh at lunchtime, as soon as I had an hour free. I was still keen to wangle more information from Kirsten if I could. The fact that she was having a clandestine relationship with her employer was her own affair, but I reckoned she knew more about Amber than she was saying. She might even be in secret communication with her, assuming of course that Amber was still alive. I thought I might find her in the park during her lunch break, especially as she was still having to walk the spaniel Ben, but she wasn't there, so I went to see if I could catch her at the shop.

I arrived at *Horrell's Antiques* to the sound of voices raised in anger. At least, Peter's voice was raised; Kirsten sounded tearful. I walked in and for a moment neither of them noticed me.

'Didn't you see the bloody thing was missing?' he demanded.

'Well, no,' she whimpered. She pointed at a walking stick hanging on the wall between a regimental sabre and a samurai sword. 'Because whoever took it put that one there in its place.'

'Are you saying that it could have been up there for days?' He was red-faced with anger. There was nothing of the lover about him now.

She sniffed dolefully as he tutted in exasperation. 'It's very similar to the swordstick,' she told him. 'I just didn't notice. I am sorry.'

'Is something the matter?' They both turned to stare at me, aghast at being caught out once again in unprofessional behaviour, a different sort this time.

Peter uttered a curse under his breath. 'Someone has stolen a swordstick,' he muttered.

It's illegal to trade in swordsticks unless they are over a hundred years old. I had no doubt he knew this and his missing swordstick was a genuine antique. The problem was, an antique was just as deadly.

'Edwardian,' he snapped as if he read my mind. 'It was a fine Malacca walking cane with a Toledo blade inside and a silver mount on the handle.' He described it as if he were reading its description on a price ticket. 'We'd priced it at seven hundred pounds. It was mounted on that wall. Whoever took it had some nerve,' he went on grimly. 'They replaced it with an almost identical walking stick so that we wouldn't notice the loss.'

'Then you've no idea when it was taken?'

He glowered at Kirsten, whose eyes were shiny with tears, but she just shook her head and sniffed into a tissue.

'Then you'd better call the police,' I told him.

'They won't do anything,' he scoffed, and made to take the walking stick down from the wall.

'I wouldn't touch it,' I warned him. 'The man found dead in the boot of Amber's car was killed with a long blade and the police haven't found the murder weapon yet. If you're saying that swordstick could have been missing for some time . . .'

Kirsten's eyes widened in horror as the significance of what I was saying sank in. 'Oh my God,' she murmured and began sobbing.

Peter looked shocked. 'Are you saying the swordstick could be the murder weapon?'

'The police haven't found it yet, so it's possible. And whoever took your swordstick and left this walking stick in its place could have left their fingerprints on it.'

He hesitated. Clearly, he didn't want to involve the police.

'I'll phone them if you like,' I offered.

'No, I'll do it,' he growled, resentfully giving in. 'I'll make the call in the office.'

As he strode off into the adjacent room, I looked around at the cameras.

'Perhaps the CCTV will show us something,' I suggested.

Kirsten didn't look convinced and snuffled into her tissue. 'Depends,' she said and blew her nose. 'The trouble is, the cameras automatically record over the footage every seven days, so if the swordstick was taken before then . . .' Her little face crumpled. She was about to burst into tears again. 'You see, that walking stick is so very similar. Same Malacca cane and silver top. I only noticed today it didn't look quite right. It could have been taken weeks ago, to be honest. I've been so busy, you see, too busy to notice.'

'Well, Peter didn't notice it either,' I reminded her, in an attempt to make her feel less responsible. I could hear him complaining loudly on the phone. If the police were about to put in an appearance, it might be just as well if I wasn't found hanging around. I gave Kirsten's arm a sympathetic squeeze. 'Cheer up! It isn't your fault. Why don't we have coffee and a chat sometime this week?' I asked and she nodded.

Peter came back into the room at that moment. 'I'll get out of the way,' I told him. 'I only came in to ask if there'd been any news of Amber.'

'None.' He rapped the word out, impatient for me to be off. He clearly didn't like me any more than I liked him. He followed me as I left, shutting the main door firmly behind me and turning the sign on it to CLOSED. I fetched Van Blanc from the car park and as I drove back past the building a few minutes later, I saw a police car drawing up outside and Cruella climbing out of it. I was glad I'd decided not to linger.

'I'm very impressed with your balsam bashing efforts, Miss B,' Daniel told me later that evening. I'd sent the video to his phone. 'You deserve a medal.'

'Hardly.' I regaled him with the tale of my long day pulling up plants. I didn't tell him about Kirsten's affair with Peter, or my subsequent visit to *Horrell's Antiques* and the missing swordstick. Nor did I divulge that, at the moment, I was waiting for a call back from Dean Collins, having left a message for him to phone me. I yawned theatrically.

'Sounds like you should be heading for bed,' he said.

'I am tired.' I yawned again, wide, like a hippo.

He laughed softly. 'I'd better let you go then. No news on the missing Miss Horrell?'

'No,' I told him truthfully, 'nor on the identity of the dead man.'

'Well, something will turn up,' he said, stifling a yawn of his own, and we wished each other goodnight.

'I don't know much about swordsticks,' Dean admitted when he eventually phoned me back.

'The defensive weapon of choice for gentlemen of fashion for centuries,' I told him. 'Very handy if you are set upon by footpads.' There was a moment of baffled silence. 'Muggers to you,' I added.

'And containing the kind of blade that could have skewered our man in the car?' he asked.

'Undoubtedly.'

He didn't sound impressed. 'So now we're looking for a missing swordstick. Whoever took the one from the Horrells' place did it more than seven days ago. There's nothing on camera.'

'That must be why they replaced it with the walking stick,' I said. 'Playing for time. They knew that if the theft wasn't discovered for seven days, the footage would be recorded over.'

'Not only that, but there was no sign of a break-in, the alarm wasn't set off and nothing else was stolen. All of which points to it having been an inside job. Someone with a key. And apart from Peter Horrell and Kirsten Blake, the only person who had a key, and who knew the combination for the alarm, was Amber. If she wasn't in the frame for this murder before, she is now.'

'Unless she was stealing it for someone else.'

'Like who?'

'Tristan?'

'Bloody Tristan,' he muttered. 'Tell me, what do you think is the most common name in the UK?'

'John Smith?' I suggested.

'Used to be. Now it's David Smith, just beating David Jones. And guess what that little toe-rag Tristan Horrell changed his name to?'

'Er, David Smith?'

'Bang on. And do you know how many David Smiths there are registered in the UK?'

'Lots?'

'Over six thousand.'

'But if the probation service has let you have his name, didn't they give you an address?'

'They did, but once his period of probation had run out, he could live where he liked. Even an official register wouldn't have his previous name. He's managed to ditch his original identity completely. Run all the David Smiths in the country through a computer, you couldn't find Tristan Horrell. And as you can guess, the boss isn't keen on me wasting time trying.'

'Bugger,' I said.

'There is one thing though,' he added, sounding more cheerful. 'We might have a lead on the dead man. A woman got in touch after seeing the news item about him. She rents out holiday cottages.'

'Where?'

'Never you mind. The point is, she let one out to a man who looks like our photofit and had a South African accent. He wanted a long-term let.' He chuckled grimly. 'Fat chance of that around here in the holiday season. The longest she would let him have the place for was a month, and only if he agreed to pay up front. She hadn't seen him for a week and thought he might have hopped it. But when she gets into the cottage, she finds his clothes are still there and there's plenty of food in the fridge. He'd stocked up and it didn't look like he was intending to leave. I'm going there to see her in the morning.'

'Sounds hopeful,' I said. 'Perhaps we'll finally find out who he is.'

'Yeh. Then all we've got to do is find out who killed him and why.' He gave a gargantuan yawn. 'Goodnight, Juno.'

'Goodnight,' I said.

CHAPTER THIRTEEN

Amber Horrell turned up safe and well the following day, driven home by what she described as *all the fuss*, in her interview with Detective Inspector Ford. How I wish I could have been a fly on the wall for that one! As it was, I had to make do with what Dean told me later. She had not, she insisted, been aware the police were trying to find her until the day before, when she started receiving *embarrassing* messages from her friends on social media, telling her she was national news.

She knew nothing about any dead man in the boot of the car she'd sold. How could she? And she'd never heard of Patrick Neil Mulder, which turned out to be the dead man's name. She had never laid eyes on Patrick Neil Mulder. And she didn't know anything about any bloody stolen swordstick either. When asked where she had been since leaving the steampunk festival in Bristol the previous Monday, she replied she had been with a friend. Asked for the friend's name, she refused to give it. She didn't need an alibi, she asserted, because she had done nothing wrong. She grudgingly consented to having her fingerprints taken and giving a sample of her DNA. Although, as Dean admitted glumly, seeing as she'd been driving her father's car around herself for years, even finding her fingerprints in the boot would prove nothing, unless they were found on the dead man and covered in blood.

'What about this Patrick Mulder?' I asked. 'Have you found out anything about him?'

'We found his passport in the pocket of a coat at the cottage he was renting. He was fifty-six and originally a citizen of South Africa. According to the woman who owns it, he didn't chat much, but she seemed to think he'd been in this country for a few weeks. She didn't think he had any family, or at least he didn't mention any. We're contacting the authorities over in Cape Town to see what else we can find.'

'And what happens to Amber now?'

Dean shrugged. 'Depends on what forensics turn up. She's been warned not to leave the area.' He chuckled. 'That went down well.'

I thought that was all the information I was going to get, but then I received a surprise phone call from Amber herself. She wanted to know more about the discovery of the dead man, as the police had told her very little. Did I fancy a drink that evening?

I did, I told her, and I would bring a bottle to Langworthy Hall, as we didn't want her to get into trouble for drink-driving, did we? No, she agreed, we didn't.

As I drove up to the Hall, I passed the turning that would take me up to Halsanger Common and Daniel's place. I felt a stab of guilt. He'd given me a key to the

145

property and I was supposed to be keeping an eye on how the building work was progressing. I'd forgotten all about it. I hadn't given a thought to his rotting staircase. Daniel hadn't mentioned it on the phone, which meant he probably hadn't given a thought to it either. But I must try to get up there during the day sometime so I could have a word with Howard, his project manager, and see how things were going.

Amber was already most of the way through a bottle of Pinot Grigio by the time I arrived. 'It's Ashburton's own Miss Marple,' she told Ben as she swung open the door, and I gave a sour smile. She was leaning her body against it a touch heavily, I thought, as if it was holding her up. Then she added to me, 'Good to see you. Come on in,' and slouched away into the living room.

I followed, Ben padding along beside me. Amber had thrown herself down on the couch. With her cheeks flushed, her eyes glittering with drink, I was struck again by how extraordinarily pretty she was. I noticed a second empty bottle on the iron-bound chest next to the one she was in the process of emptying. She was already way ahead of me in the drinking department. She mussed a hand through her short hair and sighed deeply. 'Tell me something,' she asked, speaking with the deliberate slowness of one who feels slightly tipsy. 'Do you honestly believe I would have driven a car from here to your fella's place at Moorview Farm if I had known there was a dead body in the boot?'

'It doesn't sound likely,' I admitted.

'Well, that's what the police seem to think. I mean,

if I'd killed the man, and then managed to get his body into the boot of a car, I'd drive him somewhere where I could hide him, wouldn't I? I wouldn't just dump him there for anyone to find.'

'Why did you bother, by the way? To deliver the car, I mean.'

She shrugged. 'I felt vaguely guilty about going off to Bristol and not being here for you to collect it when I said I would. Especially as I was going to be away for the whole weekend. I thought it was the least I could do, to be polite.'

'Well, thank you. Shall I?' I asked, indicating the bottle I'd brought with me.

She nodded. 'Please.'

I dealt with the bottle and looked around for a glass for myself.

'Kitchen,' she told me. 'Sorry.'

I fetched a clean glass from the draining board. 'You must have walked back then?'

She squinted as if she was trying to remember some event from long ago.

'When you'd delivered the car,' I prompted.

'Jogged,' she said at last. 'It isn't far.'

'And this was Thursday morning?'

She nodded as she watched me pour. 'So, was it awful?' she asked, after accepting her glass. Her eyes glinted with an odd relish. 'Finding the body? I mean, was there a lot of blood?'

'It wasn't actually me who found it,' I told her.

'Oh?' She looked surprised, almost disappointed.

'It was my fella, Daniel. And I think it was pretty

awful, yes. Although I didn't ask him about the gruesome details.'

'So, who was he? The police didn't tell me much. On the news it said something about a tattoo.'

'It's South African. Mean anything?'

She shook her head. 'All I know is I had that car valeted the morning after we'd struck the deal, and he certainly wasn't in the boot when I collected it.'

'When was that?'

'Oh, I don't know. To be honest, I didn't open the boot again after I'd checked it had been cleaned properly. I mean, why would I?'

'And where was it parked, when the garage brought it back?'

'The police wanted to know that too.' She took a sip of wine and giggled. 'That Sergeant deVille is a cow, isn't she?'

'Cruella?'

Her smile widened. 'That's not her real name?'

'No. Her name is Christine really.'

'Amazing colour eyes though, sort of violet.'

'Yes. Going back to the car . . .'

'Pity about the mouth.' She flapped an arm at me and laughed. 'I brought the car back. I wanted to park my Mini in the drive, so I drove the boring old Bora up the track a bit – it leads to the field.'

'And it stayed there until you drove it to Daniel's place on Thursday?'

'Yes. I told the police. I drive my own car back and forth to work.'

'So, it was left there unattended for two days?'

'It was.' She stared broodingly into her wine glass. 'Bloody cheek, someone dumping their dead body in my car.'

'Daniel's car,' I pointed out. 'And you didn't see any strangers hanging around your property?'

'No, the police asked me that too.' She shrugged carelessly. 'No. No one . . . Oh,' she cried as if suddenly remembering. 'They kept on asking if anyone else had been sleeping here. They seemed keen to know if someone had been sleeping in the second bedroom?'

'My fault, I'm afraid. I told them about the ghostly footsteps.'

'Well, it was me. I sometimes sleep in there if my bed is in too much of a mess.'

I didn't even like to think what that meant.

'So, how did he die?' she persisted. 'The man in the boot?'

I hesitated for a moment. 'Didn't the police say?' If they hadn't told Amber, perhaps they didn't want her to know. If they really suspected her of murder, they might hope she would betray herself by revealing some knowledge she could only have if she'd killed the man herself. Perhaps, I realised, I shouldn't be talking to her at all. 'I understand he was stabbed,' I told her cautiously.

She pointed at me with a slightly wavering finger. 'And there's a swordstick missing. *That's* why they're making such a fuss about it! Well, I didn't pinch the thing.' She considered in silence for a moment. 'Someone's trying to frame me,' she muttered darkly. 'Someone's trying to frame me for stabbing Patrick Bloody Somebody who I've never even heard of.'

'Who would do that?' I asked.

She pouted like a child. 'Peter, I suppose. He hates me. It's because I get to live in this place and he only got the lousy house in Buckfastleigh. In fact, if it was an inside job, it could only be him or Kirsten.'

'Kirsten?' I glanced down at Ben curled up by my feet. 'I thought Kirsten was your friend.'

'We went to the same school.'

'Oh?' Kirsten hadn't mentioned that.

'Not in the same class,' she went on dismissively. 'I hardly knew her. We didn't keep in touch when we left or anything. Then a couple of years later there was a vacancy at the shop and she applied for a job. I thought it might be fun to work with her. I'd forgotten how deplorably needy she is.' She shuddered. 'I can't stand clingy women, can you? The ones who always want to be your friend.'

'I can't honestly say it's a problem I've encountered,' I told her, sipping my wine. I was taking it very slowly. It was in my interest to stay sober, in contrast to Amber, and not just because of the drive home. The more she drank, the more talkative she became, and I wanted to remember later what she'd said. 'So, why are you so convinced that Peter hates you?'

She gave a gurgle of laughter. 'Oh God! Don't you know about the Horrell family? We all hate each other, always have. It's written into our genes. Julian hated Peter and Peter hated Julian, probably because they were both in love with Anita – my mother,' she added, leaning forward to splash more wine, not very accurately, into her glass. She managed to slosh half of it onto the lid of the chest. 'Anita chose Julian. And Peter has always resented the fact that, as the elder son of an elder son, it was Julian who inherited the lion's share of the estate. And now it's all come to me and he hates me for it,' she finished simply.

'Can't you just walk away? Go off, do your own thing?'

She was shaking her head. 'I haven't got a bean. Thanks to my darling daddy, all my money is tied up in a trust fund. Until I'm thirty, can you believe? And guess who's the sole trustee? Dear old Uncle Pete. And he's such a bastard. He wants me to sell Granny Horrell's cottage. Well, I won't.'

'It must be worth quite a lot of money.'

'That's not the point. He wants to sell it to some builder friends of his. What's to stop them tearing the old place down and putting up some hideous modern bunker, all glass and concrete?'

'The Dartmoor National Park Authority. They would never allow it.'

'Maybe not,' she conceded. 'But the cottage is in my garden. If it were sold, then the garden would have to be carved up. The drive would have to be *shared*.' She spoke as if this were a serious affront to her civil liberty. 'I don't want neighbours. I don't want strangers living here, waving and smiling like idiots every time they park their bloody car. Especially if they are anything to do with Peter. He only wants to put his friends here to spy on me.'

Much as I disliked Peter Horrell, I very much doubted this was true. His motive for selling the place was more likely to be financial, but I knew that to suggest anything in his defence would alienate Amber, so I kept quiet, and watched her drain her glass. I let a minute go by before I asked my next question. 'Do you ever hear anything from Tristan at all?'

'Tris?' For several seconds she just stared at me, astonished, and then her face crumpled like a child's. 'Oh God, I haven't heard from Tris in years. He was such a darling. But he doesn't come near any of us anymore. Not since . . .' Her voice trailed off into silence, a large tear rolling down one cheek. 'I don't even know where he lives. My cow of a mother knows, but she wants to keep him to herself. Locked up. And he can never come back here to see me,' she finished tragically.

'And you've no idea where he is?'

She shook her head.

'Were you close, as children?' I asked.

'Yes. *We* didn't hate each other.' She got up suddenly and stumbled into the corner of the room, where she picked up a framed photograph from a table and brought it over to me. 'Look at him,' she implored me. 'Isn't he a darling?'

The photo showed me two young teenagers: clearly Amber in her younger years, her hair much longer, and a boy, a little older. They stood together with their arms about each other, both smiling into the camera. There couldn't have been more than two years between them. They shared the same elfin looks. The boy's hair was a little blonder, but otherwise they looked so alike they might have been twins.

'You can tell he's your brother,' I said. There were

a group of adults standing in the background of the picture. 'Is this your father?'

'Yes, that's Julian.'

'He and Peter were really alike too. And this older lady here?'

'Oh, that's Granny Horrell. She was a witch.' She giggled. 'Quite a funny one though. She moved into the little cottage when Grandpa died.' She sniffed and smeared the tear across her cheek, almost snatching the picture from my hand. 'Can we please talk about something else?' she asked as she teetered across the room to replace it.

'I'm sorry, I don't mean to pry.' I tapped the lid of the iron-bound chest. 'Tell me about this.'

'Oh, this thing! We can never open it because one of the keys is missing. I'll let you into a secret though.' She beckoned me closer and then pointed at the portrait of India Horrell. 'See her? Well, that thing around her neck . . .'

'The red diamond?'

'Oh, you know about that, do you? Worth squillions! Well, Granny Horrell told me before she died that it's in there.' She tapped on the lid of the chest and lowered her voice to a whisper. 'In a secret compartment.'

I looked at the chest and then back at her, and she nodded. 'If the diamond's worth squillions,' I asked, 'then wouldn't it be worth taking a chainsaw to this?'

She shouted with laughter. 'It's lined with lead. You can't even X-ray the bloody thing to find out what's inside.'

'Drop it off a cliff?' I suggested.

She shook her head. 'Honestly, I think Granny Horrell was making it up. She used to do things like that. I don't think the diamond is in there, not really. But if it is, it's safe. No one can get at it. Not even Peter.' She leant back against the sofa cushions and closed her eyes. She looked in danger of nodding off.

'So, how was the steampunk festival?' I asked, in an effort to keep her awake.

Her eyelids snapped open and she grinned. 'Fabulous!'

'Were you there to sell clothes?' I asked.

She nodded, suddenly wide awake, her eyes dancing. 'Want to come upstairs and try some on?'

We climbed a creaking, twisty corkscrew of a staircase that wouldn't have been an original feature. A longhouse is traditionally single-storey. The upper floor would have been opened up a couple of centuries later, as the family became more affluent, and it led directly into the roof space, open to the rafters in every room. The floor on the landing had a decided slope, which didn't help Amber's attempts to wobble along it, and she was giggling like a pixie by the time we reached her bedroom door.

Once inside she flung herself down on a chaise longue, clutching the now empty wine bottle. She waved an arm at a mound of steampunk costumes which lay piled on the cover of her four-poster bed, those which hadn't already made it to the floor. I could see now why she sometimes slept in the other room.

'Help yourself,' she said generously. 'They're all my own designs, you know. I get a woman in Ilsington to make them up for me.'

In other words, she had the creative ideas but got someone else to do the dirty work. It was the same arrangement she'd wanted with Ricky and Morris. I grabbed the garment on top of the pile, a deep-red dress overlaid in spotted black netting, and held it up against myself. As Victorian costumes went, it wasn't quite complete. There was a bodice and sleeves, and a bustle bunched up at the back, but where an ankle-length skirt should have been, there was only a short net petticoat, in pink. All of it clashed horribly with my hair.

'That looks brilliant on you,' Amber told me. 'You should try it on.'

'Don't think so.' I laid it back on the bed and picked up an ankle-length coat in chestnut velvet, embellished with military-style frogging. 'This is more my style.'

'That's for a man . . . oh no, you look bloody wonderful!' she cried delighted as I slipped it on. 'You are lucky being so tall. You just need a hat.'

Reluctantly, I took the coat off. I didn't intend to buy anything and it was time I headed home. As I laid the coat back on the bed, I noticed a box on the floor full of steampunk comics. I picked one off the top. The cover showed me a character in a top hat, fair hair hanging down to his shoulders, the lower half of his face concealed by a black mask, over which his dark eyes burnt fiercely. *Syrius Blade* was splashed across the front in jagged red lettering. 'Can I buy one of these?' I asked, thinking of Olly. 'I've got a friend who might like it.'

She waved an arm at me. 'Take it, take it. I've got

loads.' She pressed a hand against her forehead. 'You know, I've got a bit of a headache. I think I might close my eyes for a bit.'

'Definitely time you went to bed.' I glanced at the mound of clothes on the coverlet. She was probably better staying where she was. Ben had climbed up on the chaise with her and she was cuddling him to her chest like an old cushion.

'Would you like some aspirin or something?'

'Yes please.' She flapped the empty wine bottle in the direction of the door. 'There's some in the bathroom.' I took the bottle from her limp fingers and found the bathroom. When I opened the cabinet above the basin, a small avalanche of pill packets fell from the glass shelf where they had been inexpertly stacked. I went through them, most of them uppers or downers, trying to find the painkillers. I extracted two paracetamol and filled the bottle up with water. She already seemed to be asleep when I returned to the bedroom.

I poured her a glass, which I placed beside her along with the pills, ready for the ghastly moment when she returned to consciousness. It was a warm night and she didn't need covering up. She was more or less lying in the recovery position, so I left her as she was, propping the door open so that Ben could go back downstairs if he needed to.

As I crept along the landing, I began softly opening doors to look into the other bedrooms. The bed was unmade in one, the duvet thrown back, a dent in the pillow. But you can tell when a room's been left empty. You can sense the absence. And if Amber or anyone else had been sleeping in that bed in the days before she went away to Bristol, there had been no one there since.

I spent an hour before bedtime reading about the exploits of scarred, masked, tormented hero Syrius Blade. A story told almost entirely in pictures, with the occasional caption or speech bubble, was something I hadn't read since my childhood comic days, but it was dramatically illustrated in stunning detail and had me gripped. The hero's weapon of choice, I noticed, was a swordstick. The author of this genuinely intriguing and exciting piece of literature called himself – or herself – *Y. Knott*. Which is kind of clever. Anyway, it was all good swashbuckling stuff in which Blade defeated all kinds of unspeakable evil, despatched villains, rescued his lady love and saved the world. It was probably a lot less corroding to the teenage imagination than most of the computer games Olly and his friends played. I'd give it to him. As soon as I'd finished reading it.

CHAPTER FOURTEEN

Much to Olly's disgust, he did not come top in his class interview project. He was runner-up to Marcus, who had interviewed his father, not about being an accountant, but about his activities with his metal detector. 'And that's cheating,' Olly protested, 'because we were supposed to be interviewing people about their jobs, and it's not his dad's job. He only goes metal-detecting at weekends.'

Term had ended, and when I caught up with him he was packing up to go away for a week's summer school in Bude with the Dartmoor Youth Orchestra. 'I'm the only one who plays bassoon,' he told me proudly.

'Well, don't forget to pack it,' I advised him, and tossed him the Syrius Blade comic.

'Oh great!' he grinned. 'Thanks Juno. I haven't read this one.'

'There are others, then?'

'Oh, yeah.' His blue eyes widened. 'There's like a whole series. And this bloke, *Y. Knott*,' he tapped the author's name on the cover, 'that's not his real name, you know.'

I caught an amused glance from Elizabeth, who was folding laundry in a corner of the kitchen. 'Really?'

'No, he's weird, he never lets anyone see his face. One of the girls at school, her mum and dad take her to all these fantasy writer conventions and she was telling me – cos he was there, signing books – that he dresses up like Syrius Blade, with his face covered, and if you want your book signed, you have to queue up and go in this tiny tent . . . and it's all like dark, just an oil lamp really low, and he won't let you take any photographs.'

'Sounds like a good gimmick.'

'Yeh,' Olly nodded enthusiastically. 'I'm gonna go next year.'

'Well, we'll talk about that. In the meantime,' Elizabeth suggested, 'perhaps you could get on with your packing? We've got an early start in the morning. If you miss that minibus . . .'

'Do you know what pieces you're going to be playing, Olly?' I asked.

'We'll be rehearsing *Peter and the Wolf* – I've got a solo in that,' he added proudly, 'and some other stuff. That's when we're not on the beach, surfing. And then, at the end of the week, we perform a concert. Lizzie's coming to it, aren't you,' he said, turning to her. 'And Tom.'

Elizabeth smiled. 'We'll be there.'

'Isn't Marcus a member of the orchestra?' I asked.

Olly sneered. 'He plays the triangle.'

I had to admit the thought of chunky Marcus tinging away on a tiny triangle was funny.

'He plays percussion,' Elizabeth corrected him, 'not just the triangle.'

'He's hopeless.'

'He's obviously not, or he wouldn't be in the orchestra,' she chided him.

'Just cos his dad had dug up a few boring silver coins, and a belt buckle,' he muttered.

'Don't be a sore loser.'

'Well, I was loads better than him! But it was cos of that stupid lot at the back of the class I didn't win,' he complained. 'Every time I said the words "bog burst" they fell about laughing.'

I still hadn't caught up with Kirsten. But I'd managed to catch up with Daniel's project manager, Howard, who told me work on replacing the rotten staircase was progressing and should be finished in a few days. The problem then would be that an official from Dartmoor National Park Authority would have to come and inspect the work before it could be signed off. Which was all very right and proper and stopped anyone like Amber's neighbours from building eyesores on the moor, but meant renovating existing properties like Daniel's took far longer, and cost far more, than needed. At least, according to Howard.

I went up to Moorview Farm to take a look. No sign of dead bodies in cars this time. From the outside it was easy to see how much time and money had already been spent. The newly slated roof was finished, and the repointed chimney. The new sash windows, which had to be made of timber like the ones they'd replaced, had cost a fortune, as had dealing with the damp interior walls. And there was still the staircase and a cracked roof beam in the kitchen to be paid for, as well as electrical rewiring. Inheriting property, Daniel has often lamented, is not all it's cracked up to be. But I knew that, I'd inherited *Old Nick's*.

Halsanger Common is wide and open, scoured in winter by cold winds. But at least the house was now weatherproof. No keening wind would find its way through gaps in the old stone walls, or between missing tiles, or whistle through cracks in rotting window frames. Despite its stone floors and bare walls, its empty rooms, the house had lost the sense of abandonment I'd felt on previous visits. The activity within had given the place a new energy. For the first time it seemed possible that Daniel might live there one day.

I'd also caught up with Maisie who, she informed me, was not looking forward to her ninety-eighth birthday party the following week. She didn't know what all the fuss was about. At her age, a birthday didn't mean anything and was better forgotten. I'd love to see her reaction if it was.

'I've lived too long,' she declared tragically.

'Now, you know you want that hundredth-birthday telegram,' I told her.

'I wanted one from Her Majesty Queen Elizabeth,' she told me with great dignity. 'Now she's gone, God bless 'er, I don't care anymore.'

'Well, you'd better hope you pop off before it arrives, then.'

'Cheeky hussy!' she spat, making a feeble attempt to slap my hand. 'Janet . . . Jacko . . . Juno!' I knew she'd arrive at the right name eventually. 'Get off and take that dog out, and while you're about it you can buy me some sweets for your cheek.'

'Acid drops?' I suggested.

She began to smile then, in spite of herself. 'Just for that, you can buy me a bar o' chocolate. Proper chocolate, you know, milky, sweet. I don't want any of that dark, bitter stuff.'

I dropped a kiss on the top of her head. 'Well, you don't need it, do you darling?' I patted her shoulder and made my escape while she was still thinking about it.

It was when I was walking Jacko through the town towards *Moor Chocolate* that I was accosted by the small but officious figure of Detective Sergeant Cruella deVille, who called my name several times before running up to me and blocking the pavement, seemingly determined to make me stop. I stepped back, worried she might get me in a headlock. Jacko, obviously a good judge of character, growled and bared his teeth. She demanded to know why I had been talking to a suspect in a murder case. No one had told me not to, I told her, wondering how she knew. I'd phoned Dean and given him a brief description of what Amber had said. He must have ratted on me. I'd deal with him later. And anyway, I told her, Amber had asked me to visit. She wanted to know more about the dead man. Any news on him? I asked.

Cruella visibly stiffened. 'That information is on a need-to-know basis,' she reprimanded me.

'Fair enough.' I shrugged, knowing that appearing unconcerned by her put-down would irritate her.

'So, what did you and Miss Horrell talk about?' she asked.

I could have told her that was on a need-to-know basis, but with Jacko revving up to tear a chunk out of her ankle, I thought I'd better keep the conversation short. 'Not much. She was already drunk when I arrived. She thinks someone's trying to frame her for the murder of Mr Mulder, most likely her cousin Peter.'

Cruella treated this information with the contempt she felt it deserved, giving a short, irritated gasp.

'I wouldn't take it too seriously,' I recommended. 'Like I said, she was drunk.'

'And she didn't say anything about the missing swordstick?'

'Only that she thought its disappearance was part of the attempt to set her up.'

'So, let me get this straight.' Cruella wisely edged into the gutter, out of range of Jacko's snout. 'She's saying Peter Horrell, stole a swordstick from his own shop in order to stab a complete stranger and put him in the boot of the car, in an attempt to frame her for murder?'

I had to admit it didn't sound likely. 'She may not say the same now she's sober. Although,' I added after a moment's thought, 'we don't know for certain this man Mulder *was* a complete stranger.'

Cruella frowned, her little mouth pursed in concentration. 'No, that's the problem. If we could establish a connection, we might have some clue as to motive.' She stopped short, realising she had expressed thoughts she had not meant to share with civilian lowlife like me. She bade me a brisk good afternoon, and bustled off across the road.

'Bye!' I called to her retreating back. 'Nice talking to you.'

After I'd delivered Jacko and the chocolate to Brook Cottage, I walked back to *Old Nick's*. Sophie was packing up her art portfolio, embalming it in layers of polythene against the possibility of dirt getting into it. She was clearly stressed and wheezing slightly. I glanced at Pat, sitting in her corner threading beaded earrings, and she rolled her eyes towards heaven.

'What are you doing, Soph?' I asked.

'She's getting in a state,' Pat pronounced glumly.

'I don't want to miss the next bus.' Sophie glanced at her watch. 'There's only one an hour.'

'Where to?'

'Seth's uncle's place. I want to give him these final paintings.'

'He's in Buckfastleigh, isn't he?'

She nodded, hunting around her desk for something she'd lost.

'You don't need to get the bus. I'll run you over there. It'll only take a few minutes. If Pat doesn't mind holding the fort,' I added.

Pat shook her head. 'It's alright with me.'

Sophie found her bag and straightened up. 'Are you sure?'

''Course,' I told her. 'No trouble.'

Fifteen minutes later, I dropped her off at her

164

destination. 'I'll park in the car park,' I told her. 'Any idea how long you'll be?'

'About half an hour?' she suggested tentatively.

'Right. See you back here in half an hour.' I looked at my watch. While I was waiting, I thought I might kill time and stroll around to *Horrell's Antiques*, see if Amber had survived her hangover.

But when I arrived, she wasn't there. Peter Horrell looked less than pleased to see me. 'Amber phoned in sick this morning. Migraine, apparently,' he added and stalked off up the stairs.

'Good afternoon to you too,' I called after him.

'I'm sorry about that,' a small voice said behind me, and I turned to see Kirsten standing in the doorway holding a highly decorative piece of porcelain. She placed it down on the surface of an octagonal table and hurried over to me. 'Peter is so irritated by all this business of the dead man in Amber's car.'

'Irritated?' I repeated. 'He thinks a man's murder is *irritating*?'

Kirsten looked flustered. 'Well, you know, we've had a lot of police here asking questions about Amber disappearing and now she's back again, she's not exactly being helpful. And then with the missing swordstick and everything. And Peter thinks you only come here to . . .' She faltered, obviously embarrassed.

'To what?'

'To snoop,' she whispered, her eyes downcast.

'Well, he's right,' I said frankly, 'I do. Amber's alright though, is she?' I added. 'You've spoken to her yourself?'

'Yes. She knows it's usually me, not Peter, who answers the phone.' She giggled. 'She didn't sound as if she'd quite sobered up.'

'She probably hasn't,' I agreed, remembering how much alcohol she'd consumed the night before. I moved over to the window, momentarily distracted. The room we were standing in would originally have been a reception room, and the windows at the back looked into a pretty courtyard garden, a wrought-iron spiral staircase descending into it from Peter Horrell's flat above. In the corner of the courtyard was a white-painted outhouse, the door painted in a tasteful pale green to match the garden table and chairs that stood in its centre. I watched as Peter Horrell came down the staircase and unlocked the green door with a key. He cast a glance over his shoulder which I could only describe as furtive, and disappeared inside. Was he really the kind of man to steal a swordstick from his own premises, and run Patrick Mulder through with the blade? If he was, he must have had a motive. Or Amber was right. He was trying to frame her for the crime.

'Are you alright?' Kirsten asked, as I was standing there, lost in thought.

'Pretty garden,' I said, turning to smile at her. 'What's in the shed?'

'Nothing, just a few garden tools. That little building next to it is the customer toilet.'

Peter Horrell emerged from the outbuilding a few moments later and locked the door again. It seemed a lot of trouble to go to for a few garden tools.

'I don't suppose the swordstick has turned up?' I asked.

'No.' Kirsten blinked at me. 'Do you think it was really the murder weapon?'

'I don't know. But unless someone can find it, I don't suppose we ever will.'

'It's just I didn't like to say this to the police when Peter was here, but Julian had a whole collection of swordsticks. All perfectly legal, all antiques,' she assured me, her words tumbling out in a rush. 'He'd sell the odd one now and again. He'd bring it here to display it, but mostly, he kept them at home.'

'At Langworthy Hall? Aren't they dangerous things to have around?'

'Only if you know what they are. Most of them look like ordinary walking sticks. Unless you knew otherwise, that's what you'd think they were.'

'Do you know where he kept them?'

Kirsten shrugged. 'In an umbrella stand, I think. They weren't all terribly valuable or anything.'

I wondered why Amber hadn't mentioned them. She must have realised their significance. But she'd been in too much of a drunken state the previous evening to realise anything much.

'Do you think I should tell the police about them?' Kirsten asked, fixing me with anxious blue eyes.

'Yes, I think you should.'

She bit her lip. 'Won't they think it's odd that I didn't tell them before?'

I shrugged. 'Tell them you only just remembered them.' They were going to think it a lot odder, I thought to myself, as I made my way back to the car park and the waiting Sophie, that Peter Horrell hadn't mentioned them either.

CHAPTER FIFTEEN

'You ratted on me,' I accused Dean as I accosted him outside of the chippie the next day. 'You told Cruella I'd been to see Amber.'

He looked guilty, and not just because of the carton of chips in curry sauce he was carrying. 'I have to share any information I learn about a case with my superior officers, you know that.' He grunted. 'Even if it is just a load of drunken gossip.'

'Well, you should make an effort to pass your sergeant's exam,' I told him sharply. 'Then she wouldn't be your superior any longer.'

He nodded gloomily. 'I know. The boss is always on at me about it.'

'D'you mean Inspector Ford or Gemma?'

He gave a rueful grin. 'The pair of 'em.'

'It's my turn to rat now. Has Kirsten been in touch with you?'

'Kirsten Blake, the girl who works in *Horrell's*?' He frowned. 'No. Why?'

'There was something she was supposed to tell you.' I explained about Julian's swordstick collection.

'And he kept them at Langworthy Hall? And none of our people at the scene picked them up?' he asked, looking horrified.

'I understand he kept them in an umbrella stand or something. They look like ordinary walking sticks.'

'But aren't they valuable?'

I helped myself to one of his chips and blew on it gently. 'Not necessarily. Some of them might be. Point is, you broke into the place looking for Amber. Didn't you notice them?'

'I didn't even notice an umbrella stand.'

'It's not the sort of thing you *would* notice, is it?'

'But one of those swordsticks could be the murder weapon.'

'Exactly.' I extracted another chip, dipping the end in curry sauce. 'You'd better get someone up there. They need to go to forensics.'

'Too right,' he muttered, shoving the carton of chips into my hands. 'Help yourself,' he muttered and strode off in the direction of the police station, slipping his phone from his jacket pocket as he went. I watched him jab the screen with his forefinger and tucked into the rest of his chips, secure in the knowledge I had done my civic duty.

'What the frigging hell, Juno Browne?' Amber screamed at me down the phone later that evening. She was shouting over a cacophony of loud music from somewhere in the background. 'I've had . . . Alexa!' she roared. 'Will you shut the fuck up?' This resulted in a sudden and slightly offended silence. 'I've had the police here,' Amber went on more quietly, 'searching the place for swordsticks.' Clearly, she was not amused.

'Sorry. But I only told them what Kirsten told me, that your father used to collect them. And in view of the way Patrick Mulder was killed . . .'

'Kirsten's a moron!' Amber pronounced her verdict with icy fury. 'There are no swordsticks. My father used to collect them, years ago, mainly because my brother was fascinated by them and he wanted to encourage his interest in fencing. After what happened at Tris's school he decided to sell them, for what I would have thought were blindingly obvious reasons. You can ask the police, if you like. They didn't find any here.'

'Amber, I'm sorry. I was only passing on information I thought might be important.'

She wasn't listening. 'I nearly told them to fuck off and come back with a search warrant. But then they'd only think I had something to hide.'

She made me feel like an interfering busybody. 'Kirsten obviously doesn't know the full story.' And you don't know the full story about her either, I added privately.

'Kirsten needs to wind her neck in,' Amber muttered venomously, 'or I might just wring it for her.'

I didn't envy Kirsten her next encounter with Amber, even if she had landed me in it for passing on duff information and wasting police time.

'Can I ask you something?' I ventured, after she'd carried on about what a blithering muffin-brain Kirsten was for another full minute.

She hesitated a moment. 'Go on then,' she consented warily.

'Do you believe Tristan killed that boy?'

She drew in a shocked breath. 'Of course not. I've never believed it.'

'Why not?'

'Because he told me he didn't, and Tris wouldn't lie to me.'

I wasn't sure it was a sufficient reason to take his word, myself. 'Are you sure about that?'

'Of course,' she told me, a tremor of sadness in her voice. 'He couldn't have done it. Tris was gentle, lovely. He wouldn't hurt a fly.'

Kirsten was on the phone to me next day, sounding more than a bit tearful. 'I am so sorry,' she'd snivelled. 'I had no idea Julian had disposed of his swordstick collection.'

I couldn't feel cross with her. It wasn't her fault. I was the one who'd told the police, and it sounded as if she'd already received a tongue-lashing from Amber about poking her nose in where it didn't belong. 'I wouldn't worry about it,' I told her. 'The police have to follow up a lot of leads that go nowhere.'

But there had been some progress on the mystery man in the boot of Daniel's car. Apparently, Dean's South African colleague had been doing some digging. The dead man had been born in Johannesburg and was Dutch on his father's side, hence the name Mulder. Originally, he had worked in a diamond mine and after a spell in the army, that's what he'd returned to. He was divorced, with no children. No one the police in Cape Town had talked to seemed to know what he was doing in this country, but they were hoping to interview his ex-wife who was out of the country, on holiday, as soon as she returned.

I'd also done some digging of my own. I didn't know much about trust funds, so I rang an old university friend of mine who works in finance. She told me that if Peter Horrell was Amber's sole trustee, then he had complete control of all her inheritance until she reached the age of thirty. He was only supposed to use the money in her interest but basically, he could do what he liked with it as long as he could justify the expenditure. He didn't even have to tell her about it. In theory, he could sell that cottage of her grandmother's over her head. He could, if he were so inclined, steal from her. And if anything should happen to Amber, for instance if she took an overdose or met with an accident, there was no reason why he couldn't become her beneficiary.

Of course, there was no reason to suppose Peter Horrell had any evil intentions towards Amber. He was probably just trying to stop her pissing away her inheritance on drugs and booze. I still didn't like him though.

Ricky regarded me suspiciously, his light-coloured eyes narrowed against the smoke drifting up from the cigarette he held between his fingers. 'Favour,' he repeated. 'What kind of favour?'

'*Horrell's* are holding an auction next week,' I told him. 'They've got a viewing day tomorrow. I just want you to come.'

'Well, we never mind looking over auction lots, do

we?' Morris placed a slice of apple pie on the table in front of me, unconvinced by my claim that I'd already eaten supper. 'I don't expect you bothered with dessert, did you, Juno love? Would you like cream or custard with it?'

I took a look at the pie, the golden sugary crust with its crimped edges, the work of Morris's own fair hand. Resistance was futile. 'Cream please.'

'Right.' He bustled off towards the fridge and came back. 'I'm afraid we've only got clotted.'

'But why do you want us there, Princess?' Ricky asked.

'I don't know how many people will be turning up tomorrow for this viewing, but I want to make sure there will be enough there to keep Horrell occupied.'

He gave a wolfish grin. 'Giving you a chance to snoop around?'

I was momentarily distracted by a mouthful of warm apple pie and melting clotted cream, and it's rude to speak with your mouth full. I flapped my hand in a delaying gesture. 'Sort of,' I managed eventually. I wanted another chance to watch the Horrells in action. I didn't mean Kirsten and Peter. I didn't want to watch their kind of action. But I was curious to see how Amber fitted into the picture at work. I couldn't imagine her working alongside Kirsten and Peter and not knowing what was going on between them.

'The Horrells are weird.' I went through everything I knew about them, going back to the death of India Horrell; the brothers long ago who couldn't trust one another; Tristan's murder of the boy at his school;

174

Julian's wife deserting him and their children; and Peter and Amber's apparent extreme dislike of one another. I also threw in the fact that Peter held the reins of Amber's inheritance. I didn't mention his affair with Kirsten.

Ricky frowned. 'What has any of this got to do with this dead man in the boot of the car?'

'I don't know,' I admitted, 'perhaps nothing. But there's the theft of that swordstick. There's something odd there.'

'Because it had to be an inside job?' Morris asked, staring at me earnestly.

'Something like that.' Secretly, I had a suspicion it hadn't been stolen at all. In fact, I wouldn't have been surprised to find it locked in that toolshed in Peter Horrell's garden. In which case, what the hell was he up to, pretending it had been stolen? 'And I reckon Kirsten knows more than she's saying,' I added.

'Well then, *Maurice*,' Ricky addressed him, flicking ash from the end of his fag, 'it seems we're off to Buckfastleigh tomorrow. This'll cost you a day here unpacking costumes, Princess,' he added, pointing his cigarette in my direction. 'We've got *The Gondoliers* arriving on Monday.'

'Sounds nasty,' I said. 'But *The Gondoliers* it is.'

CHAPTER SIXTEEN

As it turned out, I needn't have worried. *Horrell's Antiques* was enjoying a busy viewing day. The Japanese screen was attracting great attention, as was a dainty diamond bracelet, estimated value thirteen thousand pounds. Other star attractions were a rare Montblanc fountain pen, a nineteenth-century mahogany *étagère* and a serpentine rosewood credenza – or cupboard to you and me – a mere snip at an estimated three thousand.

I arrived separately to Ricky and Morris, and we had decided to behave as strangers when we met. I glimpsed their arrival, or should I say entrance, after I'd been there about ten minutes. They were dressed for summer, Morris wearing a cream linen suit, with a yellow silk handkerchief flowing from his breast pocket, and a Panama hat. Ricky was resplendent in a blue silk Nehru shirt, and knee-length shorts. They looked eccentric enough to be rich.

'Well, she's no better than she should be,' I heard Ricky declare in his best posh actor's voice. He was looking at an art deco bronze statuette of a dancer flinging her legs in the air. I hid a smile and moved on into the adjoining room, where Peter Horrell was locked in earnest conversation with another dealer about an inlaid table. It was here I also located Kirsten and sidled up to her. The one person I could not see was Amber.

'Oh, hello.' Kirsten was chewing her lip like a frightened rabbit, and cast a nervous, sideways glance at her boss, as if she wasn't sure she should be talking to me. 'I wasn't expecting to see you here today.'

'I'm always interested in antiques, as you know,' I told her. 'Lusting after things I can't afford. No Amber today?'

Kisten flicked another glance at Peter Horrell and then lowered her voice. 'She turned up this morning wearing one of her steampunk dresses. Peter was furious, told her she wasn't being seen by our clients looking like . . .' She raised her hand to stifle a giggle. 'Like some bedraggled tart from a Wild West saloon. He sent her home and told her not to come back unless she changed her clothes.'

Which, I imagined, was exactly what she wanted. Aware of being watched, I turned to find Peter staring at the pair of us. 'Here again, Miss Browne?' He wore a fixed grin but the cold hostility in his eyes was unmistakeable. 'Here to look at something to buy for your little shop? I doubt you'll find anything you can afford.'

I smiled at him sunnily. 'Oh, you never know. I understand you used to do business in my shop yourself at one time, when Mr Nikolai was alive.'

He continued to smile. 'I don't know where you got that idea. I've never been through the front door.'

I looked him in the eye. 'It was more the back door I was thinking of.'

His smile vanished. 'I don't know what you're insinuating.'

'Oh, I think we both do.'

For a moment he looked thunderous, but just then, Morris, who'd been lurking nearby as if he was trying to eavesdrop, claimed his attention by asking about the portrait of India Horrell. Shame, really – I would like to have heard his response.

'Any sign of the missing swordstick?' I asked Kirsten, loud enough for Peter to hear as he led Morris away.

'Well, no,' she whispered. 'I'm afraid not.'

I looked through one of the windows overlooking the courtyard, and at the green door of the toolshed. I could clearly see an iron key sitting in the lock. How very careless of someone. I turned back to Kirsten and smiled, pointing. 'Did you tell me the other day there's a toilet out there?'

She nodded. 'Just go through the glass door there and follow the path.'

On my way, I bumped into Ricky. 'How's it going, Princess?' he muttered from the corner of his mouth.

'I was hoping Amber would be here.' I looked him up and down. 'I'm not sure about the Gandhi impersonation.'

He grinned. 'Don't you believe it. Old Horrell was eating out of our hands just now. He thinks we're big bidders.'

'Keep him occupied if you can.' I nodded in the direction of the glass door. 'I'm just off to visit the facilities.'

I stepped out into the sunny courtyard. For a few moments I paused to enjoy the warmth of the sunshine and admire an ancient olive tree, its leaves casting dappled shadows over the rough flagstones. This must have been a pleasant place to sit when the business of the day was done. Not to be distracted, I carried on down the path and into the white-painted building with the sign for TOILET on the door. After making quick use of the spotlessly clean facilities and helping myself to a generous dollop of hand cream, I opened the door and looked out. Across the courtyard the auction rooms were heaving with people. I couldn't see anyone looking in my direction, so I sidled up to the green door of the toolshed and placed my hand on the handle. I turned it, the door opened, and I slipped inside the shed. It wasn't even locked.

It was dim in there, almost dark after the bright sunlight outside and cool, a gloomy green glow coming in through one narrow window near the ceiling, its glass obscured by the foliage of a climbing plant. For a moment I stood blinking, trying to accustom my eyes to the low level of light. For a toolshed, it was altogether too tidy and contained precious few tools. A stiff garden broom leant against one wall, and a rake for fallen leaves, while a trug containing a trowel, a fork and a pair of barely soiled gardening gloves stood on the floor in one corner. On a shelf sat a ball of green garden twine, a pair of deadheading snips and a carton of rose-feed. No sign of any swordsticks. It was deeply disappointing.

What took up most of the space in the shed, emitting a low electric hum, was a large chest freezer. I looked around and saw a light switch by the door but didn't dare flip it on. Instead, I lifted the lid of the freezer to see what was inside. Well, you would, wouldn't you? I mean, who wouldn't? Anybody would.

The concrete floor heaved like a wave. I staggered back, stifling a scream as a shudder of revulsion ran through me. The thing inside the freezer was shrouded in black plastic, the head and torso closely wrapped, the stiffly upraised arms tightly bound. The rest of the body was missing.

For a moment, I couldn't process what I was staring at. A corpse, half a corpse. My mind reeled. Could this be Amber? She'd returned safely after being missing for days. Perhaps she wasn't supposed to. Had Peter killed her when she'd turned up this morning? No. That was impossible. He could not have done it. This would have taken time, this thing, mummified in black plastic. Perhaps he had killed her in the night and Kirsten was lying to cover for him. I didn't believe it. It couldn't be Amber. But if it wasn't her, who was it? I reached out with shaking fingers and touched the head. I could clearly trace through the plastic the curved outline of an ear, frozen hard, and drew back my fingers as if they'd been burnt. I swallowed, taking a ragged breath, and dug my fingers into the plastic, ready to rip it apart.

The door of the shed was flung open. Peter Horrell stood in the doorway, a dark silhouette against the bright sunshine outside. For a moment, he and I stared. Then, with a gasp of impatience, he pushed me roughly out of the way, grabbed the plastic between his own fingers and tore it open. I found myself staring at the head of a Buddha, eyes closed, its serene features not frozen but carved in a pale shade of wood.

'Seen enough?' he demanded scathingly. He knocked at the head with his knuckles. 'It's made of wood. Touch it!' he ordered, and when I hung back, he shoved me forward, grabbing my hair and pushing my head down into the freezer. Seizing my wrist, he forced my hand down onto the hard, wooden head. 'It's a half-length statue and it has woodworm! Do you know how we cure woodworm in the antiques trade?' he snarled in my ear. 'Or is that something Old Nick neglected to teach you?'

'You wrap it in plastic and put it in a freezer,' I gulped faintly.

'That's right,' he nodded, sneering, and released his hold on me, letting me stand up. 'Now what the hell are you doing in here?'

I was still trying to catch my breath. 'I was looking for the loo,' I explained brokenly, 'and I wandered in here by mistake and . . .'

'It's all lies. I don't want to hear it.' He grabbed me by the arm. 'C'mon! Out!'

I yanked my arm away. I'd had enough of him pushing me around. But he grabbed me again, dragged me outside and began to march me across the courtyard. 'I want you off my property,' he yelled, loud enough for everyone inside to hear. Already I could see people

181

gathering to look out of the windows, and my cheeks burnt with humiliation.

His fingers were digging into my arm. 'Ow!' I protested. I didn't try to fight him off even though I could have done. A tussle would only create a worse scene, and I was already the centre of too much attention.

'If I ever find you in here again, I'll call the police,' he warned savagely as he thrust me through the door before him and into the house. Inside there was a murmur of shocked voices as people drew back to let us pass. A few of the people watching began to eye me with disgust. I suppose they thought he'd caught me stealing.

'There's no need to manhandle the lady,' I heard Ricky's voice protest loudly as I was dragged through the salesroom towards the front door. 'I'm sure she's willing to leave.'

'Oh, I bet she is!' Peter ejected me out into the street, pushing me across the pavement. I staggered to a stop in the gutter, a passing cyclist just missing my toes. The strap of my bag slid from my shoulder and landed on my foot with a thump. I heard Morris's voice as he rushed out after me. 'I'll pick it up, Juno love.'

A moment later I felt Ricky's arm slide protectively around my shoulders. 'Did he hurt you?' he demanded in a furious whisper.

'And you two!' Peter Horrell was spitting in fury as he pointed at them both. 'I knew there was something fishy about you two. You stay away as well, d'you hear me, or I'll call the police.'

'Only too happy to, mate!' Ricky yelled back at him. 'If this is the way you treat your customers.' His arm around me tightened. 'You'll be lucky if this lady doesn't sue you for assault.'

Peter Horrell barked with laughter. 'That's no lady.'

'Leave it,' I begged Ricky in a whisper as I felt him tense, ready with an angry retort, 'please just leave it.'

Morris was peering at me anxiously. 'Are you alright, Juno?'

I heard the door of *Horrell's Antiques* slam shut. 'I might die of shame,' I whispered hoarsely as tears of humiliation gathered in my eyes. 'Otherwise, I'm okay.'

'What on earth happened in there?'

I shook my head. 'I feel so stupid,' I breathed. 'I just want to go home.'

'Nah! What you need, Princess, is a stiff drink,' Ricky pointed up the road. 'Come on, the nearest pub is this way.'

'Cheer up,' he said, as I moped at the pub table, staring into the brandy Morris had insisted on buying me. 'It's not that bad!' I raised my eyes to his and he grinned. 'It's bloody funny, actually.'

I shook my head. 'I feel such an idiot.'

Morris, sitting next to me, patted my hand. 'It *is* quite funny really, you know, Juno my love. Try not to take it so hard.'

'No, no,' I sighed. 'I must try to see the funny side of becoming a complete laughing stock in the local antiques community.' Because everyone would soon know what had happened. There had been far too many people packed into that auction room witnessing my ignominious exit for word not to spread. It might even spread as far as the police station. Inspector Ford and Cruella would hear about it, and Dean. I groaned. Ashburton's amateur Miss Marple thought she'd discovered a dead body in a freezer, and it turned out to be a statue with woodworm. They'd all be laughing their heads off. The only person who wouldn't see the funny side of it would be Daniel, who'd be furious with me for going into the shed in the first place. I just had to hope no one would tell him.

But I deserved what I'd got. I had no evidence Peter Horrell was involved in any wrongdoing, beyond the fact that he was having an affair with a younger woman and I disliked him. I'd let prejudice colour my judgement and had made a blundering error.

'Mind you,' Morris went on indignantly, 'he could have just asked you to leave. There was no excuse for him throwing you out like that. I think you'd have grounds for assault.'

I took rather too large a sip of brandy and shuddered as it burnt my throat. 'No,' I croaked. 'It's not worth it. Forget it.'

Ricky was still grinning. 'I reckon you're right about him being a wrong 'un. Nasty piece of work if you ask me.'

'Can we talk about something else?' I asked. 'Or preferably, not talk at all.' A few moments of hush followed, allowing me to wallow in my misery for a short while, before I felt compelled to break the silence myself. 'You see, what I don't understand is his attitude to Amber. Her mother abandoned her when she was very young, and her brother got locked up for killing another boy.

She recently lost her father and she lives all alone in that longhouse. She's obviously not happy and on all sorts of pills, and yet Peter Horrell doesn't seem to be remotely concerned about her welfare. Perhaps he's hoping she'll do herself in.'

'You don't know that's true, to be fair, Juno love,' Morris pointed out. 'Maybe he just doesn't show his feelings.'

I didn't believe it. He'd been showing them well enough in that toolshed.

'I expect he's had enough of her over the years,' Ricky added.

'I'm sure she's tried his patience sorely,' I conceded, 'but even when we found the body in her car and she was missing for days, he didn't seem to worry about her. He seemed far more concerned about his missing swordstick.'

'Amber herself told you they were a strange family,' Ricky reminded me. 'Perhaps they really do hate each other.'

'She told me she thought Peter was trying to frame her for murder.'

'Whose?' Morris blinked, confused.

'The man in the car.'

Ricky snorted in disdain. 'She might be paranoid. She could believe anything.'

Morris gave a decisive nod of his head. 'I think you should stay away from all of them from now on, Juno love.'

'I intend to,' I assured him. At least Peter Horrell and his rotten antiques shop, I added privately. 'But what about poor Mr Mulder?'

Ricky frowned. 'Who's he?'

'The dead man in Daniel's car. The police have got nowhere. He was murdered, far from home, and no one seems to care. Someone should be hunting for his killer.'

'Indeed, they should,' Ricky nodded as he raised his glass to his lips. 'But it doesn't have to be you.'

CHAPTER SEVENTEEN

I wanted to lie low for the rest of Saturday, but I had to go back to *Old Nick's*. Sophie had volunteered to mind the shop for the morning so I could go to the auction viewing, but I'd promised to relieve her when I got back. She listened to my tale of woe with parted lips, her dark eyes round as an owl's. Until I reached the moment when the corpse in the freezer turned out to have woodworm. Then she covered her mouth with her hands, and started giggling. 'I'm sorry,' she gasped. 'But it *is* funny.' She became serious again when I told her how Peter Horrell had thrown me out into the street, but even then, she kept biting her lip and her shoulders would shake now and then with suppressed laughter. I told her to go away and never darken my door again and she left, still smiling. At least I'd cheered her up a bit.

But news of my mortifying experience at *Horrell's* spread faster than a nasty disease. I'd known it would. Even Mitch, the editor from the effing *Dartmoor Gazette*, phoned. I told him what he could do and slammed the phone down. It didn't stop word spreading though. I wasn't surprised to see Dean Collins appear in

187

the doorway later in the afternoon, a big grin plastered across his face and his blue eyes dancing with merriment. He tried to speak but apparently, the look on my face was as funny as anything else he'd heard that day and he burst out laughing. I felt the heat rise in a tide up my neck. 'It's all around the station, then? That bastard Horrell reported me.'

Dean wiped tears of laughter from his eyes as he pulled up a chair and sat down. 'He did.'

'Oh fuck!' I moaned. 'The bloody *Dartmoor Gazette* has been on the phone as well. I can just see the headline. "*Local Amateur Detective Juno Browne Finds Corpse Murdered by Woodworm*".'

'Luckily for you,' Dean went on, finally controlling his mirth, 'you haven't committed any crime. Cruella gave it her best shot, wanted to arrest you for breaking and entering.'

'I didn't break, I only entered!' I protested. 'The door wasn't even locked.'

'The boss told Peter Horrell to calm down, said we wouldn't be charging you with anything. And if he wanted to keep you off his property, he'd better seek a court injunction.'

I always knew Inspector Ford was a lovely man.

'But,' Dean went on, wagging a thick forefinger, 'you stay away from there, Juno. This comes straight from the inspector. I don't know what you thought you were after, but leave Peter Horrell alone. The boss told me to tell you, just because you've given him the best laugh he's had in years, doesn't mean he'll go easy on you if you step over the line.'

'Did he laugh?' I asked. The inspector could be very stern.

Dean grinned. 'He ended up with hiccups. But he means it, Juno,' he added more seriously. 'Leave Horrell alone. He's not a suspect in this case.'

'I know. I just don't like him, that's all.'

'Not a good enough reason to harass the man.'

'I don't think I've been harassing him exactly. Before today, I mean. I've just been there a couple of times to enquire after Amber.' I scowled. 'Is that what he said, that I'd been harassing him?'

Dean pulled a face. 'Trouble is, Miss Marple, you've got a reputation.'

'Which,' I told him, tapping my finger on the counter, 'is only a problem if you've got something to hide.'

Dean leant forward confidentially. 'Make me a cup of tea and I'll forget you said that.'

'Deal!' I told him, getting up. 'Any more news on Mulder?'

'No.'

'But you must have found out something,' I objected. 'We know he'd been in the country some time before he was killed. Where has he been? How has he been getting about?'

'We have been able to track his movements,' Dean said piously. 'We know which hotel he stayed in when he arrived in London – where, incidentally, he reported the theft of a laptop—'

'What was on it?'

He rolled his eyes. 'Well, we don't know, do we, because it got stolen.'

'Right.'

'And we now know where he was staying at the time he was murdered.'

'Where?'

'None of your business. Where's this cup of tea?'

'I'm just getting it,' I told him. 'But you're not getting any of my biscuits.'

Between Daniel's farmhouse on Halsanger Common, and Langworthy Hall where Amber lived, there were several buildings that had used to belong to the old Horrell estate and had been sold off years before when it was broken up. I found them on the map and spent an hour looking up their names online, to establish which ones were now operating as holiday accommodation. There were several, converted barns and farm buildings mostly, from grander places offering self-catering accommodation for parties of sixteen, down to cosy shepherd's huts, perfect for two or one. Patrick Mulder had stayed at one of these, I was sure. Dean might not be prepared to tell me the address, but I reckoned for the man to turn up dead in the car at Langworthy Hall, he had to be staying nearby. Also, judging from their websites, all the accommodation available was high-quality and costly. Mulder had wanted a long-term let, which in the summer months would have been eye-wateringly expensive, had it been available. But we knew he'd had money. And if he'd wanted to rent long-term, it seemed as if he'd been intending to stick around.

I began phoning the various establishments,

concentrating first on those which had smaller properties to rent. It was the same story at nearly all of them, nothing available now until October. No last-minute cancellations? I asked hopefully, and got the same sad reply: no, nothing. Except at one. The woman on the end of the phone hesitated, explaining she did have a one-bedroom cottage, The Piggery, which was currently unoccupied. It was an awkward situation, she explained, because it had been rented out to a guest who had passed away – he hadn't died *in* the property, she hurried to assure me, but he had paid until the end of the month. The police were still investigating his death and she didn't know when she'd be allowed to rent the place out again. Meanwhile, she was hoping someone would come to take away his things.

I sympathised with her predicament. Do you think it would be possible for me to come and look at The Piggery, I asked, even if it's not actually available? I had to find somewhere for a friend coming later in the year, I told her, and it sounded as if it might be perfect. Well, she responded, if I wanted to pop around for a look, she supposed it would be okay. The police hadn't told her she *couldn't* show it to anyone. Well, it wasn't actually a crime scene, was it? I pointed out. No, it wasn't, she agreed emphatically. Good, I said. How about tomorrow morning?

The Piggery, though small, turned out to be luxuriously appointed. Whether my fictional friend could afford this level of rustic chic was something I didn't discuss with the owner, Diane, who was very pleasant. I thanked her for giving me her time and letting me see the property on a Sunday morning.

Whatever the police might have told her about keeping the place as he'd left it, it was clear it had been thoroughly cleaned and emptied since Patrick Mulder had been staying there.

'Did he leave a lot of stuff for you to clear up?' I asked.

'No, just his clothes, and I've packed those away in his suitcases. He has an ex-wife back in South Africa, I'm told, so I'll have to await instructions from her, I suppose, as to whether she wants his stuff sent back or disposed of.'

'This is a lovely place,' I said, remembering what I was supposed to have come to look at. 'It looks very comfortable. No wonder he wanted a long-term stay.'

Diane smiled. 'I wondered if he might have been looking to buy a property in the area, although he didn't say so. He didn't say much, to be honest. But quite a few of our guests come here to stay when they're looking for second homes,' she told me sunnily. Ain't that the truth? I thought. Just ask the locals what they think about second-homers pricing them out of the market. I didn't comment. Instead, I murmured complimentary remarks about the king-sized bed and the tiled wet-room. 'Well, there's certainly room for two in here,' I said. 'But you say this, er . . . deceased gentleman was here on his own?'

'He was a bit of a mystery man to be honest,' she told me. 'There was one funny thing, though.' She reached in her pocket and pulled something out. 'We found this in the kitchen when we were clearing up.'

'A credit card? Surely the police want that.'

'No,' she laughed. 'It's not a credit card. It's a library card.'

'Library card?' I repeated. 'For Devon Libraries?'

'He used to go to Newton Abbot, spend hours there in the library.' She frowned. 'Don't you think that's odd? If you're staying here on holiday? The weather's been beautiful. Most people want to spend their time on the moor or on the beach, not shut in a library. In any case, if he wanted something to read, we've got shelves full of books in the games room for when the weather's wet.'

'Perhaps he was fussy about authors.'

'Well, he was a bit cheeky because he would have needed a home address in Devon to qualify for a card, and I bet he used ours. I can't imagine the police will want it,' she said, dropping it onto the kitchen table. 'I might as well throw it away, I suppose . . . Oh, Hildegarde, no!' she cried, dashing forward as some posh-looking breed of hound nosed her way in through the open door and loped into the kitchen. 'Out!' Diane cried, clapping her hands and shoving the reluctant Hildegarde before her. 'Out!'

I hurried after them, pulling the door shut behind me. I made a great fuss of Hildegarde, who seemed overjoyed to meet me, thanked Diane profusely for letting me take up so much of her time, and promised to get in touch once I'd discussed the details with my fictional friend. Hopefully she would forget all about the library card, now safely lodged in my jacket pocket. I didn't find it as difficult as Diane to imagine why someone like Patrick

Mulder might want to join the local library, even if he was only here on holiday. But then, she didn't know he'd had his laptop stolen.

Later that evening, my phone rang. I almost didn't answer it. I was dreading a call from anyone who might have found out about the incident at *Horrell's Antiques*. Particularly if they found it funny. Even worse if they didn't. But when I picked up, it was Kirsten's gentle voice at the end of the line.

'Hello Juno. Are you okay?'

I breathed a sigh of relief. 'Yes, thanks. I'm okay.'

'I wanted to phone you last night, but I couldn't. I am sorry about what happened yesterday.'

'Well, it was my own fault,' I admitted. 'I shouldn't have been snooping.'

'I think some of the people there were quite shocked at the way Peter behaved towards you, because he's usually so charming to customers. Some of them left soon after.'

'Really?' That would make me even more popular with him.

'The trouble is,' Kirsten went on with an irritating slowness, 'Peter has quite a nasty temper. When Julian was alive, it was awful, they would quarrel all the time.'

'What about?'

'Oh, I don't know,' she sighed. 'It seemed like the most trivial thing would set them off. Amber says they've always been the same. She calls it the curse of the Horrells. She says Peter resented his cousin because her mother chose Julian instead of him. Then, when

Anita left him for this yoga instructor or whoever he was, Peter never stopped goading him about it.'

'Did you ever meet Anita?' I was curious about the woman who could have inspired two brothers to become such bitter rivals.

'Not really. I mean, I'm sure she must have come to sports days and plays and things at school,' she said breathily, 'but I never really met her, not properly. Amber says that Peter thought he might be in with a chance with Anita when she left Julian, and when he realised she still wasn't interested he became more bitter still. But she thinks Peter didn't really love her. He only wanted the satisfaction of stealing her from Julian.'

'What was Julian like?'

Kirsten let out her breath in a thoughtful sigh. 'He was always nice enough to me, quite charming really. In fact, he was fine with everyone when Peter wasn't around. Amber says he was never the same after Tristan . . .' She hesitated awkwardly. 'Well, you know. I thought he was a bit sad. But Amber could wind him around her little finger, get anything she wanted. He always gave in to her. I wonder sometimes if he was trying to make it up to her for her mother going away.'

'But presumably Amber could have gone to live with her mother if she'd wanted to?'

'Oh, I don't know about that. Peter once said to me Julian had turned Amber into a spoilt brat and her mother was glad to get away from her.'

'That's a bit cruel.'

'Yes, well.' Kirsten hesitated. 'Peter can be like that . . . and Amber has a terrible temper too. Sometimes.'

'You mean she can give as good as she gets?'

Kirsten hesitated and then giggled. 'Well, yes, I do.'

'But if Peter and Julian really hated each other so much, why did they stay in business together?'

'I understand they'd each tried to buy the other out in the past, but couldn't agree on a deal. And Peter said something once about keeping your enemies closer than your friends. I think they were afraid to turn their backs on each other, if you know what I mean.'

I thought about those three quarrelsome brothers and their father long ago, who all had to be present before the Horrell chest could be opened. 'And has Peter never married?' I asked.

'No. He doesn't believe in marriage. Anyway,' she said, in the voice of someone who wants to bring a conversation to a close, 'as long as you're alright, Juno. I was worried about you.'

'I'm fine,' I told her, and thanked her for her call. She might have been a bit dim but she really was very sweet.

CHAPTER EIGHTEEN

Sophie and Pat were both in *Old Nick's* when I called in at the end of the day. 'I don't know why we bother to open on Mondays,' I heard Sophie telling Pat as I walked in. Her cheeks blushed pink when she saw me.

'I don't know why we bother to open at all,' I told her frankly. 'I take it we haven't sold anything today?'

'No,' Pat confirmed, jerking her knitting so that her ball of wool rolled onto the floor. She seemed to be creating some kind of animal. Pink. A pig, possibly? An aardvark? She was good at knitting quirky-looking creatures. She sold a lot of them. 'But there is a customer out the back there. At least I think she's a customer, she's waiting for you.'

'Who?' I mouthed.

She and Sophie both shrugged, Sophie making circles with one finger next to her temple, to indicate that she thought whoever was back there was insane. I could hear a lot of rustling as I approached and found Amber standing in front of the cheval mirror, admiring herself, wearing a man's tailcoat with a top hat perched on her head and a stiff net petticoat pulled on over her jeans.

'I'm having these,' she announced as soon as she saw me.

They would go well with all her steampunk gear. I was about to tell her so when she suddenly doubled up, convulsed by a shriek of banshee laughter. 'Well done, by the way! You really rattled Peter, the bastard. I haven't laughed about anything so much in years.'

'You and everyone else,' I muttered.

'Bravo, I say!' She flung the coat and top hat aside and struggled into a long-sleeved Victorian nightshirt, trying to wriggle it over her top. 'I'm taking this as well,' she informed me after gazing at her reflection for a moment.

At least we were going to sell something today, even if the profits would belong to Ricky and Morris. I watched her hold up a silk waistcoat, head on one side as she considered. She looked a lot better today than the last time I had seen her, as if she'd managed a couple of decent nights' sleep. 'I thought you might have been there on Saturday,' I said.

She laughed, putting down the waistcoat and picking up another. 'I wish I had been. I missed all the fun. But I was sent home,' she said, rolling her eyes dramatically. 'Dismissed, like a naughty schoolgirl.'

I smiled. 'Had you been naughty?'

'Peter thought so. He is such a bastard,' she added bitterly. She began to struggle out of the nightdress. 'All I want is some space in the shop to sell my stuff and he won't let me have it. I just want one room to display my own designs.'

'But he's not keen?'

She laughed. 'That's putting it mildly. My freakish old tat, as he calls it, has no place in an establishment selling antiques and fine art.' She flung herself down in a leather armchair and ran a hand through her hair. 'I'm supposed to be a partner in this business and I get no say at all.'

It was on the tip of my tongue to say that I had two empty rooms upstairs, just waiting to be rented out, but I held back. The thought of Amber up there was not something I was sure about. For a start, I'd expect her to put in some time minding the shop and I wasn't convinced she'd be reliable. I wasn't sure what Sophie and Pat would think about her either.

'So, where do you sell your stuff?' I asked.

'Fairs, concerts, conventions, anywhere there are likely to be steampunk fans. I'm doing a big one at Biddlecombe House this weekend.' She shot an impish glance at me. 'Why don't you come?'

'Thanks, I might.' I had to admit to being curious. 'Do I have to dress up?'

She shrugged. 'Your choice.' She began to gather up her purchases. 'I'd better pay you for this lot. And I want to look at some of that weird knitting woman's jewellery,' she added as she loped towards the main shop. I smiled as I followed. Weird Knitting Woman would be delighted, I was sure.

I tell awful lies sometimes. The library card, I informed the lady at Newton Abbot Library next day, belonged to a friend of mine who'd moved away and accidentally left it behind. I was glad Mr Mulder had patronised this library and not the one in Ashburton. I'm too well known to the volunteers there, they'd know I was up to something. At least, I *thought* it was him it belonged to, I carried on as I held the card out to her. 'Could you find out if it's really his?'

She took the card from me silently. I was probably asking her to break privacy rules or data protection or something. But she scanned it. 'What name do you think it is?' she asked, flicking me a searching glance.

'Mulder,' I told her, 'Patrick Mulder.'

She nodded. 'This is his card.'

'Can you tell me what books he borrowed?'

'I'm afraid I can't do that.'

'You don't keep records?'

'I don't mean that.' She lowered her voice. 'The library has the right to track anyone's computer usage. Just to make sure there is no *improper* use, you understand.'

'Porn and stuff?' I whispered back.

She tried not to smile. 'Or any other illegal activity.'

'And would it be possible to . . . er . . . view . . . what he was looking at?' I asked.

'We're not supposed to do it unless we are requested by the authorities, or we have suspicions ourselves about what's being viewed.'

'He's lost all his research notes, you see,' I told her. 'And now he can't remember what books he took out.'

'He would be able to access his borrowing record, but only he can do that.' She directed me a straight look. 'Unless you know his password.'

I cursed inwardly and held out my hand for the card. 'He'll just have to come back again and look for himself,' I said, smiling. She gave it back to me, a touch reluctantly, I thought.

'Thank you.' I moved away and began mooching along the shelves, turning my head to read titles on the spines and occasionally picking out a book for a closer look. After a few minutes the library assistant became busy with people at her desk. I dived around the back of the shelves to see if any of the computer terminals were free. There was one with no one sitting at it, so I hastily plonked myself in the seat and inserted Patrick Mulder's card into the card-reader. After a few moments the screen flashed up a *Welcome to Devon Libraries* and the message *Enter Password*.

How many goes at entering the password did I get, I wondered? I used up six, just experimenting with his name. I tried putting his Christian name first, then his surname; I tried including his middle name, then leaving it out. Should I put dots between his names? Next, I tried his surname with initials. As yet, I hadn't been locked out, but I reckoned I didn't have many chances left. I sat drumming my fingers on the desk while I pondered. Was the password case-sensitive? I tried *ThePiggery* and found myself staring at a list of borrowed titles.

My moment of triumph was short-lived. I began to scroll my way down the list and it wasn't inspiring. Most of it was just local history and information about the area. Nothing called *How to Get Murdered in Devon*, but I could probably have written that one myself. The list covered the last three weeks which was roughly the period I knew Mulder had been here. There were no titles that stood out.

As I sat there staring at the list glumly, the library assistant appeared in front of me, making me jump. 'I'm glad you're still here,' she said in a low whisper. 'It seems Mr Mulder has failed to return some items he borrowed.'

'I'll tell him,' I lied, although it would be a bit difficult getting through to him without assistance from a medium. 'Is there a fine to pay?'

'It's not quite as simple as that. These were items from the reference library. He was supposed to return them to the reference librarian when he'd finished looking at them. Reference books are not to be taken away,' she added severely.

He'd stolen them, in effect. In which case, they must have contained something important. 'I'm sure he misunderstood,' I said.

'We would have allowed him to photocopy whatever pages he needed,' she added sadly.

'Can you give me the titles?' I asked.

She'd already written them on a piece of paper for me. She pointed at the first title. 'This was a pamphlet.'

'*The Feoffee Chest*,' I read. 'What's that?'

'You can see it, just across the road, in the museum,' she whispered almost chattily. 'That's what's so annoying. He could have got all the information he needed about it from there. He didn't need to steal our pamphlet.'

'Is the museum still open?'

'It closes at four.'

I glanced at my watch. I reckoned I could just about get there at a quick sprint. I almost snatched the piece of paper from her, ripped the library card from the reader, grabbed my bag and ran. I could hear her tutting behind me because I hadn't stopped to close down the computer screen properly.

The museum had been recently rehoused in the old St Leonard's Chapel. Although it was literally yards away, getting to it involved crossing a busy road. But the little green man was glowing at the traffic lights, and I raced across just before he stopped beeping and turned red. As I got to the museum door, a man with a *Newton Abbot Museum* logo emblazoned on his sweatshirt was just in the process of locking it.

'Are you closing?' I asked breathlessly.

He was an upright, fit-looking man, grey-haired, with a definite look of security guard about him. 'Open again at ten tomorrow,' he told me with a smile.

'Oh dear.' I drooped with disappointment. 'I just wanted a look at the Feoffee Chest.'

'I'm sorry, love, I can't let you in now.'

'It's for my son's school project,' I told him, looking dejected. 'I promised I'd take a photo of it for him.' I am such a liar.

He definitely hesitated a moment. I gazed at him with my best helpless female expression. If I'd been Sophie Child, he wouldn't have stood a chance. But I'm a bit too tall and solid to convince in the helplessness department, and I don't possess her orphaned seal eyes.

'Sorry, I can't let you in. But tell you what.' He held up a finger and beckoned me into the lobby. 'Hold on there a minute.' He unlocked the glass door that led into the hall full of exhibits and slipped inside, where he collected something from a desk near the entrance. 'Will this do?' he asked. 'It tells you all about the chest. And there are photographs.' He handed me a pamphlet, probably the self-same pamphlet, I suspected, that Mulder had stolen from the library.

I could have kissed him. 'Oh, thank you so much, Mr . . .'

'Bolt,' he told me, twinkly-eyed. 'Mr Bolt.'

'Thank you, Mr Bolt.' I shook his hand, then fled, hearing him chuckle to himself as he locked the door after me.

Back in the car park, sitting in the driver's seat of Van Blanc, I unfolded the pamphlet about the Feoffee Chest. The first picture showed me a portrait of a group of distinguished-looking gents, roughly seventeenth-century, soberly clad in black and sporting beards and long mustachios. These were the foeffees, or trustees, the pamphlet told me, and there were eight of them. They were responsible for good works in the town and looking after the needy of the parish. There was also a photograph of the chest itself, where all the civic documents had been stored. It was similar to the oak chest in Amber Horrell's living room, except that it was massive by comparison and secured by no fewer than eight locks. The chest could only be opened when all the feoffees were present. In 1612 the names of two new trustees, John Reynell and Nicholas Par, had been inscribed on the lock-plate, and there was a close-up photograph of these too.

Why was this subject of so much interest to Patrick Mulder? I glanced at the piece of paper the librarian had given me, to see the title of the other item he'd nicked. I recognised it, because I remembered looking at it myself when I'd been in the library in Buckfastleigh. It contained the history of Gadd House. Something finally woke up in my brain. Patrick Mulder hadn't simply been collecting information about the local area. He'd been researching the Horrells.

What I should do, I told myself as I drove back to Ashburton, was to let the police know what I'd discovered, that Mulder had an interest in the Horrell family and maybe it was what had got him killed. But Inspector Ford had already warned me about my investigating activities. Perhaps I'd keep this information to myself for a little longer, at least until I could see where it was leading.

So, the sight of the inspector sitting waiting for me at the counter in *Old Nick's* flooded my face with a hot blush of guilt. My look of horror made his lips twitch with amusement as he stood up. 'It's alright Juno, I haven't come to tell you off.'

'Thank God for that,' I told him frankly, wondering how long he'd been waiting.

'I just wanted a word.' He nodded in the direction of the back room. 'Perhaps in the back room, if Miss Giddings will excuse us?'

I glanced at Pat, sitting knitting in the corner. She'd begun counting her stitches in the manner of someone not remotely interested in what was going on. 'You carry on,' she said, without looking up. I knew her ears would be on stalks.

I followed the inspector's solid form into the back room and indicated that he should sit in a Windsor chair. I took a seat on an old piano stool.

'Very comfortable, these old chairs,' he said, settling himself and running his hands along its wooden arms.

'English elm wood,' I told him sadly. 'Can't make them out of that anymore.'

He stretched his legs out in front of him, crossing his ankles. 'I have a question for you,' he began.

I waited.

'Who, apart from Mr Thorncroft, knew you were going to buy that car? Had you told anyone?'

I shrugged. 'I don't think so. I might have mentioned to Sophie or Pat that I was going to look at a car but to be honest, I don't remember.'

'Hmmm.' The inspector fell to silent musings.

'Is it relevant?' I asked after he'd pondered for a few moments.

'You're sure you didn't discuss it in a pub or somewhere where you might have been overheard?'

'I don't think so.'

'You see, the question which occurs to me, Juno, is why that car? Why hide the body of a murdered man in that particular car?'

I shrugged. 'Perhaps it was handy.'

'Handy to the scene of the crime?' He raised his eyebrows. 'Where was that? We've found no evidence of crime at Langworthy Hall, or at Mr Thorncroft's property on Halsanger Common. As far as we know, the only other place that car had been driven to was the garage where Miss Horrell had it valeted. And according to her, she checked the boot when she brought it back.'

'What about the place where Mulder was staying?' I asked. 'Is it possible he could have been murdered there?'

'Again, we've found no evidence of that.' He was silent for a while. You get used to silences with Inspector Ford. 'And was it clear to Miss Horrell, d'you think,' he continued eventually, 'that you were buying the car on behalf of Mr Thorncroft?'

'I'm sure it was. We had to fill in the paperwork with his name on it.'

He nodded. 'Of course. But I can't help wondering if she told anyone else that she was selling her father's car to the famous Juno Browne.'

I began to catch on at last. 'Are you saying you think that whoever murdered Mr Mulder put his body in that boot because he thought *I* would be the one to open it?'

'Not knowing the car was intended for the unfortunate Mr Thorncroft,' the inspector added. 'You see, Juno, you do have a reputation for finding dead bodies. Our murderer must have had a motive for killing Mr Mulder, but he might also be possessed of a macabre sense of humour.'

'What a damned cheek!' I breathed.

'Indeed,' the inspector agreed solemnly.

A nasty thought occurred. 'Does this mean the murderer is someone who knows me?'

'Now, there's no need to become alarmed. I'm not saying that. But someone who knows *of* you through reports of your exploits in the local paper, knows your reputation as it were – that is possible.'

I was speechless. I puffed out my cheeks in astonishment.

'But if you're sure you didn't mention the purchase of the car to anyone else,' the inspector went on, 'then I'd better go and talk to Miss Horrell.'

He heaved himself out of the comfortable Windsor chair, rather reluctantly, I thought. 'Good afternoon, Juno,' he said politely. And I was left there, struggling to remember everyone I had talked to between that Monday and the Friday, and wondering whether I had mentioned the car.

I told Daniel about the inspector's visit when he phoned that night. I didn't mention anything about library cards, statues with woodworm or my other investigating activities. But relaying the inspector's theory did not involve me in any subterfuge. After all, he'd come to me with it.

Daniel sounded serious. 'I'm not happy about this, Miss B. If the inspector is right, then this is all too personal for my liking.'

'It's someone's idea of a joke,' I said.

'It's a murderer's idea of a joke,' he answered gravely, 'and it must be someone local. Too close for comfort.'

'Not necessarily,' I pointed out. 'The inspector thinks it could be someone who's read about me in the *Dartmoor Gazette*, and that covers a large area.'

He didn't sound reassured. 'I'll see if I can get a flight over this weekend.'

'You'll get dragged to Maisie's birthday party, if you do,' I warned him.

'That's a sacrifice I'm prepared to make, Miss B.'

'Well, don't say I didn't warn you.'

'Don't you want me to come?' He sounded slightly hurt.

'Of course I do. But I'm sure there's nothing to worry about.' I could hardly tell him I didn't want him to scupper my chances of going to the steampunk festival at Biddlecombe House on Saturday night. 'And should you be taking time off again so soon?' I asked. The slight pause at the end of the line suggested I'd made a valid point. 'Look, really, I don't think there's any reason to worry,' I argued, pressing my advantage home.

He didn't sound convinced. 'Haven't the police made any progress on finding this man's killer?'

I brought him up to date with everything I thought I could safely tell him without revealing my involvement. 'The South African police are waiting to interview Mulder's ex-wife,' I said, 'to try to find out what he was doing in this country. That might help establish a motive. But the truth is, he may just have been an unlucky tourist, the victim of a random mugging that went wrong.'

'Up on Dartmoor? Run through with a sword?' Daniel sounded sceptical. 'Doesn't sound very random to me.'

'Well, we don't know where he was killed,' I pointed out, 'only where his body ended up. Besides, have you seen the kind of blades criminals carry around these days? Zombie knives and machetes, even kids carry them.'

'And I'm not supposed to worry?'

'All I'm saying is that for some wrongdoer to carry a long-bladed weapon is not particularly unusual these days. It could have been used in a random attack.' I tried to change the subject, telling him about Olly's school talk and how indignant he was at coming second place to his friend Marcus.

'The one with the boring accountant father?' Daniel sounded indignant as well.

'Ah! But he goes metal-detecting at the weekends and has made a few interesting finds,' I explained. 'Now, if you'd managed to come up with a bog body . . .'

'Yes, I see. Well, the best I can do is finding one in the boot of my car.'

We were back to that again. It took me another half hour to persuade Daniel I was not in any danger and, much as I would love to see him, there was no need for him to rush back to Devon on the next available flight. He was still sounding less than convinced when we ended our call. But I thought I'd managed to put him off. Not that I wouldn't have loved to see him. In fact, right then and there in the bedroom would have been perfect. But I wanted to check out this steampunk event. And I thought he might get in the way.

As I drifted off to sleep, it came to me out of the blue what a wonderful name Bolt was for a man who locks places up.

CHAPTER NINETEEN

One of the nice things about Ashburton is its independent shops. Walk along West Street, and within the space of a few yards of pavement you pass a craft-makers' gallery, a guitar shop, an artisan bakery and a bookshop dedicated to comics and graphic fiction. And that's without crossing the road. It was at the last of these shops, *Gnash!*, where I stopped to look in the window, my attention caught by a large poster. *Graphic Fiction Convention*, it proclaimed, at Biddlecombe House, this weekend, and illustrated by a picture of, among others, Syrius Blade.

The door of the shop was always open, so I popped my head inside. The owner, Jenny, was standing before her computer terminal with her back to me. Despite her swingy silver hair, her cool green trousers and negligently tied scarf, she was wearing the air of someone in more than a slight frazzle. I stood patiently for a moment, gazing at the artwork on the books around me. A lot of it was edgy, dangerous-looking. Graphic fiction, as Jenny will tell anyone who comes into her shop, is not just about comic books; it is a complex and sophisticated method of communication through the visual rather than the written word. 'This damn thing!' she cursed without looking over her shoulder. 'Hello Juno.'

'What's up?' I asked. Not that I could be of much help when it came to computers.

'I'm trying to order in some last-minute stock for this graphic event at the weekend, and this blasted machine is not helping. I think it might be the wholesaler's website that's at fault.' She turned to look at me and smiled in spite of herself. 'What can I do for you?'

'Nothing really. This event at Biddlecombe House at the weekend is a graphic fiction convention, then, is it? I thought it was a steampunk thing. Amber will be there, selling her clothes and stuff.'

Jenny shrugged. 'There will be a lot of steampunk fans going, because *he* will be there.' She nodded in the direction of a poster, the figure of Syrius Blade scowling down at us, swordstick in hand. 'There will be other authors and illustrators there, but Y. Knott will be the big draw.'

'Is it true he never lets his face be seen?'

She smiled. 'He's a recluse apparently. He wears a mask, hides in his little dark tent. It's a great gimmick. His fans love it.'

'And *Y. Knott* is a clever name,' I added. 'I thought I might go and get a book signed for Olly. He's a Syrius Blade fan. He'll love it.'

'In that case, I'll see you there,' she said.

'Are you sure about this, Princess?' Ricky asked as I stood in front of the mirror in the workroom at Druid Lodge.

I surveyed my reflection through the smoked lenses of the wire-rimmed spectacles I wore on the bridge of my nose. My hair was tucked up out of sight beneath a top hat. The corset I wore was too tight and revealing, but it looked great with brown leather trousers. 'I'm sure.' I had phoned Ricky and Morris to tell them what I wanted.

'We've got some beautiful Victorian dresses,' Morris told me, blinking, 'if you'd rather.'

Beautiful was not the look I was aiming for. More incognito. With my hair swept out of sight and wearing the smoked glasses, and a military-cut coat, I wasn't immediately recognisable. And the pilot's goggles perched on the brim of my hat and the watch chain looped across my corset were authentic steampunk accessories.

'You need a walking stick,' Ricky told me and handed me a Malacca cane, its brass handle shaped like the head of a greyhound.

'It's not a swordstick, is it?' I asked.

He frowned. 'Why, d'you need one?'

'I hope not.'

'Are you going to this thing on your own, Juno love?' Morris sounded worried.

'I asked Sophie if she wanted to come, but she's already got a ticket to see the flamenco dancing at the Arts Centre tonight.'

'Flamenco?' Morris clapped his hands in delight. 'How exciting! Are you sure you wouldn't rather go to that?'

'Flamenco dancing!' Ricky sneered. 'All that stamping about! Any fool can do it. All you need is an infestation of cockroaches.'

213

'It's only a graphic fiction convention,' I told Morris. 'Nothing sinister. Just a chance for people to meet some authors and illustrators and buy their books.'

'So why are you going?'

'Amber invited me, and anyway I'm curious.'

'She'll be there flogging her clobber there, will she?' Ricky was almost strangling me in an attempt to tie a silk scarf around my neck. 'I thought you were staying away from the Horrells.'

'I am. Except for Amber.'

'How do you know Peter Horrell won't be there?'

'Believe me, he won't be. This is not his kind of thing at all.'

Ricky stepped back to admire the effect of the scarf. 'Too dull,' he decided, pulling it off roughly and throwing it aside. He held out an arm imperiously. '*Maurice*, pass me that scarlet one!' I was subjected to another neck-winding before he stood back again. 'Much better!' he pronounced, looking me up and down. 'You look fabulous, Princess. Like a lesbian incarnation of Jack the Ripper.'

'Take no notice of him, Juno!' Morris cried, scandalised. 'You look wonderful! Are you sure you wouldn't rather wear a dress?'

'No thank you, I still haven't forgotten the tartan crinoline you saddled me with at the Christmas Fair last year.'

'You looked lovely in it,' he protested.

'Well, it didn't feel lovely. That damned hooped petticoat was like wearing a birdcage.'

Ricky was still surveying me critically, his eyes

narrowed. 'I still think there's something missing.' He held up a finger. 'Jewellery! She needs more jewellery!' He disappeared and we heard him rooting around in drawers at the end of the workroom. He came back with a jewellery box and began pinning a series of brass badges onto the lapel of my coat. 'This is what you need,' he added as he pinned on a medal.

'She's got the wrong hat!' Morris cried suddenly.

'I like this one,' I began but he had already disappeared.

Ricky shook his head. 'He's as mad as a hatter . . . Ah!' he called out, as if he'd suddenly caught on to what Morris was getting at. '*Maurice!* You're a genius!'

Morris came back into the room proudly bearing a top hat with a price ticket and feather shoved into its band, and perched on the brim, an old-fashioned alarm clock. 'You wore this in *Alice in Wonderland*,' he reminded Ricky.

'I did,' he grinned.

'You played the Mad Hatter?' I asked. 'What a surprise.'

'And I was the White Rabbit,' Morris added.

'No, you weren't, you clot,' Ricky told him. 'You were the Sleepy Dormouse.'

'I was the White Rabbit,' Morris insisted. 'Little Jenny Smith was the Sleepy Dormouse.'

'So she was,' Ricky acknowledged. 'I stand corrected.'

I removed the hat I had been wearing, unleashing my hair, and took the new hat from him before an argument had time to develop. I placed it on my head. The clock was a master stroke. Morris removed the goggles from the hat I had been wearing. There was no room for them on the brim of the new one. 'Put these around your neck, Juno love. That's where a lot of people wear them. On top of the scarf, that's it.'

'Leave your hair down,' Ricky ordered as I began to tuck it back under the hat. 'You look amazing.'

It blew my disguise, my attempt at incognito, but I had to admit he was right. The hat perched perfectly on top of my mass of hair. Somehow the odd mixture of Victorian, gothic and military worked. I had the look of a mad Victorian inventor about me; a ravishingly attractive one, obviously.

'I think you'll do,' Ricky announced, satisfied.

'Yes,' I agreed. 'I think I'll do, too.'

Biddlecombe House is a small stately home just off the A38 near Exeter, long ago sold off by its aristocratic owners to the National Trust. It sits in the midst of attractive parkland, with wide rolling lawns dotted with centuries-old oak trees, a deer park and an ornamental lake. On this particular occasion, the fine Palladian house was closed, and the centre of activity was a large cobbled courtyard, surrounded by buildings that had once been stables and coach houses before they were turned over to plant sales, a café and a gift shop. It was in this space that the various sellers of graphic fiction, picture books and comics had set themselves up, with guest authors and illustrators chatting to the eager fans who crowded around their tables. I could see Jenny, busily selling to customers at her *Gnash!* stall; and in the furthest corner of the courtyard, clothes rails sagging beneath the weight of steampunk costumes, was

Amber, the tables before her piled with hats, goggles and other strange accessories. She was shouting with laughter at something a man in a top hat was saying to her. Someone else was behind the table with her, I noticed, helping to serve the customers. It was Kirsten. She wasn't dressed in steampunk attire herself though, just jeans and a T-shirt. She looked nervous and I got the impression she might be an unwilling volunteer.

By the time I'd arrived, the sun was already sinking and the courtyard was lit by strings of electric lanterns. I was surprised to see the place was still so busy. This event had been going since the morning and it wasn't showing any sign of slowing down yet. Just outside the courtyard, set slightly apart from all the activity, was a tiny tent like a fortune-teller's, striped in red and white. The long queue of men, women and children snaking towards its dark entrance, clutching their latest Syrius Blade purchases, told me this was the lair of the mysterious Y. Knott.

The smell of pizza and street food, mingling with the aroma of hot coffee, drew me towards a line of catering vans against the courtyard wall. Music from a fiddler and a girl with a squeeze-box added to the jolly atmosphere and I made my way around the courtyard slowly, trying to take it all in. I took time to look around the bookstalls, working my way to Jenny's, where I picked up a copy of the latest Syrius Blade adventure. She grinned as I handed her my payment. 'You wouldn't like a signed, limited-edition T-shirt to go with it?' She held up a garment with Syrius Blade's image emblazoned on the front.

I looked at the price. 'No, I wouldn't,' I told her frankly. 'Have you sold many of those?'

'Yes, it's been a fantastic day! Are you going to get that book signed?'

'Of course.' Olly would never forgive me if I didn't.

She pointed in the direction of the queue for the tent. 'It looks like you've got a long wait.'

'It'll be worth it, I'm sure.' I was surprised by how many of the people around me had dressed up for the occasion, particularly the girls in their tightly corseted dresses and extravagant hats. Watching a stunning ensemble in bronze silk go by, I began to wonder if I shouldn't have worn a dress after all.

I headed towards Amber's little empire in the corner. She was wearing a green dress with a bustle, lace mittens and a three-cornered pirate hat. She saw me approaching and pointed. 'Juno Browne!' she yelled. 'Don't you look amazing?' She cackled with laughter, puffing on a vape clutched in one mitten. 'My God, woman, you pack a lot into that corset!'

'Too much,' I admitted.

'No, flaunt it, don't hide it!' she recommended. She pointed to the Syrius Blade book I was carrying. 'Aha! Have you had it signed?'

'Not yet. I'm about to. I'm intrigued to meet the mysterious Y. Knott.'

'Well, you'd better get in the queue if you want it signed before midnight,' she told me, and turned her attention to Kirsten and a man trying on a waistcoat.

I headed for the queue, but first went to buy a coffee and a carton of sugary churros to help me stay awake while I waited.

I started to feel nervous as the queue crawled closer

to the tent. Silly really. Perhaps I was picking up the excitement of the people in the queue around me, all dedicated Syrius Blade fans, many of them wearing their hero's T-shirt. I began chatting to the couple behind. Did they know what the author's real name was? I asked. It was a closely guarded secret, they told me. The woman in front of me turned around to say that she'd heard several names put forward, some of them famous ones, and probably none of them were the truth. Spreading rumours about his real identity was good publicity, it added to the mystery. It was like wearing the mask. Did he wear it just to preserve his privacy, or because, like the hero of his stories, he was scarred and disfigured? Or did he just want his readers to believe he was? There was a lot of chatter about this, which helped the time to pass.

It was another twenty minutes before I reached the tent. A guard stood at the door, a burly individual in a bowler hat and waistcoat, a kerchief knotted around his neck and a heavy truncheon in one fist, which I hoped was just for show. He looked like one of the characters in a Syrius Blade book, the lowlife type Syrius might employ if he needed some skulduggery carried out on his behalf. His job here seemed to be to keep the queue moving and to discourage fans from lingering too long in the tent as they tried to wring a few words from their favourite mystery author. No one was allowed to stay in there long, I noticed, before they came out again clutching their newly signed book.

Then it was my turn to step inside. I received a nod of consent from the bulldog in the bowler. The interior was dark, the canvas walls draped in black, and it was suffocatingly hot, the air smoky from the brass oil lamp that burnt on the table. Its low flame gave just enough light to make out the shadowy figure of Y. Knott sitting at his table in his mask and top hat, his long fair hair hanging down to his shoulders. Only a pale strip of his face was visible above the black scarf that covered him from nose to chin, and that was shaded by the brim of his hat.

I placed my book on the table and he slid it towards him, opening it at the flyleaf. His fingers were long, I noticed, his hands white and delicate. 'What name?' His voice sounded hoarse behind the mask. He must have been breathing in this smoky atmosphere all day, repeating the same question hundreds of times. He picked up a pen. It was a Sharpie but fashioned to look like an old-fashioned quill. I had seen some like it for sale on Jenny's stall.

'It's for a friend,' I explained. 'Could you please sign it *To Olly*.'

He flicked a glance up at me, his dark eyes burning in the glow from the oil lamp. 'Olly?' he repeated softly.

'Yes,' I told him brightly. '*To Olly with Best Wishes*.'

He lowered his burning gaze and wrote, signing the name with a flourish that came with long practice. He handed me back the book and didn't look at me again. I was dismissed.

'Thank you,' I said. He only grunted in response. I had planned to try to get him to talk a little, pretending I was his greatest fan, as so many in the queue before me had done. But in the end, I didn't want to hang around any longer than I had to in that stifling atmosphere, with the bowler-hatted henchman by the door eyeing me up as he swung his truncheon. I went out, and gratefully breathed in the fresh evening air.

I wandered off around the back of the tent, away from the lights and chatter of the courtyard, and stared out across the open parkland. The sun had long dipped below the horizon, leaving only a smear of bloody red beyond faraway hills, and turning the evening to twilight. I could make out the silhouettes of roe deer wandering in the park, but soon these too would be lost in the dusk. Crickets had begun their evening chorus, a repetitive, rasping orchestra in the long grass.

I turned around and the queue had cleared – there was no one waiting outside the tent. A moment later a figure emerged, not from the front, but through a flap in the back, taking off his bowler hat as he struggled to lift aside the canvas. He stood for a moment, turning to look all around him, his eyes scanning his surroundings as if he was searching for something. He didn't see me lurking in the shadows and, curious, I kept still.

'It's alright, mate,' I heard him mutter to the man inside. 'The coast is clear.'

A moment later, Y. Knott himself stepped out into the dusk and took off his hat. His fair hair clung damply to his forehead as he passed a hand across his glistening brow. Then he pulled aside his mask and took in some deep breaths. He seemed exhausted, like someone at the end of a long day. He stood for a few moments, sagging against the canvas of the tent behind him, breathing in deeply, before he accepted a cigarette from the packet offered him by his bowler-hatted friend, and placed it between his lips. I heard the striking of a match, saw it flare and as the flame was held towards his face, saw him clearly. He had a straight nose, finely chiselled cheekbones and a strong, clean jaw. There was no scarring or disfigurement I could see. He was a beautiful young man, with fair hair and burning brown eyes, and so like his sister, they might have been twins. He might call himself Y. Knott but there was no doubt in my mind that the face I was looking at belonged to someone I had once seen in a photograph. Tristan Horrell. I heard him speak, his voice soft and gentle, but I could not make out his words.

'Don't worry,' Bowler Hat replied. 'She's across the other side of the courtyard.' He must have been asking where Amber was.

The flame guttered and died, and the two men were hidden in the shadows. I must have drawn in a breath, because suddenly Bowler Hat glanced sharply in my direction. 'Someone's here,' he hissed, and Y. Knott flung down the cigarette, pulling the mask back over his nose as the two of them hurried away.

I started to follow them, back in the direction of the car park. But any thought I might have had of giving chase was foiled by the dark figure of a man striding towards me, effectively blocking my way. He was tall, wearing a long black coat with shoulder capes. For one dreadful moment I thought it might be Ricky. He and Morris had been concerned about me coming here on my own. They hadn't followed me, had they? Then I realised it was worse than that. It wasn't Ricky. It was Daniel.

CHAPTER TWENTY

Still reeling from the shock of seeing Tristan Horrell, I wasn't quick enough to get my head together. 'Daniel!' I cried, aghast. 'What are you doing here?'

'Good to see you too, Miss Browne with an e,' he said, grabbing me by the arm. 'And I might ask you the same question.'

'What I mean is,' I began, trying to recover from my surprise as he drew me close to him, 'how did you get . . . I mean, how did you know I was here?'

His response was to kiss me firmly. I felt a soft laugh go through him. 'You've got sugar on your lips.'

'Churros,' I admitted guiltily as we kissed again.

'After our last conversation I decided to catch the next flight,' he murmured. 'I thought I'd give you a surprise.' You certainly have, I thought.

'I bummed a lift from the airport with a man I'd got talking to on the plane. He was heading for Plymouth and he dropped me off in Ashburton.' He paused for a moment, unable to keep his eyes from straying to the contents of my corset. 'Dear God, Miss B!' he breathed huskily.

'Never mind that!' I snapped, trying and failing to button my coat across my chest. 'How did you know I was here? And where,' I added, taking him in more fully, 'did you get that fantastic coat?'

'Same place you got yours,' he responded, grinning. 'When I got to your flat and you weren't there, and Kate and Adam didn't know where you were either, I decided the next stop was Ricky and Morris's place.'

'Right. But how did you get to Biddlecombe House?' I stopped in horror as I realised. 'They brought you. They're here, aren't they?'

Daniel laughed and took my arm, steering me back towards the courtyard. He pointed. 'Can you see the fellow in the black coat and top hat, looks like an undertaker? And over there, the rather stout flying ace in a leather helmet and goggles?'

'Oh my God!' I groaned. 'So, you all arrived together?'

'Curiosity, Miss Browne with an e. We were all curious about what you found so attractive about this event.'

'You mean, you're checking up on me.'

'You can put it that way if you wish. You do look adorable when you frown.'

I ignored this. 'Look, for a start, Amber invited me. And I wanted to get the latest Syrius Blade book for Olly. He's a big fan and he'll love having this signed copy.'

As I spoke, I was still keeping an eye out for Tristan Horrell. Where had he disappeared to? Had he left the event or was he hiding somewhere? Suddenly, Amber's presence at the festival made more sense. She and that bowler-hatted bulldog with the truncheon must have been sheltering her brother, colluding in the creation of the fictitious character that kept his true identity a secret. But why had she lied to me, told me she hadn't seen her brother in years? What was the point of that? And what about Kirsten? She'd claimed she didn't know Tristan or where he was. Yet she was here now with his sister. Did she really not know of the connection between Amber and the mysterious Y. Knott? She must do, I decided, if she'd ever seen his face.

'You seem a little distracted, Miss B,' Daniel observed, frowning. 'Is something the matter?'

'No, I'm fine,' I lied. We seemed to be hurrying across the cobbles. 'Where are we going?'

'To that pizza van first. I'm starving. And then I think it's time I finally made the acquaintance of Miss Amber Horrell.'

'Of course, you've never met her. I'd forgotten that.'

'No, I haven't. And I'm curious to meet the woman who sold me a car with a corpse in it.'

Pizza took priority. We sat at a picnic table in order to manage tomato sauce and melting cheese with some degree of decorum, or at least without ruining our clothes, and downed two bottles of lager while we watched the graphic fiction fans go by. The crowd was thinning out now, the event beginning to wind down. I spotted Ricky and Morris chatting to Jenny, but I was still scanning the crowd for a glimpse of Tristan Horrell.

Over at Amber's stall, I could see Kirsten had become aware of Daniel's presence. She would remember him from our visit to *Horrell's Antiques* and was staring at him, open-mouthed. When she saw me looking at her, she turned away, but a moment later I saw her whisper to Amber, who swung her head in our direction.

Daniel was oblivious of all this. He'd wiped his greasy fingers on a napkin and was studiously absorbed in the most recent adventure of Syrius Blade. 'This artwork is superb,' he muttered. He turned the page, frowning, and then turned back. 'The backgrounds in these pictures, these rocks that this character is standing on, look familiar somehow.'

I stood up and peered over his shoulder. 'It would. That looks like Sheep Tor.' I pointed at another picture. 'And that's definitely Hound Tor in the distance.'

'Is Y. Knott a West Country writer then?'

'I don't know,' I answered vaguely, 'but he's obviously been to Dartmoor.' I patted him on the shoulder. 'I'm just going to the loo.'

'Don't go opening any freezers,' he responded without looking up.

I gaped at him for a moment. He *knew*. 'They told you, didn't they?' I glared across the courtyard at Ricky and Morris. 'Those two gossiping old windbags told you what happened.'

He looked up, grinning. 'I was in their company for at least an hour, my darling. You can't expect them to keep a secret that long.'

I eyed him suspiciously. 'And you're not angry?'

'Oh, I am angry,' he answered calmly. 'But not with you.'

I stood for a moment, wondering what he meant.

'Pop along, then,' he recommended, jerking his head in the direction of the sign pointing to the toilets.

'Right, I won't be a tick.' I didn't need to use the facilities at all, but with Daniel watching me, I was forced to head off in their direction and then work a convoluted route back to where I really wanted to be.

'Hello, Juno love,' Morris greeted me as I arrived, a little breathlessly, at Jenny's stall.

'Don't you *Juno love* me!' I told him fiercely. 'Which one of you two told Daniel what happened with Horrell's freezer?'

'Oh, well . . .' Morris faltered.

Ricky came to his rescue. 'We both did, Princess. Sorry.'

'It just sort of slipped out,' Morris added lamely.

'I fail to see how it could have,' I retorted. 'You're a pair of . . .' I paused, groping for the right word. 'Traitors.'

Jenny was struggling to smother a smile, which reminded me of the reason I'd come to her stall. 'Do you know who the guy in the bowler hat is?' I asked. 'The one who acts like a bodyguard to Y. Knott.'

'I think he's his manager,' she answered vaguely. 'At least, he always seems to be with him at these events. He always brings over the stock and the merchandise. But I think he acts as his security guard as well.'

'Does he need one?'

She shrugged. 'Some of the fans can be pretty intense. Why d'you ask?'

'He's just a bit intimidating, that's all. Standing there with his truncheon.'

She just laughed. 'It's all part of the theatre, I expect.'

Ricky nudged me. 'Lover boy's coming over.' I turned to see Daniel strolling towards us, Olly's book tucked under his arm. 'You've got to admit, he looks good in that coat.'

'Fits him beautifully across the shoulders,' Morris agreed admiringly.

'It does,' I admitted. He ought to wear it all the time. I'd known the Victorian look would suit him. He was at home in it. 'But if you think that's a reason for me to forgive you for blabbing, then you need to think again,' I told them and strode off to meet him.

Together, we turned towards Amber's stall. As we approached, she greeted us with a luminous smile. By now, she had obviously learnt from Kirsten who Daniel was, and didn't seem in the least wrong-footed at the thought of meeting him. In her situation I'd have wanted to curl up and die.

'Sorry about the car!' she called out before he'd had a chance to introduce himself. 'I don't usually throw in a free dead body. I hope you're not going to ask for your money back.'

Even from someone a little the worse for alcohol or some other kind of stimulant, Amber's remarks were massively insensitive. After finding a corpse in the boot, Daniel might have been suffering from post-traumatic stress for all she knew. But he didn't miss a beat. 'I won't,' he responded, 'but don't expect a rave review in *Exchange and Mart*.'

She cracked up with laughter. 'Fair enough.'

'It's good to see that you haven't become a victim

of whoever killed the unfortunate Mr Mulder,' he continued. 'I suppose you can't shed any light on his presence in my car?'

'I'm afraid I can't.'

'I thought not.' He smiled. 'I was hoping your Uncle Peter might be here this evening.'

She giggled. 'Hardly.'

'Well then, perhaps you could convey a message to him?'

I frowned. I had no idea what he was about to say.

Amber shrugged. 'Okay.'

'Tell him if he ever lays a finger on Miss B again, I will personally punch that expensive dentistry of his down his throat,' he told her with perfect calm. 'Can you tell him that?'

For a moment Amber's lips parted in surprise. Then she laughed again, delighted. 'I bet you would too,' she grinned, her eyes bright. 'I'd buy a ticket to see that.'

So, I added silently, gazing at Daniel with astonishment, would I.

'Thank you,' he said, and gripping my hand tightly, pulled me away from the stall. I turned back to see Amber still laughing and Kirsten gazing after us in open-mouthed stupefaction. 'Stay away from her, Miss B,' Daniel whispered fiercely as we moved away. 'She's dangerous.'

'Amber?' I almost laughed. 'She's a bit high at the moment, it's true.'

He turned to face me and his frown was troubled. 'She's as rotten as that damned uncle of hers. Stay away from both of them.' I thought he was wrong about Amber, or at the least he was overreacting, but to save an argument I just shrugged. He smiled, his voice softening. 'Is your van parked somewhere near here?'

'It is. Why?'

He slid his arms around my waist. 'I think we can both agree that you look magnificent in these clothes, Miss Browne with an e.'

'I do rather,' I admitted modestly. 'And so do you.'

'Excellent,' he murmured, his lips nuzzling my ear. 'Let's go back to your place and take 'em all off.'

CHAPTER TWENTY-ONE

As soon as Daniel slipped into the shower next morning, I crept into the living room and grabbed my phone. Amber didn't pick up but I hadn't expected her to. Her phone went straight to voicemail. 'I know who your brother is,' I hissed. 'We need to talk.' By the time I'd got into the kitchen and filled the kettle, the phone was buzzing in my dressing gown pocket and I slid it out.

'Please don't tell anyone,' Amber begged as I answered. She sounded pitiful, like a little girl.

'You know the police want to speak to your brother about the death of Patrick Mulder.' I paused a moment. 'He's not there with you now, is he?'

'No, I told you, Tris never comes here.'

'You also told me you hadn't seen him in years.'

'I know,' she admitted miserably. 'I'm sorry I lied. Look, I know I've got some explaining to do, but please don't tell anyone you've seen Tris,' she said, her voice close to tears. 'Give me a chance to explain.'

'Alright,' I relented. 'But only until tonight. I'll come and see you. Will you be at home?'

'Yes, yes, I'll be here, I promise.'

231

'Right, I'll see you later.'

As I disconnected, Daniel wandered into the kitchen, a towel around his waist, his dark hair damp and tousled. 'Someone on the phone?' he asked innocently.

'Just Our Janet,' I lied, smiling. 'About this afternoon. Oh my God! That reminds me,' I cried, clutching my hair. 'I haven't collected the cake!'

Maisie's ninety-eighth birthday party was held in St Andrew's church hall, which had been decorated with banners and balloons by her friends from church; and by members of her family, including Our Janet, who had made the long drive down from Heck-as-Like in honour of the occasion. By the time I arrived with Daniel, after a hasty trip to Buckfastleigh to rescue the cake, the guests had already begun to assemble. Maisie was in the seat of honour at the head of a long table, as yet covered only in a white tablecloth, its snowy surface sprinkled with tiny glittering sequins shaped like nines and eights. Two similarly shaped balloons floated on ribbons tied to the back of her chair. She was wearing a clean blue dress, forced upon her by a determined Janet, and her apricot curls were permed tighter than ever.

'Hello, Doctor!' she cried brightly, on seeing Daniel. 'Good of you to come.'

'This isn't the doctor, Maisie,' I explained. 'This is Daniel, my friend.'

'Oh, you're him, are you?' She sniffed, looking him up and down. 'You're a tall one, aren't you? Mind you,' she added, pointing in my direction, 'you need to be with a great long wench like that one there.'

'It's lovely to meet you, Maisie,' he responded gravely, with only the slightest tremor at the corner of his mouth. He shook her hand. 'Happy birthday! I've heard so much about you.'

She frowned darkly. 'You don't want to believe all of that, neither.'

'I only believe the good bits.'

She cackled with laughter. 'You going to make an honest woman of her?'

He glanced at me sideways. 'Do you think I should?'

'It's about time somebody did. Stop her getting up to all her nonsense.'

Rather than listen to myself being discussed in this fashion, I slipped into the kitchen, carrying the cake in its box. Our Janet looked relieved to see it. 'Everything's under control,' she assured me with a determined smile, despatching teenage grandchildren into the hall with trays of glasses and canapés. She had only been in Ashburton for a matter of hours but already wore the look of the last survivor of a month-long siege. We both held our breath as we took the lid off the cake box. But Angela had done a beautiful job, created perfection in peachy pink.

'It's lovely, Juno. Look at Mum's name all picked out in tiny flowers.'

'It's a relief,' I admitted. We'd nearly ended up with a Mary in green.

'Is there anything else I can do?' I was feeling guilty. So far, I'd taken little part in the preparation for Maisie's birthday party beyond booking her an appointment to get her nails done, sorting out the cake and ferrying her

233

to the hairdresser for her perm. The friends from church had helped with all the food.

'You do enough,' Janet breathed, fanning herself with a tea-towel. 'And your friend seems to be keeping Mother sweet,' she added, glancing into the hall, 'for the time being at least.'

'She seems on fine form.' I grabbed a glass of prosecco from a passing tray.

'Oh, she is!' Janet agreed. 'I'm just glad we decided to book rooms at the hotel instead of trying to cram ourselves into her cottage.'

I didn't know how many of Maisie's grandchildren and great-grandchildren Janet had brought with her, but the cottage would have been quite a squash.

'And of course, I'm in trouble because I insisted that we left Jacko behind this afternoon,' she continued, still flapping the tea-towel. Her cheeks were hot pink and I guessed she was experiencing a power surge. 'Mother wanted to bring him to her party, but you know what he's like when he gets overexcited. He'd only end up biting someone.'

I nodded sympathetically. Janet was probably right. He'd certainly make a nuisance of himself trying to cadge sausage rolls or bits of sandwich, or anything else he could blackmail people into dropping in his direction. I took a quick glance into the hall to see how Daniel was holding up with Maisie. They were still deep in conversation. I hadn't said a word to him about seeing Tristan Horrell the previous night.

'You'd better go and rescue him,' Janet murmured, nudging me.

'Yes, I think I'd better.'

'It's all a fuss about nothing,' I could hear Maisie telling him in her loudest voice. 'The only reason they're having this party is because they don't think I'm going to make it to ninety-nine and they're trying to keep me sweet.'

I went to join them, stepping carefully over a toddler in a bow-tie and best togs who was rolling his toy tractor around the carpet.

'Is he yours?' Maisie asked loudly, pointing at him.

'No, Maisie. He's one of yours. Great-grandchild, I think.'

She scowled. 'Well, how many is that, then?'

'Don't ask me,' I told her frankly. 'I've lost count.'

She tutted and turned to Daniel. 'I don't know why they keep having all these children. I don't want 'em. Do you know,' she went on, her voice rising in indignation, 'they're all staying in some posh hotel? My place isn't good enough for them.'

I stifled a smile.

'But would you really want all these grandchildren and great-grandchildren in your lovely cottage,' Daniel asked reasonably, 'filling the place with noise and toys and dirty nappies?'

Maisie frowned for a moment, struggling to think of a good reason to continue feeling aggrieved, but was forced to give in. 'You're right,' she admitted. 'I wouldn't. And Jacko wouldn't like 'em either.'

'And he's the most important one,' Daniel reminded her. 'He'll still be there when everyone else has gone back to . . . er . . . home.'

'You're right,' she agreed, patting his hand approvingly. 'He will.'

'I must bring Daniel around to your place sometime so that he can meet Jacko,' I said to Maisie, anticipating with a certain perverse relish the inevitable attack on his ankles. More guests came to greet the birthday girl at that moment, allowing us to make our escape. 'Crawler!' I hissed as we found ourselves seats further down the table.

'Not at all, Miss B, I was merely wooing her with my devastating charm.'

'Huh! She'll have forgotten who you are by the time we leave.'

Mountainous platters of sandwiches began arriving on the table, causing a momentary distraction, together with plates of sausage rolls, scones and dainty cakes. Maisie's neighbour Bev came to sit next to us, and as we were all busy stuffing ourselves with fat and carbohydrates, Ricky and Morris turned up to provide the entertainment.

Ricky played the piano while Morris sang songs from Maisie's youth, roughly Second World War era, until she insisted he sing 'My Way'.

What with the focus on the 'end', they were not the jolliest lyrics for a ninety-eight-year-old's birthday party. But she announced she wanted it played at her funeral, along with 'Onward, Christian Soldiers'.

'She would,' Our Janet muttered.

The lights in the hall were suddenly dimmed as one of Janet's daughters arrived bearing the birthday cake, loaded with as many flaming candles as could be crammed on. Maisie had to have several attempts at blowing them out while we all sang 'Happy Birthday', and eventually it was one of her grandsons who finished off the blowing when she ran out of puff. Then of course, despite being stuffed full already, we all had to have a piece.

Cutting the cake up took ages, but the boredom was relieved by a speech from the minister, talking about Maisie's long association with St Andrew's Church and how beautifully she had always kept her husband Bob's grave. With fresh flowers every Sunday, he told us, until Anno Domini and severe arthritis had got the better of her, and that job was passed over to one of the churchyard volunteers. He went on to extol her virtues as the matriarch of her family, a tower of strength, he assured everyone, to her children, grandchildren and great-grandchildren, beloved by all the generations, and loving in return; although judging by the expressions on their faces, this was news to some of them. During this long speech one of the youngest of Maisie's descendants, a tiny babe in arms, began to cry, and her recommendation that someone should shut that squealing brat up while the vicar was speaking only proved how accurate his estimation was.

'This is wonderful, Miss B,' Daniel whispered from the corner of his mouth. 'I haven't enjoyed myself this much in ages.'

Alas, all good things have to come to an end, and soon after, the guests began to escape, leaving Janet and her family to clear up and cart Maisie home with a mountain of wrapped parcels. I wondered what was in them all. What do you buy a ninety-eight-year-old, apart from flowers, chocolates and cardigans? I'd commissioned Sophie to paint a portrait of Jacko from photographs I'd taken. She'd done it for me on the cheap but had made a great job of capturing his character. You could almost smell him.

'I'm sorry I can't stay and help clear up,' I apologised to Janet as we made to leave, 'but I have to get Daniel to Exeter in time for his flight back to Donegal.'

'That's alright, Juno. It was good of you to come, especially when he's here on such a brief visit.' She sighed. 'Seeing as we still can't persuade Mother to shift from Ashburton and come to live near us, I suppose we'll just keep carrying on with things as they are.'

'I suppose we will,' I agreed. 'We seem to manage between us.'

Daniel, meanwhile, was saying goodbye to the birthday girl.

'Thank you so much for coming, Doctor,' she was telling him. 'Especially on a Sunday.'

'My absolute pleasure, Maisie,' he responded.

'While you're here,' she went on, clutching at his sleeve, 'I could do with some more of that stuff for my piles.'

He patted her hand in a doctorly fashion. 'We'll ask Juno to get you some, shall we?' He slanted a wicked glance at me. 'I'm sure she'll be able to sort you out.'

'Practising your bedside manner, Doctor?' I whispered as we made our escape from the hall.

He glanced at his watch. 'Alas, Miss B, we don't have time for playing doctors and nurses. I really have to catch this next flight if I'm to be back at work tomorrow morning.'

He was right about the time. We were cutting it fine. I got him to Exeter airport with just ten minutes to check in. Our goodbyes were as passionate as the departure lounge allowed and over too soon.

'Brief encounter again, Miss B.' Daniel gave me a final hug.

'Thank you for coming,' I murmured. 'It's been so lovely to see you.'

'Worth the trip for the sight of you in that corset,' he grinned. He began to walk away and then turned to look back. 'If you talk nicely to Ricky and Morris, they might let you keep it.'

'You try wearing the damn thing,' I muttered and headed for the exit.

There was no sign of Amber when I arrived at Langworthy Hall. The front door was locked and she didn't respond to my banging. She'd probably gone out to avoid talking to me. 'I know you're in there!' I yelled, although I didn't know any such thing. I went around the side of the building, stopping to peer through French doors into what seemed to be a dining room. Nothing to see but an oak table set with candlesticks and four empty dining chairs. I carried on until I came to the back door, which was unlocked, and open. I stepped inside and peered about me.

After the brightness of a sunlit evening, it seemed gloomy inside, almost dark. I hunted around for a light switch and flipped it on. Something long and dark was hanging from a beam at the end of the kitchen. My heart lurched in shock, my hand flying to my mouth. But it was just a dress, one of Amber's steampunk costumes, dangling from a hanger. I felt my body flood with anger. Amber knew I was coming. Had she put it there deliberately just to give me a fright, to make me think she'd hanged herself? It was a pretty tasteless joke. I went to the garment and grabbed a handful of the skirt. The fabric was damp, as if it had been washed and hung from a convenient hook to dry, but I still wasn't convinced. And where was Amber?

I went into the hall and yelled her name. No answer. Was she hiding upstairs? As I turned back into the kitchen I saw her through the open door, strolling across the lawn. As she saw me, she raised her hand in a careless wave, as if she didn't have a trouble in the world, Ben plodding by her side. 'Juno!' she called out cheerily. 'Come and see the garden.'

'I've been knocking,' I told her, between gritted teeth, as I bent down to smooth the dog's head.

'Sorry, I was down by the stream. I find it very calming down there.' She slid an arm companionably through mine. 'Come and see.'

I didn't intend to let her distract me but I never pass up a chance to look around a garden, especially one as large and beautifully kept as this.

'I have a gardener who does all the work,' she said, as if she read my thoughts. 'I don't look after all this myself.' She laughed lightly. 'Peter insisted I kept him on after Dad died. He doesn't want the place going to rack and ruin, he says, so he spends my money on its upkeep.'

'He's right, don't you think,' I suggested, looking around me at well-tended flowerbeds, trained fruit trees and rose arches laden with blossoms. Obnoxious as Peter Horrell might be, in this case I had some sympathy with his point of view. I allowed Amber to lead me down to a tiny stream, burbling pleasantly over mossy rocks and splashing into a pool.

'We used to keep koi carp. But after Dad died, I kept forgetting to feed them,' she told me heedlessly, 'so Peter got them taken away.'

I glanced down at Ben. At least he could bark when he was hungry.

Amber sat on the grass, gazing down into the pool, and after a moment I sat down beside her. 'It's lovely here, isn't it?' she asked. There was a bird feeder hanging from the branch of a nearby apple tree, and for a moment we watched chaffinches flitting back and forth. Across the stream, on the far bank, I could glimpse the pink flowers of Himalayan balsam peeping through the bushes.

'It is lovely,' I agreed, 'but it's not what I'm here to talk about.'

She frowned and began fiddling awkwardly with blades of grass. 'Look, what you need to understand is . . . when Tris was locked up, accused of killing that boy . . .'

'What was his name?' I interrupted her. 'The dead boy?'

She shrugged. 'I don't remember.'

I didn't believe that. If your brother gets put away for murdering someone, there's no way you're going to forget the victim's name. 'Christopher someone,' she admitted, after I'd been waiting a moment. 'I'm not sure I was ever told his last name, to be honest. Anyway, I was never allowed to visit Tris after he was taken away. And when he came out, I wasn't even told, wasn't allowed to know where he was. He and I had been so close.' She stopped speaking, concentrating on ripping blades of grass from the lawn.

'It must have been hard,' I said softly.

'Tristan had a new identity, Dad told me. A new name. He wanted to break completely with his past. With us. We must forget him. Just as if . . .' Her voice broke tragically. 'Just as if he was dead.'

Like poor Christopher, I added silently. 'Didn't he get in touch?'

'He couldn't,' she whispered miserably.

'Then how did you make contact with him?'

Amber turned to look at me. Her eyes were bright with tears but her expression was triumphant. 'I found him. I tracked him down.'

'How?'

'Through Syrius Blade,' she said excitedly. 'As soon as I saw that first book I knew it was Tris's work. We used to draw together all the time when we were children. And even back then, before he was sent away, Tris had these amazing characters in his head, characters like Syrius. He used to show them to me. And he would sign them. *Y. Knott*. I realised he was writing the books as a way of reaching out to me, so I could find him.'

'But he knew where you were,' I pointed out warily. 'If he wanted to get in touch, why didn't he do it?'

'Because *she* wouldn't let him.' Amber looked suddenly vicious. 'It was on the back of the book, in small print, the name of the publisher. *Aquae Sulis*.'

'That's the Roman name for Bath.' I frowned, puzzled.

'Exactly!' Her face was bright and fierce. 'That's where she lives.'

'Who?' I asked, still in the dark.

'Anita!' She spat her mother's name. 'I looked up the publisher's name at Companies House. *A. Horrell* was listed as the managing director.'

'Just slow down a moment,' I said. 'You're saying that your mother is listed as the publisher of Tristan's books?'

'Yes, it all happens in Bath. That's where the books are printed and everything.'

'And is it where Tristan lives?' I asked.

She shook her head. 'Anita won't tell me where he lives. I went to her house once and demanded that she tell me, but she wouldn't. It's almost as if he's still in prison. She wants to keep him under lock and key. She employs that Neanderthal to keep watch on him.'

'You mean the guy in the bowler hat?'

She nodded. 'His name's Roger.'

'But Tristan is a free man now. He can do what he likes, surely?'

'You don't understand! Tris is not like other people. He's always been vulnerable. And after being in an institution for so long, he can't cope on his own any more. He needs someone to live with him, to look after him. He needs *me*,' she cried, jabbing her fingers at her own chest as the tears ran down her face.

I was silent a moment, not sure what to say. I wasn't quite sure how much of what Amber was saying was true, how much her fantasy. 'So, is that why you go to these steampunk festivals, so you can be near Tristan?'

'They are the only places where we can see each other, get a chance to talk.' She grinned suddenly. 'When we can manage to outwit Roger for a bit.'

'Don't you ever talk on the phone?'

She shook her head. 'Tris doesn't have a mobile. He doesn't trust the modern world. He lives in Syrius's world. Drawing is all that makes him happy. But you see, he couldn't have killed that man Mulder because he was in Bristol. I was there with him at the festival.'

I knew that wouldn't work as an alibi. Patrick Mulder was murdered sometime between the Tuesday and the Thursday. Amber couldn't have met her brother in Bristol until Thursday evening at the earliest. Being at the festival didn't let Tristan off the hook. But it was what Amber wanted to believe, and for the moment I wasn't going to challenge her.

'How much of all this does Kirsten know?' I asked.

'Kirsten?' Her face twisted in scorn. 'She doesn't know anything.'

'But she was there with you the other night at Biddlecombe House, when Tristan was there. Doesn't she know who he is?'

'No, she doesn't,' she smirked. 'And I didn't ask her to come. She volunteered to help. I know it was Peter who sent her to spy on me.'

'Spy?'

'Kirsten is sly,' Amber sneered. 'She was always sneaky at school.'

She was certainly having a sly affair with Peter, something Amber didn't seem to know about. 'So, you're saying Tristan was not here when Patrick Mulder was killed? He wasn't staying here with you?'

'No!' she almost screamed at me. 'I told you. Tris hasn't been home since . . . since before that thing at his school happened. He wasn't allowed to come home. And afterwards . . .' She shook her head sadly. 'He didn't want to come.'

'And you have no idea where he is now?'

'I wish I did.'

'After the festival in Bristol,' I went on, 'you didn't come home. As far as the police were concerned, you were missing. You said you stayed with a friend, but wouldn't tell them who.'

'I wasn't with a friend,' she admitted. 'Roger was there with Tristan in Bristol and I hardly got a chance to speak to him. When the festival ended, he took Tris away. I went to Bath and stayed at a hotel just across the road from where Anita lives. I was keeping watch on the place. I followed her from there a few times, and once I saw Roger go in and come out. I followed him too.'

'You thought he might lead you to Tristan?'

She nodded. 'But Roger spotted me and I had to run. Then Kirsten started messaging me about the dead man in the car, so I came home.'

'And did you get a chance to talk to Tristan at Biddlecombe House?' I asked.

'No.' She gave a bitter laugh. 'Roger was on full alert.'

I left her in the garden, wondering as I drove Van Blanc down the hill how much of what she had told me was really the truth. But if Tristan Horrell had killed Patrick Mulder, would he come back to Devon, to Biddlecombe House, a place so close to the scene of the murder? And so soon after the event? Even in disguise it seemed a risky thing to do. But there are murderers who turn up at their victims' funerals, if I'm to believe what I see on television. They enjoy the frisson of danger involved in returning to the scene of the crime. Perhaps Tristan Horrell was one of those.

CHAPTER TWENTY-TWO

Monday was full-on, with Domestic Goddess cleaning jobs one after another throughout the day. It was hot and muggy with the threat of thunderstorms and difficult to work with any enthusiasm. I scrubbed my way around the Brownlow family's kitchen. The Brownlows – husband and wife, both doctors – live in cheerful chaos with their three growing children. Chris, the eldest, is away studying at university and helps Adam out at *Sunflowers* when he comes home for the holidays, serving and washing up. I don't know if he was responsible for the chaos in the kitchen but someone had cooked a roast the day before, and left all the washing up for me. They'd also had dessert, judging by the jug of congealed custard sitting on the windowsill.

As I scraped plates and loaded the dishwasher, my mind kept returning to Tristan Horrell, and that footstep. The one I had heard coming from the floor above my head, on my first evening at Langworthy Hall. Whatever Amber said, someone had been up there. She insisted that Tristan hadn't been back home for years, but I suspected this was a lie. It could have been Tristan staying in that spare room. But if it had been him, and he'd killed Patrick Mulder for God knows what motive, then why dump his body in Daniel's car?

A slurping noise close to my foot alerted me to the fact that the Brownlows' golden retriever, the imaginatively named Goldie, was helping me with the cleaning, licking splashes of gravy from the skirting board. Sighing, I reached for the mop. None of this answered the question of what Mulder had been doing in the area in the first place, apparently looking into the history of the Horrell family.

'Nothing makes any sense.' Goldie licked her chops and stared at me hopefully, in case I might have food concealed about my person. Why was a diamond miner from South Africa researching the fluctuating fortunes of a family who had enjoyed wealth and privilege centuries ago but had since, by their standards at least, fallen on hard times?

'Perhaps that's it.' Goldie's interest in my story was clearly waning in favour of trying to paw open the door of the pantry. Perhaps it was not the Horrell family Mulder was interested in, but that famous red diamond, brought back by the ill-fated India; a diamond Peter Horrell claimed had been lost years ago. Mulder had worked in a diamond mine. Would he have known about the Horrell diamond, out in South Africa? Just how famous, I wondered, was this thing?

If I wanted to find out about red diamonds, there was only one person in Ashburton who would be able to help me: Reuben Lenkiewicz. He'd helped me out with pricing more than once, on those rare occasions I got my hands on jewellery that couldn't trace its origin to a Christmas cracker.

'What can I do for you, Juno?' he asked, as I walked into his shop. He spoke in the patient voice of one who knew I hadn't come in because I was in the market for precious jewels.

I took out my phone and showed him a photo of the India Horrell portrait. 'Do you know this picture?'

'Of course. It's India Horrell. The artist is unknown but it's a fine example of eighteenth-century portraiture.'

'Isn't the necklace unusual in a portrait of that era? In most of the portraits I've seen from the period, the women's necks and shoulders are bare.'

'It was the fashion,' he admitted. 'Look at this one, for example.' He pointed at a portrait hanging on the wall, of a young girl dressed in yellow silk. 'All her glowing white skin on show is supposed to be a sign of her good health, to show she's a good marriage prospect. And the little posy of lily-of-the-valley she's carrying represents her purity.'

'So, this picture is telling us she's a virgin and ripe for the marriage market.'

'Exactly,' he confirmed. 'Now India Horrell was already a married woman when her portrait was painted, so this picture reflects the family's wealth. That's a very rare jewel and the Horrells wanted to show it off.'

'The red diamond?'

'Indeed.' He raised his brows, looking vaguely impressed. 'Most people think it's a ruby.'

I confessed that Peter Horrell had told me. 'I know it's very rare.'

'It certainly is. Fewer than thirty pure red diamonds have ever been found. In terms of dollars per carat, they are the most expensive diamonds there are.'

'How expensive is most expensive?' Diamonds are not something I usually shop for.

He pushed back a flowing lock of silver hair and pondered. Like Inspector Ford, Reuben is not the sort of person you can hurry. 'The biggest red diamond ever found would probably be the Moussaieff diamond,' he decided after a moment. 'It sold quite recently for around eight million dollars.'

'So even a small one would be worth killing for,' I muttered.

He looked vaguely alarmed. 'Well, I suppose.'

'Sorry, just thinking aloud.' I moved on hastily. 'What makes a diamond red? Is it some sort of mineral?'

Reuben was shaking his head. He indicated a delicate-looking Sheraton chair and invited me to sit. I did so carefully, not sure that such a fragile stick of furniture could take the weight of a healthy woman. He took a more solid-looking porter's chair and paused reflectively for a moment, steepling his fingers. 'It's an imperfection, a deformation, if you like, in the crystalline structure. It affects the way light passes through the gemstone and hence the way we see it. Sometimes this results in a brownish or orange-red colour, but it's the true blood-red diamond which is the most valuable.'

'Where do they come from?'

'Australia, mostly, in the Kimberley region. But they've also been discovered in Brazil.'

'South Africa?' I asked and he nodded. South Africa, where Patrick Mulder came from. Interesting. 'But India Horrell came from, well, India,' I pointed out.

Reuben smiled. 'And her diamond almost certainly came from the Golconda mines, in a region that is now part of Hyderabad,' he went on knowledgeably. 'Mining was at its peak there in the seventeenth and eighteenth centuries.'

'That would fit in with when she married into the Horrell family.'

'Some of the most famous diamonds in the world have come from the Golconda mines,' he added. 'The Daria-i-Noor, a pale pink diamond, came from there. It weighed in at one hundred and eighty-two carats.'

Carats don't mean much to me. Reuben smiled and made a circle with his forefinger and thumb, indicating the space he'd created, about the size of a pigeon's egg. Now I understood. In diamond terms, that thing was big.

'Another interesting point about the Golconda diamonds,' he went on, 'is they are said to be cursed.'

'Cursed?' I repeated. 'Really?'

Reuben laughed. 'Some of the people who have owned them have come to unpleasant ends. But to be honest, they probably would have done anyway, considering the kinds of people they were. Pirates and thieves, a lot of them.'

'No one knows what happened to the Horrell diamond.'

He shrugged. 'I doubt if it was really lost. Far more

likely it was secretly sold to pay off family debts. Some private collector has probably got it somewhere.'

'And would whoever it was sold to have bought the curse as well?'

'I imagine so.' He smiled. 'I've never been tempted to buy one.'

'I don't think I'm putting one on my Christmas list either.' I thought for a moment, remembering what Sheila in *Keepsakes* had told me. 'Do you know the Horrell family?'

A shadow crossed his usually amiable features. 'I have dealt with them in the past.'

'But not now?'

He shook his head. 'Julian Horrell screwed a dear customer of mine over a portrait. Told her it was valueless and paid her a few hundred pounds, then took it to auction where it sold for seventy thousand.'

'And he knew its true value?'

He gave a bitter laugh. 'He'd been in this business too long not to know.'

'And the lady who sold it to him had no redress?'

'Difficult to prove Julian didn't buy it in good faith. It would have meant a court case and the lady wasn't up to it. Her health wasn't good. She died shortly afterwards.'

'I'm sorry.'

Reuben shrugged. 'Well, Julian got his just deserts, I suppose.'

'You mean his accident?'

'He came to an unpleasant end.' He nodded gravely. 'Like the pirate and thief that he was.'

* * *

The next morning, I woke up to thick mist. The hot weather had broken in the night with dramatic rolls of thunder over the moor. Then heavy rain had pelted the roof for hours. The leaky gutter outside my bedroom window created a waterfall that spattered noisily onto the glass of the ramshackle lean-to conservatory beneath. How many times had Adam tried to fix it? To be fair, he's not good up ladders, but I would be submitting a complaint in triplicate next time I passed the kitchen door.

By dawn the rain had stopped. The mist hung low, the pointed tops of fir trees on the hills above the town lost, the light blotted out by a smothering duvet of damp grey. The air was still, with no breath of wind to blow the mist away. The dogs didn't mind. After a spell of hot, dry days, the gurgling streams and splashy puddles, the dripping trees, damp cushions of moss and muddy paths through the woods were a paradise of fresh, earthy smells, requiring much licking, sniffing and snorting. Nookie the husky and Dylan the German shepherd bounded ahead, the first dogs to disappear into the mist, followed by Boog and E.B., with little Schnitzel's short legs bringing up the rear. I strolled along behind them, thinking.

Daniel had phoned last night, and sent me a lovely video of Lottie frolicking around with her new friend, black Labrador puppy, Albert. I'd told him all I'd learnt from Reuben about red diamonds, although I hadn't divulged that I'd gone into his gallery to find out about them. It might count as poking my nose into a police investigation. I pretended I'd bumped into him outside his shop. I'd also told him what Reuben had told me about Julian Horrell.

'I told you they were a bad lot,' Daniel had said. 'Stay away from them, Miss B. And I mean all of them.'

'I'll do my best,' I promised. I had to admit I had started to think he was right. I was sorry for Amber, who obviously had problems, but I was beginning to wish I'd never had anything to do with her. I certainly wished I'd never bought Daniel that damn car.

Fortunately, he changed the subject. 'Did Olly like his copy of the Syrius Blade book?'

'He loved it. I gave it to him last night when he came back from music school. He had a wonderful time. Now it's just the anxious wait for the exam results.'

Daniel laughed. 'He didn't seem very anxious about them the last time we saw him.'

'But now they're getting closer. And then he'll have to decide what to do next, and that will be the difficult bit. According to Elizabeth, he changes his mind about what A-levels he wants to do every five minutes. Oh, and I returned your coat to Ricky and Morris,' I remembered.

'And the corset?' he asked wistfully.

'And the corset. I've got no intention of squeezing myself into that thing again.'

'I'm disappointed, Miss B, in your lack of perseverance.'

'Perseverance be damned, I like to breathe occasionally.'

Now, I emerged from the woods. Ahead of me the dogs had disappeared, although nearby snuffling noises and the occasional bark told me they couldn't have got far. I called and they all came, eventually, although it took a blast on the whistle before Nookie returned, appearing out of the mist like a silver-white ghost, her fur beaded with pearls of moisture. Then Dylan came bounding after her, with one ear up and one ear down, and we turned off onto the lane that would take us to the road and back into town.

'What do you mean, you *know*?' I asked Dean indignantly. I had phoned him later that morning, asking if he could come into the shop. I sat him down in the kitchen with a cup of tea, ready to astound him with all I'd learnt from Amber about her brother's identity and his possible whereabouts. I hadn't got very far before he announced that he knew all this already. 'How do you know?' I demanded, feeling put out.

'Peter Horrell. We asked him for Tristan's mother's address.'

'And he gave it to you?' I asked, astonished.

Dean grinned. 'We *are* the police.'

'Then you know Tristan is in touch with Anita Horrell?'

'Yes.' He took a sip of his tea. 'We've interviewed her.'

'You've been to Bath?'

'It's only a couple of hours away.'

'Then you know all about the Syrius Blade books?'

A biscuit disappeared into his gob. 'Ughumm,' he muttered, nodding.

'Does Anita know where Tristan is?' I asked.

He shook his head. 'Not at the moment,' he managed eventually, 'and if she did . . .'

'I know,' I predicted, disgruntled, 'you wouldn't tell me.'

'Quite right. I wouldn't, but the fact is,' he went on, holding up a chunky finger, 'he lives with her. He's lived with his mother since he was released from the institution, apparently. Calls himself David Smith, and his neighbours have never known him as anything else. But he's a recluse. They seem to think he lives in a shed at the bottom of his mother's garden. According to her, that's where his studio is. He works there, and sleeps there if he's working late, which is most of the time. Anyway, we searched the place and he's not there now. Anita Horrell says she hasn't seen him or his carer since they set off for Biddlecombe.'

'His carer?' I repeated. Amber hadn't said anything about Tristan having a carer.

'A bloke called Roger Faulkner. He lives there too. Tristan is on medication which has to be carefully monitored and this chap Faulkner used to be a psychiatric nurse, as it happens, so he helps look after him.'

This must be the same Roger that Amber had been talking about, the bulldog character in the bowler hat whom I'd seen standing in the entrance of the Syrius Blade tent. 'I saw him at Biddlecombe House,' I told Dean. 'Stocky, carries a truncheon, looks like the type you wouldn't want to tangle with.'

Dean nodded. 'Mrs Horrell says he looks like one of the characters in the books, and he enjoys acting the part. But he's there to keep an eye on the fans as well.

According to his mother, it upsets Tristan if any of them try to get too close or ask personal questions. Once or twice their van has been broken into, and they've had merchandise and personal items stolen and he's really freaked out.'

I could just imagine what a signed, limited-edition Syrius Blade T-shirt might fetch on eBay.

'Roger Faulkner phoned Mrs Horrell on Saturday night after the Biddlecombe do,' Dean continued, 'to say that he and Tristan were taking off for a few days for a bit of wild camping on Dartmoor. She says Tristan likes to retreat into the wilderness, especially after a signing, and as long as Roger is with him, she doesn't worry.'

'And does Anita know anything about the death of Patrick Mulder?' I asked.

'Never heard of him.' Dean puffed out his cheeks in a sigh. 'She swears Tristan was in Bath, at her house, all of the week preceding the festival in Bristol. But then, she would say that,' he added cynically, 'she is his mother.'

'But won't this Roger Faulkner character – manager, bodyguard, carer or whoever he is – be able to swear to it too?'

'If he ever gets back from this camping trip, we'll ask him. Just out of interest,' he added, frowning, 'what were you doing at Biddlecombe House?'

'Attending a graphic fiction festival,' I told him, snapping the lid of my biscuit tin shut. 'It's a free country.'

'Amber Horrell wasn't there, by any chance?'

'Yes. She was selling her steampunk stuff.'

He sniffed dismissively. 'I can tell you something about her I bet she hasn't told you.'

I leant towards him, curious. 'What?'

'There's a court injunction against her. She's not allowed within two hundred yards of where Tristan Horrell lives.'

I stared at him open-mouthed. 'Did his mother tell you this?'

'She did, but she isn't the one who took out the injunction. That was Tristan Horrell, aka David Smith, himself.'

I gave a low whistle. 'Did she say why?'

'She freaks him out, according to his mother. She's too excitable. He can't stand her anywhere near him.'

I thought back to that moment at Biddlecombe, standing outside the back of Y. Knott's tent, and how careful Roger Faulkner had been to make sure the coast was clear before Tristan came out. Then Tristan had asked Roger a question, something I couldn't hear. He'd replied, *Don't worry. She's across the other side of the courtyard*. I had thought Tristan had simply been asking where his sister was. Now it sounded as if he'd been checking she wasn't too close. 'No, you're right,' I said, leaning back in my chair. 'She didn't tell me that.'

Daniel phoned again later in the evening. 'You'll never guess what I'm reading, Miss B,' he said by way of a hello.

'*Fifty Shades of Porn*?' I suggested, settling myself on the sofa.

He laughed. 'No, I've read that. I'm reading a Syrius Blade adventure. I picked it up in a second-hand shop in Limerick. I think it must be one of the very early stories in the series. This Blade is a fascinating character, isn't he? Did you know he accidentally killed his best friend in a sword fight? . . . Are you there?' he asked after a moment. 'You've gone quiet.'

'No, I didn't know,' I said, as Bill leapt up and took advantage of my lap.

Daniel, who still knew nothing about the identity of Syrius Blade's author, cheerfully rattled on. 'He's also got a wicked uncle who bears an uncanny resemblance to Peter Horrell.'

'Well, he does look like a wicked uncle, you have to admit.'

'Too villainous by half,' he agreed.

'What's this book called?'

'*Syrius Blade and the Red Diamond*,' he read out. 'Olly might like it. I'll bring it over next time I come.'

He chatted on for another few minutes, but I was barely listening. Had Tristan Horrell written *Syrius Blade* as a kind of therapy, a means of dealing with his guilt about killing the boy at school? Was he trying, through his alter ego, to atone for what he'd done? All I knew was I couldn't wait until Daniel came home to get my hands on a copy of the book he was reading.

The next morning, I popped my head into *Gnash! Comics*. Jenny had just taken a delivery of new books and was working her way through a pile of cardboard boxes. She was clutching a pile of invoices in one hand, and wore the look of a woman who'd prefer not to stop what she was doing. 'Hello!' I said brightly. 'Do you know if you have a copy of *Syrius Blade and the Red Diamond*?'

'On the shelf behind you.' She nodded in its direction. 'If I've got it, that's where it'll be.' I found it, along with two other Syrius Blade adventures. I took the lot. Jenny grinned as I swiped my debit card. 'Got you hooked, has he?'

'You could say that.'

I was minding the shop that afternoon, which allowed me plenty of time to peruse my new purchases. I got stuck straight into *Syrius Blade and the Red Diamond*, in which our hero rescues a dark-eyed lady called India from being murdered by her villainous Uncle Victor, who did indeed bear a striking resemblance to Peter Horrell, and who was intent on gaining possession of the red diamond of the title. It was edge-of-the-seat stuff, and I felt quite grumpy when I was interrupted by a customer wanting to buy an ugly mahogany sideboard I'd been trying to shift for ages.

After she'd gone, I was left to reflect. Was Tristan Horrell simply calling on his family history for inspiration, or was reality and fantasy twisted in his mind? Could he tell one from the other? The swordstick was not Syrius Blade's only way of despatching villains, I noticed. In *Syrius Blade and the Moon of Death*, he locked the villain up in an iron chest with the treasure the man had murdered to obtain, a chest that required four locks. The story kept me fascinated all afternoon, while outside the rain began to pour. It was closing time before I turned to the third book, the one with the strangest title of all – *Syrius Blade and the Twisted Sister* – and decided to save it for later.

CHAPTER TWENTY-THREE

Baby Noah was in a gurgling, chuckling mood when I encountered him in the hall that evening, bouncing up and down in a kind of bungee arrangement suspended from the doorframe. I suppose it was the only place where he could keep bouncing without being in anyone's way, at least while Kate was mopping the kitchen floor. He squealed in delight when he saw me, which made a pleasant change from the pouty, red-faced, tear-sploshed greeting I so often get.

I knocked on the open door and Kate looked up from her mopping. She looked better than I'd seen her lately, not as pale and tired. Perhaps baby Noah was finally letting her get a full night's sleep. 'Hello, Juno!' she smiled, swinging her black plait back over her shoulder as she came forward. 'Come in, I haven't seen you for ages.'

'It does seem a long time,' I agreed, negotiating my way carefully around the bouncing Noah.

'Has it stopped raining?' she asked.

'Only just.' The rain had stopped, but the mist had not lifted. The air was dank and dismal and now evening was coming on.

'It's so depressing,' she went on. 'You'd never think this was summer. Cup of tea?'

While she busied herself with the kettle, I restored a discarded purple dinosaur to its rightful owner so that he could put it in his mouth and suck it briefly before flinging it to the floor again. I gave it back. If he thought I was going to pick it up a third time, he could think again. Fortunately, he returned to bouncing.

Kate and I chatted over our cups of tea, mostly about Noah and the cost of childcare. And while we chatted, Adam arrived home from the café, bearing intriguing-looking parcels wrapped in tin foil. Leftovers, unless I was much mistaken. 'Just the man I want to see,' I said, as he dropped his parcels on the table and shook off his wet coat.

He eyed me suspiciously above his bushy beard as if my desire to see him was a sign of trouble to come, which it usually was. 'What's up?' he asked gruffly.

'The guttering outside my bedroom window is what's up. There was a cataract falling onto the roof of the damn conservatory all night. Sounded like Niagara.'

'But I fixed that,' he scowled. 'Last year.'

'Well, you didn't fix it very well, because the bit where the guttering fits into the downpipe has come adrift again.'

Adam groaned. 'Get that bloke of yours to fix it,' he said grumpily. 'He's tall enough. He won't need the ladder.'

'Slight exaggeration. Anyway, he's in Ireland.'

'He's back here often enough. He can fix it in lieu of rent.'

'He's not here that often!' I protested. 'Don't be such a skinflint.'

'That's no way to speak to your landlord, especially one who feeds you spicy chickpea rolls.' He lobbed me one of the foil-wrapped parcels. 'You'd starve without us.'

'Don't think I can be bought off with mere baked goods,' I told him loftily. 'I want that gutter fixed.'

'Salted caramel brownie?' he offered, waggling another parcel suggestively.

'It might buy you some time until the next dry gutter-fixing day,' I conceded, catching it as he threw. 'But if the damn thing keeps me awake again tonight, I shall bang on the floor.'

'You'll wake Noah and set him off,' he warned me grinning, 'and then you'll be sorry.' He turned to extract his son from the bouncing bungee device and carried him into the kitchen, blowing a raspberry on his soft, chubby cheek, making him giggle with delight, and bearing him off into the living room. I heard the TV flick on and the sound of a CBeebies tune.

'Don't think you can escape that easily,' I called after him. 'I live here, you know.'

'Would you like to stay to supper?' Kate offered. 'It's only pasta.'

Only pasta would be lovely, I told her, and it would give me a further opportunity to harangue my landlord; but only if I could help.

'You can pour us a glass of wine, for a start,' Kate recommended, and we settled into a chatty and unhurried chopping of vegetables and grating of cheese as she put the ingredients of the sauce together. It was nearly an hour later when we sat around the table together and finally got to eat. Noah, in his high chair, preferred sliding pieces of fusilli around his tray with the palm of one hand, smearing the surface with tomato sauce and then throwing them onto Kate's newly washed floor. But it kept him quiet.

Just as we had started to clear up, my phone rang and I dug it from my shoulder bag. The display told me the call was from Kirsten. 'Excuse me a moment,' I said and took it into the hall.

'Kirsten?'

'Juno? I'm sorry.' She sounded breathless. I heard a stifled sob.

'Are you alright? What's the matter?'

'I think something terrible is going to happen,' she sniffed. 'It's Tristan. He's here.'

'What do you mean? Kirsten? Where are you?'

'At the shop. We stayed late, cataloguing stuff for the next sale. Tristan turned up here and had the most terrible row with Peter. He got quite violent. It was about the stolen swordstick . . .'

'Just hold on, Kirsten. Was Roger with him?'

'Roger?' She stopped short. 'Who's Roger?'

'Never mind,' I told her. 'Carry on.'

'Well, Peter accused him of having stolen the swordstick, or of getting Amber to steal it for him. He stormed out and Amber chased after him. Peter tried to follow them, but then he came back to get the car and now he's gone after them both.'

'Do you know where they've gone?'

'To Trinity Church.'

She meant the burnt-out ruin at the top of the hill. 'Are you sure?'

'Yes. Peter said he saw Amber running up the steps.'

'But why would Tristan go there?'

'Amber says he used to go there a lot. To draw,' Kirsten moaned. She sounded almost hysterical. 'I'm just so frightened. Juno, please come.'

'Kirsten, you must ring the police.'

'No, I can't,' she wept. 'Please, Juno.' She dissolved into a hiccupping sob.

'Alright, calm down,' I told her. 'I'll get to you as soon as I can.'

Buckfastleigh might only be a few miles away, but driving there through the fog was difficult, even on a quiet road. At least squinting through the murk at the red tail lights of the car in front of me stopped me wondering what I was going to do when I got there. The fog seemed to be thinning. I glimpsed the moon for a few moments, soft-edged and blurry like a swollen pearl, before it was swallowed again by cloud.

Horrell's Antiques was in darkness when I arrived. All shut up. No light showing from any windows and no sign of Kirsten. I tried the doorbell and yelled her name just in case, but I could tell there was no one at home. I tried her phone number but it went straight to voicemail. She must have followed the others to Trinity Church.

In any other weather the sensible thing to do would be to go back to the van and drive up there. But this was not sensible weather; it would be easy to miss the turning. And the flight of steps leading up the hill directly to the church was only yards away. I grabbed my torch from the glove box and prepared for a long climb.

There are one hundred and ninety-eight stone steps up to Holy Trinity Church, hemmed in on either side by a tunnel of trees and bushes. Even on a bright day it's a gloomy climb. Tonight, the tunnel was lost in darkness. I had to aim my torch beam just ahead of me, pointing the light at the stone treads that glistened wetly at my feet. Tripping and tumbling backwards down those steps was not a comfortable thought. But it was the stillness, the complete absence of any movement or sound beyond my own footsteps, my own breathing, that I found most unsettling.

I reached the iron kissing gate that blocked the path. Some kindly soul had set a bench at this spot to allow those short of breath or with aching knees a chance to rest. For this was not the end of the climb. There were no more steps, but a bare earth path continued up the rest of the hill towards the summit, a path as long and steep as the steps had been.

'Kirsten?' I yelled. Would she really have climbed these steps alone, in this fog? She'd sounded frantic with worry. Perhaps she had driven up, unable to wait for me any longer, in which case her car would be parked by the lych-gate, beyond the church, on the far side of the churchyard.

'Kirsten?' I tried again, raising my voice. 'Amber?'

No response.

'This better not be some kind of joke,' I muttered,

and struggled on up the path. Eventually, I emerged from the tree tunnel and onto level ground, stopping to catch my breath. Perhaps it was coming out from under the darkness of the trees, but I had the impression the fog was thinner here, allowing the light of the moon to show through the clouds as a soft, silver blur. Ahead of me I could make out the dark outline of the ruined church with its roofless walls and spire. Pointed archways and empty windows made pale shapes in the dark walls and showed the misty air hanging in veils within the ruin. I shone my torch around the churchyard, lighting up the crooked slabs of ancient tombstones leaning among unkempt grass. On my left loomed the solid shape of the tomb of Richard Cabell, the squire who had murdered his wife and sold his soul to the Devil. It was too foggy for him to ride his hounds across the moor tonight; better he stayed tucked up safely under that granite slab.

A scream ripped through the thickness of the fog like a blade. I dropped the torch and swore, nerves shredded, stooping to retrieve it with trembling fingers.

'Oh God! Tristan, what have you done?' It was Amber's voice, a long, thin wail coming from within the ruined walls of the church.

'Amber!' I yelled. But there was no reply beyond the swift patter of footsteps somewhere close. Whose footsteps, Amber's or Tristan's? I swept the torchlight around me and waited, my heart thumping against my ribs. I could hear nothing.

I headed for the nearest open doorway, a pale pointed arch in the dark wall ahead. 'Amber?' I called out.

There was a sound of muffled sobbing. 'Kirsten? Where are you?' Suddenly a dark figure flitted across the open archway and disappeared. I froze. Could it have been Tristan? 'Kirsten?' I yelled. The torch felt slippery in my sweaty hand, yet my throat was dry, my yell more of a croak. The sobbing cut off; again, the sound of running feet. I whirled around, blood singing in my ears. I could not tell whose footsteps they were or which way they were going. 'Kirsten!' I tried again. I passed through the archway, into the roofless nave of the church, and pointed the torch at a sign on the wall. ENTER AT YOUR OWN RISK, it warned me. 'Thanks,' I muttered.

At the western end the steeple was a pointing finger, dark against the silvery fog; at the other end a pale glow shone through three narrow pointed lancets that formed the east window. Above them the wall rose up in a steep gable topped with a stone cross. Tristan would come here to draw, Amber had said. I could see that now. Ruins like this formed the background of many of his illustrations. I ran the torch over broken pillars and arches that once would have supported the roof of the nave. Around the bare floor were scattered lumps of masonry that had fallen on the night of the fire and lain there ever since. I began to pick my way with cautious feet across towards its southern door, my shoes scrunching on grit and fragments of stone.

I stepped so close to what was lying in the centre of the nave that I almost tripped over it, and when I shone my torch on the thing at my feet, I took a shuddering step back. For a moment I almost lost my balance in the fog. I had to freeze, wait until the world swirled into stillness to stop myself from toppling. Peter Horrell's face was ghostly in the light of the torch, his eyes staring wide. His lips writhed back in a grimace, his teeth glazed with blood. From the centre of his chest a dark, wet stain spread out beneath his clutching fingers. I dropped to my knees and put a hand to his neck, feeling for a pulse. Not the faintest flicker, nothing.

The pounding of running footsteps brought me to my feet. 'Who's there?' I cried in panic, the torch in my hand sending light swooping around me in wild circles. I could hear the tremor in my voice and quite close to me, someone's sobbing breath.

'Juno?' a voice quavered, and a moment later a dark shadow emerged from the fog and stepped into the torchlight. Kirsten. She was shivering, her face and blouse spattered with blood, her chest heaving as she fought to speak. She pointed a shaking hand at Peter. 'I found him . . .' She was hauling in breath like a drowning swimmer. 'I tried to stop the blood but . . . then I heard footsteps . . . Tristan was coming back . . . so I ran.'

I laid a hand on her shoulder, tried to keep my voice as calm as possible. Tristan might be close by in this fog, still holding whatever weapon he had used to kill his uncle. 'Do you know where he is now?'

She shook her head. 'He had the swordstick.' She began to cry, gulping sobs that shook her whole frame.

I took her arm gently and pulled her a few steps away from where Peter was lying. 'Where is Amber?'

'I don't know!' she wailed. 'She went running after Tristan. She was desperate to stop him. I haven't seen her since I got here.'

'We have to call the police.' I began to dig my phone from my pocket.

She clutched at my arm. 'Please don't leave me here alone.'

'I'm not going to leave you. But we don't know where Tristan is and I think we should get out of here.'

'But we can't leave Peter!'

'He's not going anywhere,' I told her gently. I put an arm around her shoulders. 'Come along. Are you parked by the church gate?'

She pulled away from me. 'I'm not going out there. Tristan's out there.'

The thought of stumbling through a foggy graveyard to reach the church gate with Tristan Horrell lurking out there, blade in hand, didn't fill me with much enthusiasm either. But neither did hanging around inside the church waiting to be skewered. I steered Kirsten towards a corner enclosed by ruined walls, a place where he couldn't creep up on us from behind. We squatted down, our backs to the stone while I made my phone call, Kirsten shivering and softly sobbing by my side. Then we switched off the torch and waited in the strange foggy gloom that was not quite dark.

There was the sudden scamper of running feet, of heaving breath. 'Kirsten?' a voice hissed in the fog.

'Amber!' Kirsten cried out impulsively. 'Here! We're over here!'

I switched on the torch. Amber stood blanched in its white beam, a swordstick with a blood-smeared blade hanging from one hand. She seemed dazed. As if suddenly aware of what she was clutching, she let it fall to the ground, staggering back from it in revulsion. 'I found it lying out there in the churchyard. Tris must have dropped it.'

'Where is he?' I whispered.

'I don't know! I tried to follow him but . . .' She wiped a hand across her face, smearing blood on her cheek, and took in a breath. 'I saw him kill Peter. Run him through.' She closed her eyes in despair before she spoke again. 'I screamed and he turned to look at me. His eyes were mad. I called his name but it was as if he didn't recognise me. I thought he was going to kill me. I ran, hid in the churchyard.'

'And you don't know where he is now?' I moved forward and gripped her by the shoulders, staring into her face. 'Because if you do, if you have any idea where he has gone, Amber, you must tell me. You can't go on shielding him.'

She began to weep and shake her head, still weeping as she sank to her knees. Kirsten had edged forward. Fascinated, she reached out for the sword, stretching out her fingers to pick it up. 'Don't touch it!' I warned her sharply.

She pulled back her hand as if the handle had scorched her fingers. 'Sorry!' she moaned. She crouched close to Amber and put her arms around her. They clung, sobbing like terrified children. I stood apart, waiting, keeping watch, sweeping the torch around the darkness, ears straining for the lightest footfall, in case, like a panther, Tristan Horrell crept up on us, soft-footed, in the dark.

CHAPTER TWENTY-FOUR

I slept so heavily I didn't hear the phone, didn't hear Boog the Boxer's mum ringing to ask why I hadn't turned up to take the dog for her morning walk; didn't know about the call until I heard her message later. Nor did I hear the message from Dylan's dad asking the same question. I didn't know a thing until I found Kate standing over me, dark eyes round with worry, gently shaking me as she called my name. She'd let herself in with her spare key when the police had arrived. There were two officers in the living room waiting to take my statement, apparently.

I've had bad hangovers where I've woken up feeling brighter. I blinked as I tried to take in her words, groaning as I realised that I'd let five dog owners down and it was too late to do anything about it. 'Are you sure you're feeling up to seeing the police?' Kate asked in a whisper. 'I can tell them you're not well. To be honest, you don't look good.'

'Thanks,' I muttered, sweeping back the tangle of my hair. My head felt heavy and my face was hot. I groaned. 'I must get up.' I'd already told the police my story, over and over, while I was kept at the police station until the early hours, until Inspector Ford seemed satisfied with my version of events. Amber and Kirsten had been taken to hospital, both suffering with shock.

During the night it had rained, pattering against the glass of my window. Heavy rain that had kept me awake, thinking of Peter Horrell's body lying on the floor of Trinity Church, the rain washing his blood into the gritty earth.

'I'll make you a cup of tea,' Kate promised as I swung my feet to the floor, my toes groping for slippers.

I stood up and hauled on my dressing gown. I didn't bother looking in the mirror. Whoever they were, the police officers would have to put up with what I looked like. I shuffled into the living room.

'Sorry to wake you, Miss Browne,' Cruella said brightly as I plumped my body down on the sofa. She looked revoltingly crisp and freshly pressed for someone who, like me, had been up late the night before. Her violet eyes gave me the once-over and she didn't bother to hide her smirk at my appearance. I yawned, to show how much I cared. I wanted to tell her to shove off and then go back to bed, but the police needed my statement. I repeated everything I'd told the inspector the night before while Cruella's sidekick, a uniformed constable, wrote down what I said. Cruella stopped me several times, making me go over and over things, needlessly I felt, as if she was just trying to draw out the agony. It was only Kate's cup of tea that kept me going.

'Can you remember Miss Blake's exact words?' she insisted when I told her about Kirsten's phone call.

'Well, she was hysterical at the time, a bit incoherent,' I told her frankly. 'She said she was worried something terrible was going to happen. Tristan had turned up unexpectedly when she and Amber and Peter Horrell were at the shop. They'd stayed late for—'

'She didn't say how the quarrel started?' Cruella interrupted.

'She just said that Peter had accused Tristan of stealing the swordstick, or of getting Amber to steal it for him.'

'I see. Thank you.'

'I did ask Kirsten if Roger was there too,' I remembered. 'But she didn't seem to know who I was talking about.'

'This would be Roger Faulkner?'

'Yes, he goes everywhere with Tristan, or so I've been led to understand.'

'By whom?'

'By Amber. Kirsten didn't seem to know his name – but Amber told me she knows nothing about Tristan, so I suppose she wouldn't.'

'Did she say if Tristan had the swordstick with him when he entered the shop?'

'She didn't say so.' I stopped to consider this for a moment. 'Tristan must have had it with him. He killed Peter with it. I assumed it was seeing him with the swordstick that had made Peter accuse him of stealing it.' Cruella was questioning my assumption with raised eyebrows. She was obviously determined to nitpick. 'But no,' I acknowledged with a sigh, 'Kirsten didn't actually say so.'

274

'Thank you. What was said after that?'

'I asked if she knew where Tristan had gone and she told me Trinity Church. Amber had followed him and Peter followed her.' I paused, but Cruella's questioning look told me she wanted to carry on. I felt as if I were reciting a poem, I'd said this so many times. 'He came back and told Kirsten he had seen her heading for the steps. He was taking the car so he could meet them both up there. That's when Kirsten phoned me. She begged me to go over. I told her she should call the police. She didn't want to.'

Cruella frowned. 'Did she say why not?'

'No, she didn't give an explanation, but as I've said before, she was hysterical, terrified something awful was going to happen. She begged me to go.'

'It's a pity you didn't phone us yourself,' she commented.

'In retrospect, yes,' I agreed. 'Although if I had, I doubt if any of us would have arrived in time to save Peter Horrell.'

'We'll never know now, will we?' she responded lightly, lingering just long enough to be sure she had made her point. She was telling me his death was my fault. 'Right. Just one more thing,' she added, adopting a more businesslike tone. 'When you were at the church, you say you didn't get a clear sighting of Tristan Horrell?'

'Not his face, no. I saw a figure, that's all. But it was foggy and quite dark.' He had disappeared like a phantom, I remembered, like Syrius Blade.

I didn't say so to Cruella.

After she and her minion had gone, I lay spread-eagled

on the sofa in my dressing gown, too weary to move until a gentle knock sounded and Kate's anxious face appeared around the door. 'Another cup of tea?' she suggested. 'They were a long time taking your statement.'

'Weren't they,' I agreed and let out a sigh. Please God, I never have to go through it all again, I begged.

Pat gave me a lift to Buckfastleigh later so I could retrieve Van Blanc. I would need it for picking up the various members of the Tribe from their homes the next morning. I'd already made five apologetic phone calls to their owners for the walkies they'd missed, and left another apologetic message on the dog owners' WhatsApp group. Never mind the five lots of money I'd have to do without.

'Lots going on then, Juno,' Pat announced glumly as she drove me over. It sounded more like a statement of fact than a question, so I just agreed.

'How's life at Honeysuckle Farm?' I enquired. It seemed as if I hadn't seen much of Pat lately, hadn't caught up with the latest news on all her waifs and strays.

'Same as always,' she responded. 'Too many mouths to feed, not enough people wanting to give animals a home. You don't know anyone who wants to foster a retired Greyhound I suppose? Preferably two.'

'I'm afraid not,' I told her. 'I'd love to, but my rental agreement doesn't allow me to keep pets.' This wasn't quite true. It didn't specify either way. But even if it had, I couldn't see Bill welcoming the competition.

'Haven't you got a cat?' she asked.

'Well, that's the funny thing. My landlords won't let me keep a pet of my own but their cat lives with me. Actually, Kate and Adam are pretty good,' I conceded. 'They don't object to Daniel bringing Lottie to stay.'

'Well, if you do hear of anyone, they're lovely dogs. People think Greyhounds need lots of exercise cos they're used for racing, but they don't. Just one quick sprint and that's them knackered for the rest of the day. Couch potatoes is what Ken calls 'em.'

I promised I would keep my ear to the ground.

'It's the same with chickens,' Pat went on. 'People don't think of hens as pets but they can be ever so affectionate, you know.'

Bill had lost an eye in a fight with a chicken. I definitely wouldn't be taking one of those home. 'How's Sophie?' I asked. Pat was in the shop with her more than I was. 'Is she going to be okay, d'you think, if she and Seth have really broken up?'

Never one to look on the bright side, Pat shrugged. 'She hasn't got much choice, has she?'

'No,' I agreed glumly, ' I don't suppose she has.'

I phoned Kirsten later to see how she was. I had no idea what her domestic arrangements were, but the woman who answered the phone turned out to be her mother. She told me Kirsten was still very shocked after what had happened and the doctor had given her some pills to help her sleep. She was in bed now. I said I'd phone back another time and didn't mention how much I envied her somnolent state. I felt I could sleep for a week.

I wasn't going to get the chance. I'd been back at

home for just a few minutes when there was a knock on my door and I found Ricky and Morris standing on the landing. 'What the hell's going on, Princess?' Ricky demanded as I let the two of them inside.

'Kate let us in and she said the police have been here,' Morris added.

Thanks, Kate, I muttered inwardly. 'There are all kinds of rumours flying about town,' Ricky prattled on as they both settled themselves on my sofa. 'They say Peter Horrell's been murdered.'

'It's true,' I said, taking the chair. There was no point in denying it – it would be all over the news soon enough. Whether Tristan would be named as his murderer was not so certain, but I knew I must be careful not to say too much. Even Kate didn't know where I'd gone the night before, and so she'd told the police when they'd asked her. I'd had a phone call and went rushing off, was what she'd told them: I hadn't told her where. She couldn't tell them anything except to confirm that I'd left at around eight o'clock.

Morris blinked at me like a worried owl. 'What happened?'

'I believe he was stabbed.'

'In the post office someone was saying the police are all over Trinity Church,' Ricky went on. 'They say it's a crime scene.'

'That's where it happened . . . apparently.' I knew they'd be upset with me later for holding out on them, but, for the moment at least, I couldn't tell them I'd been there at the scene of the crime.

'But do the police know who did it?' Morris asked.

'Do they think it's the same person who killed that man in the car?'

I just shrugged.

Ricky frowned. 'So, what were the police doing here this morning, Princess?'

'They wanted to ask me about my argument with the victim.'

Morris looked shocked and I held up my hands in a gesture of innocence. 'It wasn't me, just in case you're wondering. I didn't kill Peter Horrell, even if he did throw me out of his shop.'

Ricky grunted. 'Wouldn't blame you if you had.'

'But surely they don't suspect you?' Morris asked, horrified. 'Not really?'

I smiled. 'No, of course not, but I suppose they have to talk to anyone who he might have quarrelled with lately.'

Ricky gave a crack of laughter. 'That'll be a bloody long list.'

'Are you alright, Juno love?' Morris asked. 'You're looking peaky.'

'I'm tired,' I admitted. 'I'm looking forward to an early night.'

'You don't want to come to supper then?' He sounded disappointed.

'No, I think I'll pass, thank you.' Not that I wasn't tempted. But if I was too long in their company there was always the chance I would let slip something I shouldn't. Besides, I had spicy chickpea rolls and a salted caramel brownie to look forward to.

* * *

It wasn't long after I'd demolished these, and was thinking about a bath and an early night, when Dean turned up. 'Cruella's already taken my statement,' I told him wearily.

'I know that,' he answered. 'I've come to check on the welfare of my child's godmother. It was pretty grim last night. Are you alright?'

'I have had better days, since you mention it. I think I've bent my fairy wand.'

He grinned. 'Yeh, you look a bit rough.'

'Thank you. I suppose you want a cup of tea?'

'No thanks. As it happens, there are one or two things I need to go through with you.' He sat down and reached for his briefcase, taking out a sheaf of paper. With a groan of resignation, I thumped myself down on the sofa. 'What?'

'It's actually your earlier statement we're concerned with, not the one taken from you today. It's the statement you made when the body of Patrick Mulder was found in the boot of Daniel's car. You said it was the Monday evening when you first visited Amber Horrell at Langworthy Hall. Is that correct?'

'Yes,' I said, irritated at having to repeat it. 'You know it was.'

'And it was while you were there on the Monday evening, that you heard noises from above, noises that convinced you someone else was upstairs. Can you confirm that?'

'Yes, of course I can. Look, why are we going through all this again?' I sighed. 'What's going on?'

Dean sighed briefly. I recognised that sigh. It was

usually accompanied by a worried frown and preceded his telling me that he shouldn't be telling me what he was about to tell me. He frowned, but he didn't bother with the rest.

'This afternoon Amber Horrell confessed that her brother Tristan had been there on that Monday evening and on the next day, he fatally stabbed Patrick Mulder.'

'What?' My voice came out in a whisper.

'It seems he turned up on the Monday afternoon, having given Roger Faulkner the slip. He'd hitchhiked, seemingly, but according to Amber, he was in a confused and distressed state and couldn't remember much about how he'd got there. She reckoned he hadn't taken his medication for a day or two, and he didn't have any on him when he arrived. She persuaded him to go to bed and slipped him some sleeping pills. She intended to phone you and cancel your appointment to see the car, but by the time she'd got him bedded down, you'd already arrived.'

'So, it was him I heard in the room above?'

He nodded. 'Next morning she gets up and he's still dead asleep. She thinks it's safe to leave him, so she drives the Bora down to Ashburton to get it valeted, picks it up when it's ready and then drives it home. Only, when she gets there, she finds Tristan raging around the lawn, wearing nothing but a dressing gown and brandishing a swordstick. Patrick Mulder is there, stone-dead on the lawn. He thought he'd killed a government spy, apparently.'

'But what did she do?' I asked, horrified.

'Well, he was off his head, shouting about infiltration

by government assassins and waving this swordstick about, and she was terrified, as you might imagine. She tried to reason with him, to get the weapon off him, but he just became more violent. She felt she had to do whatever he told her or she could end up like the dead man on the lawn.'

'Did she know who he was?'

'No, says she never laid eyes on him before. He had a rucksack, so she thinks he was some poor bugger out for a walk who must have wandered into the garden for some reason, probably to ask for directions.'

'Was it Tristan's idea to put his body into the boot of the car?'

'According to Amber. They stripped him of his ID first, and the rucksack, and rolled him onto a tarpaulin to drag him up the garden to the car.'

'But why did they drive the car to Daniel's place?'

'Amber's idea. She knew the body would be discovered soon enough, but by then all she cared about was getting her brother away from the scene of the crime. She realised if he was accused of murdering Mulder, he'd be locked up forever. She loves him, she says, and couldn't bear the thought of that happening to him. So, after she'd returned from leaving the body outside Daniel's, she set to destroying the evidence, burying all Mulder's belongings in the woods. Then, she drove Tristan back to Bath, dropped him off at his mother's house, and went straight on to Bristol.'

'But didn't Anita tell you Tristan had been with her for the entire week?'

Dean laughed. 'That's just it. Amber says whatever

Tristan had done, she believed she could rely on Anita to lie to protect him.'

'So Anita was lying?'

'Looks like it.'

'What will happen to Amber now?'

'She's been warned she's likely to be charged with perverting the course of justice and being an accessory after the fact. Of course, there are mitigating circumstances. But tomorrow she'll be taking us to those woods to show us where she buried that rucksack.'

'I see.'

'And there's something else.'

'What?'

'We found a glove, a blood-stained glove.'

'Where?'

'In Trinity churchyard. The killer must have dropped it when he fled the scene. Forensics have got it now, testing to see if the blood is a match with Peter Horrell's. Apart from Amber's statement, it's the first bit of luck we've had. Mind you, we still have to prove the glove belongs to Tristan,' he added.

'I don't suppose there's much doubt about it, is there?'

'Not much, but it's a pity you didn't get a clear sighting of him.' He frowned, thoughtful for a moment. 'Tell me, this Syrius Blade character he writes about, is he some kind of phantom or what?'

'Phantom?' I repeated. 'No. He's just an ordinary human being. He doesn't have any superpowers or anything. He has a brilliant, if slightly twisted, mind and he's a skilled swordsman. Why do you ask?'

'Well, like I said, this glove is the first bit of luck we've had. The rain last night didn't help, washing footprints away, but it's almost as if he was never there.'

'But it's not Syrius Blade you're chasing. It's Tristan Horrell. And you've got his glove.'

'Yes, but it would be good if forensics turned up something on the body. Anyway,' he added as he began to put his papers away, 'the local force in Bath has put a watch on his mother's place in case he turns up there.' He stood to leave. 'By the way. The hunt is on for both Horrell and Faulkner but we're keeping it quiet for a day or two. Nothing's being released to the press as yet.'

'But isn't Tristan considered a danger to the public?'

'Yes. But if some reporter starts digging and finds a connection between Tristan Horrell, David Smith and this Syrius Blade character, the press will have a field day. And a lot of speculation on social media is more likely to hamper the investigation than help. We've had experience of that before.'

I was still thinking about Amber, about how coolly she'd lied to cover up for her brother, the lengths she was prepared to go to. 'But what made her suddenly tell you all this?'

He rubbed the side of his nose, thoughtfully. 'Perhaps it was seeing him kill her uncle. Don't forget Mulder was a complete stranger. He meant nothing to her. And he was already dead when she first laid eyes on him. Till then, perhaps she'd been trying to deny to herself that her brother really was a killer. But seeing him stab Peter, she couldn't deny it any longer.'

'Perhaps,' I agreed.

'And she said it was because of what you'd said to her.'

'Me?' I frowned. 'What did I say?'

'Something about not being able to shield him any longer. She realised you were right.'

I doubted whether I'd been responsible for her change of heart; it was more likely that witnessing the violent death of her father's cousin had the desired effect, as Dean had indicated. 'But what about Roger Faulkner?' I asked. 'Anita told you he'd taken Tristan camping.'

'Well, Tristan must have given him the slip somehow before he turned up at Buckfastleigh and confronted Peter Horrell,' Dean answered uneasily. 'Which makes me wonder if Faulkner's not lying dead in the boot of a car somewhere.'

'Yes,' I said, biting my lip. 'I was wondering that too.'

CHAPTER TWENTY-FIVE

After all that had happened, trying to slip back into any kind of normal routine was difficult. Dean had warned me to stay away from Amber. She would be going back at Langworthy Hall for the time being, but police would certainly want to interview her again. Likewise Kirsten, who had gone home to Buckfastleigh.

I tried to go about my usual business. On Friday I was in St Lawrence Lane, after coming out of the post office, when I bumped into Sheila from *Keepsakes*. She wanted to chat about the murder, rumours of which were all around town. She had always predicted Peter Horrell would come to a nasty end, she said. 'Did you ever get around to asking Reuben about the Horrells?' she asked.

'I did. He said Julian had cheated one of his customers, bought a painting from her for less than it was worth, then made a massive profit at auction.'

Sheila was frowning. 'That's not what I was thinking of. I thought there was something else.' She put a hand up to her mouth. 'Oh dear, I wonder if I've got it wrong.'

'He didn't mention that Peter was involved,' I added.

Sheila was still pondering. 'I thought it had something to do with his father.'

'Reuben's father? You mean, Robert Lenkiewicz?'

'Yes, I'm sure it was.' She shook her head. 'Oh, well!' She laughed at her own forgetfulness. 'Never mind!' And she went on her way, having aroused my curiosity, then failed to satisfy it. There was only one thing to do, I decided, and that was to go straight to the horse's mouth. But Reuben was busy with a customer when I headed into his gallery, a lady trying on seriously expensive jewellery. I decided to leave and come back later.

I went back to *Old Nick's*. Pat would be busy at the animal sanctuary, it being a Friday, but Sophie was not planning a trip to Wales this weekend. She had still heard nothing from Seth, and had been in the shop all morning, working on a portrait of a Dalmatian puppy called Dot. Or she should have been. There was no sign of her in the shop. Elizabeth was tidying paperbacks in the book exchange and cast me an amused glance as I walked in. 'She's up in the kitchen,' she told me before I asked.

'Ah,' I said.

'With Seth.'

'Oh. He's turned up, has he?'

'He arrived about an hour ago. Perhaps now is not the time go up there to make a cup of tea.'

'Best not,' I agreed. 'An hour, you said?'

'Hm. I haven't heard any screaming or shouting so far, so I assume things must be going well.'

'Let's hope so.' I held up crossed fingers. I didn't want

Sophie upset by Seth again, just when she seemed to be getting over their break-up.

'I hear Peter Horrell's been murdered,' Elizabeth added conversationally.

'Yes, I heard that too.'

She slid a sharp glance at me. 'And you know nothing about it?'

'Why would I?' I asked, trying to look innocent.

'Because the car you bought from his niece turned out to have a dead man in the boot and he threw you out of his shop. Now he's been murdered. I thought you might take an interest.'

'I might. But the police have other ideas.'

This would hardly satisfy Elizabeth. She knew me too well to be deceived by my feigned lack of interest, and on top of that, she was shrewd. But I was saved from any further explanation by the opening of the kitchen door upstairs, and the sound of Seth's voice raised cheerfully. 'I'll come back for you about six, then.' Then the door half closed again and I heard a lot of whispering. A moment later he bounced down the stairs and through the shop, grinning like a man who'd just won the lottery. He acknowledged me with a wave, and a nod to Elizabeth, before he was out of the door and gone.

She and I stared at one another, wondering whether one of us should go upstairs and see what kind of state Sophie was in. But there was no need. A minute later, she came downstairs, rather more slowly than Seth, her eyes shiny with tears and wearing a radiant smile.

'Oh, hello, Juno,' she said simply, then sat at her

easel, picked up her paintbrush and began to paint as if absolutely nothing had happened.

'Everything alright, is it?' I asked, after she'd carried on this pantomime for a few more moments. 'Between you and Seth?'

'Yes, thank you.' She glanced uncertainly at Elizabeth, who is never slow to pick up a cue.

'If you want me to go . . .'

'Oh, no, I don't mean . . .' Sophie began, her cheeks turning pink.

'It's alright,' she assured her, holding up a hand in surrender. 'I'll go up and make some tea. Juno and I have been gagging for one for the last ten minutes.'

As soon as we heard the kitchen door close behind her, Sophie turned to me, favouring me with another huge smile.

'Well, he took his time getting here,' I pointed out before she could say anything.

'Well, you see, after I walked out the other weekend, Imogen came on really strong to him. She went on about what a silly little fool I was and how we weren't really suited. Seth had a really serious talk with her and managed to persuade her that he wasn't interested. He says that this time she finally got the message. She called him all kinds of names and flounced off in a temper. Anyway, after all this, Seth has decided to leave St Davids. His thesis is almost completed anyway, so he's come home to finish it here. Or he will, if I want him to, and of course I do, so . . . so there we are!' she finished, beaming at me.

I got up and gave her a hug. 'I'm happy for you, Soph.'

'But you were right, Juno. What you said.' I couldn't remember having said anything. 'You said I'd let Imogen get inside my head, that she was sort of using me against myself. And you were right. Because I couldn't believe Seth would prefer me to someone like her, you see.'

'And do you believe it now?' I asked, teasing.

'Yes,' she nodded happily. 'Yes, I do.'

Just then, the kitchen door opened and Elizabeth's enquiring voice came down the stairs. 'Is it safe for me to bring this tea down?'

I caught Rueben Lenkiewicz just as he was closing his gallery. 'Did you have a profitable afternoon?' I enquired.

'I did, thank you very much,' he answered with a smile. 'My customer was here for quite some time.'

'Was she one of Dartmoor's millionaires?'

'Well, I wouldn't know,' he admitted, 'but she did buy a sapphire-and-diamond necklace. Although what she really came in for was a Rolex Submariner for her husband's birthday.'

'Oh, is that all?' I tutted. 'Did she buy that too?'

'Of course.' He smiled. 'Anyway, if you've come to ask me whether I murdered Peter Horrell, the answer is, no, I didn't.'

'So, you've heard?'

'The news of his demise has whipped around the antiques community of South Devon with unseemly speed,' he responded cheerfully. 'So far, I haven't heard of anyone shedding any tears.'

'He doesn't seem to have been any more popular than his cousin,' I said. 'Less so, if anything.'

'Ah, but Julian has already been dead a year,' Reuben pointed out, 'and distance lends enchantment.'

I laughed and then added more seriously, 'Someone told me your father had experience of the Horrells too.'

He paused, and closed the ring box in his hand with a snap. 'I wonder who that someone was.'

'Sorry. It was just idle chit-chat. If you'd rather not talk about it . . .'

'No, no. It's alright. It is quite a story.' He indicated a chair, a Victorian hall chair this time, and I sat. He drew up a padded stool and folded his hands in his lap. 'Some years before he died, my father had a painting stolen from his studio. It was worth . . .' He paused. 'Shall we just say it was worth a lot? After it had been missing for several weeks, Peter Horrell came and said that someone had tried to sell the painting to him. Knowing it was stolen, he had refused to buy it. Naturally.'

'Naturally,' I agreed.

'But he suggested to my father that he might act as a broker, allowing the thieves to return the painting without unnecessary involvement from the law. My father agreed and so Horrell negotiated a price for its return of twenty thousand pounds. This was nothing like its real value,' he added quickly, 'but there was a condition attached. If he didn't buy back his own painting, it would be burnt.'

'So, it was blackmail.'

'Indeed.'

'And did he get his painting back?'

'Yes, it was returned safely, care of Horrell himself. Needless to say, the culprits were never caught. Because of course,' he gave a wry smile, 'there were no culprits.'

'You think Peter stole the painting?'

Reuben shrugged. 'Him or his rotten cousin. Couldn't prove it, of course. But all that mattered to my father was that he got his painting back unharmed.'

'Do you think the Horrells had done this kind of thing before?' I asked.

'Possibly. Holding a valuable painting to ransom in this way is not uncommon in the fine art business. There are some quite famous cases.'

'I was just thinking, if that's the way the Horrells did business, Peter must have made a lot of enemies.'

'In which case, any number of people could have murdered him.' Reuben nodded with cheerful satisfaction. 'I couldn't agree more.'

CHAPTER TWENTY-SIX

I wasn't happy. Things weren't adding up. There were so many questions I wanted to ask Amber. For a start, why, when Tristan had turned up in Buckfastleigh, didn't Peter phone the police? Perhaps he'd thought he could deal with Tristan himself. He didn't want the skeleton coming out of the family armoire and he wanted to avoid involving the authorities. But what about Kirsten? If she was so afraid there would be violence, why was she so reluctant to phone them?

And what about Roger Faulkner? Did he have any idea what Tristan had done, either to Partick Mulder, or to his uncle? Tristan had fled Trinity Church, somehow disappeared into the fog; someone must have helped him get away. Was Faulkner now an accomplice, or was he Tristan's latest victim?

Then there was Anita Horrell. Was she lying about the camping trip? Did she really have no idea where the two of them might have gone, or was the whole story of the trip just a lie? Like Amber, was Anita prepared to say anything to protect her beloved Tristan? Some people will tell any lie to protect the ones they love, or to get what they want. Like that stupid creature Imogen, planting her necklace in Seth's bed to try to wreck his relationship with Sophie. Finally, there was Patrick Mulder. We'd never know what took place between him and Tristan that day in the garden at Langworthy Hall. Had he really come to ask directions, as Amber seemed to think? Was he just in the wrong place at the wrong time, asking the wrong psychopath? But if I was right, and he had been in the library researching the Horrell family, perhaps he had a reason for being there that day.

I pondered all this through a long and boring day in the shop. Sophie was off with Seth; Pat didn't do Saturdays and so far, there was no sign of Elizabeth. There I was, all on my ownsome, waiting in for the customers while outside bright sunshine shone on the ungodly. I occupied myself in the back room, dusting, polishing and rearranging, keeping one ear cocked for the jangling of the shop bell announcing a customer.

It didn't jangle at all until early afternoon, and then the only person it announced was Sophie, who called out as she ran up the stairs. 'I left my mobile phone in the kitchen yesterday. Can you believe it?'

'Easily,' I called back.

A moment later Seth wandered in and grinned at me. 'Hello Juno. I'm sorry, I didn't stop to say hello to you when I was in here before.'

I laughed. 'You had other things on your mind.' We came together in a hug. 'It's good to see you. How are you?'

'I'm fine.' We chatted a moment about Sophie, who seemed to take forever to find her phone; but then, her idea of searching for something is to stand in the middle of a room and wait for it to leap out at her. We talked about how brilliant her illustrations for the hedgerow book were, and then he said, 'This is a bad business about Peter Horrell.' He shook his head. 'Poor old Tristan.'

'Did you know him?' Seth had been born and brought up in Buckfastleigh, but the possibility he might know the Horrells hadn't occurred to me.

'We'd kick a football around the park sometimes in the school holidays. He was away during term-time at boarding school, and his school friends weren't local, so in the holidays he was on his own.'

I recognised this situation from my own childhood, having been sent off to boarding school myself. 'You don't remember the name of the school?'

'St Myrrins. It's somewhere near Marlborough, I think. This was before the death of that boy,' he went on. 'In fact, the last time I saw Tristan must have been the summer before it happened.'

'Really?' I asked. 'How old were you then?'

'I suppose we were about fourteen. Fifteen perhaps. Me and the other local lads used to feel quite sorry for him. His parents had broken up and he'd have to spend half the holiday with his dad, and he hated him.'

At this moment, Sophie bounced down the stairs, brandishing her mobile. 'It had got hidden under a biscuit wrapper,' she announced, blinking indignantly at me as if it was my fault, which it probably was.

I ignored her. 'This would be Julian?' I asked Seth.

'Yes. He seemed to spend all his time in their antiques

place leaving Tristan to wander round like a lost soul. Except,' he grinned suddenly, 'he always had his sister in tow.'

'You mean Amber?'

'Yeah. We didn't mind her joining in because she was pretty spectacular-looking even at that age. Not that she was interested in spotty kids like us. She wasn't much good at football either.'

'Who's this?' Sophie demanded with a slight frown.

'Amber Horrell,' he told her. 'The other girl though, she was really fast, just like Tristan.'

It was my turn to frown then. 'What other girl?'

'Kim?' he suggested vaguely.

'Kirsten?'

'That's it. We used to laugh about her and Amber. The terrible twins, we called them. They were inseparable. It was like Amber only had eyes for her brother and Kirsten only had eyes for Amber, if you know what I mean.'

'Amber told me Kirsten was clingy,' I remembered. 'It sounds as if she couldn't shake her off.'

'It all sounds a bit weird to me,' Sophie observed, obviously impatient for her and Seth to be on their way.

But he wasn't in a hurry. 'Tristan and Kirsten competed at county level,' he went on, 'so I suppose that's how they knew each other.'

'Competed at what?' Sophie asked. 'Football?'

'No. Fencing. They represented their schools in county championships. Tristan represented St Myrrins and Kirsten represented some Devon school.'

'Are you sure?' This was something she had never mentioned to me.

'Yes. They used to joke about whose team had won the most trophies.'

I was puzzled. Kirsten had given me the impression she had never known Tristan. And she'd certainly never mentioned that she fenced herself.

Sophie grabbed Seth's arm. 'Let's go.' She nodded in my direction. 'Look at her. She's gone all quiet and mysterious. She's detecting in her head. She'll be like this for hours.'

'Yeh, sod off, the pair of you,' I recommended. Seth gave me a brief, brotherly kiss on the cheek before Sophie steered him towards the shop door. I was glad to be left on my own. I had a lot to think about.

I was still thinking about it when the shop bell tinkled about an hour later. This time in came someone I didn't know, or at least, someone I didn't recognise immediately. He was a tall man in his sixties, cropped grey hair just visible under a baseball cap, and accompanied by a white English Bull Terrier with a brown patch around one eye. 'If he's not called Bullseye, I'll eat my hat,' I said approvingly, bending down to stroke his lovely sloping nose as he wagged his tail at me.

'Got it in one,' said his owner, whom I hadn't really paid much attention to yet. 'How did your son's project go?'

I was at a loss, for a moment, before it dawned on me where I had seen him before. He was the man who'd given me the leaflet about the Feoffee Chest at Newton Abbot Museum, the man who'd been just about to lock the place up. 'Mr Bolt,' I remembered, staring. 'Um, as a matter of fact . . .'

He gave me a twinkly-eyed smile. 'It's alright, I know you haven't really got a son. I recognised you, you see, on the day you came to the museum.'

'Did you?' I asked, feeling a little uneasy.

'You're Juno Browne. I've read about you several times in the *Dartmoor Gazette*, you and all that stuff you get up to. Seen your picture. And you're not difficult to find. Mention your name around here and . . . Oh, don't worry!' he said suddenly, reading the look of dismay on my face.

What was running through my mind was what Inspector Ford had said to me, about how the person who'd dumped Mulder's body in the car might have known me from the newspaper.

'I'm not a stalker!' he assured me, looking genuinely concerned. 'I don't want you to think I'm creepy or anything. Mrs Bolt is waiting for me in *Taylors* café. I can give her a call if you like, get her to come round here.'

'No. No, please don't bother your wife,' I said, relaxing. 'In any case, I don't think stalkers usually bring their bull terriers with them.' I indicated the nearest chair. 'Please have a seat. What can I do for you, Mr Bolt?'

'Frazer, please,' he insisted. 'Now you settle down, Bullseye!' he told the dog at his feet. 'I don't know if you can do anything, really . . . may I call you Juno?'

'Yes, of course.'

'Well, Juno, it's just after you'd gone off with the leaflet that day, I was thinking to myself that it wouldn't have hurt to let you into the museum for a few minutes, just to look at the chest. Of course, it was too late by then. But it did leave me wondering why you were so keen to see it.'

'Well,' I began, wondering what to say.

'And that made me think about the chap a few weeks back,' he went on.

'What chap?'

'He turned up late in the afternoon, like you did. Very insistent he wanted to see the chest, he was, which is unusual. It's not that visitors to the museum don't take an interest in it,' he explained, 'but not many come specifically to see it, if you know what I mean. Anyway, this chap was South African.'

'Are you sure?' I asked, suddenly intent. 'You recognised his accent?'

'I recognised his tattoo,' he told me proudly. 'I've been about a bit in my time. South African Special Forces. And his accent was quite noticeable, now you mention it. A few weeks later, I read someone with the same tattoo had turned up dead in the boot of a car. Mrs Bolt told me I should tell the police I'd met the fella, but I said to her, well it's not going to do any good, is it? Even if it was him, how can the fact he wanted to look at a museum artefact help to identify him? I didn't know what his name was. But then, when you turned up wanting to see the chest as well, I wondered if she mightn't have been right.'

'Well, they have identified him now, Mr . . . I mean, Frazer. His name was Patrick Mulder and he came from South Africa.'

'So, it was him, then,' he nodded, 'with the accent.'

'Did he say why he was so keen to see the chest?'

'He said he knew of another one just like it, except with only four locks. He said it belonged to his ancestors. He'd come over here from South Africa because he'd started researching his family history online and found he was related to some people who lived not far away, people who used to have their own estate.'

'And that's why he'd come to England?'

Frazer nodded. 'He said he was planning to go and see them, give them a big surprise. Claim his inheritance, is how he put it.'

'He didn't tell you the name of this family?'

'No, no he didn't,' he admitted. 'But I said to him, just joking, they might not be too pleased to see you if you've come to ask them for a share of the inheritance. But he said, oh yes, they will, because they owned this chest with the four locks. And he had a key.'

I had to speak to Amber. And to Kirsten. But before I did, there were a few things I needed to check out. There was Patrick Mulder for a start. If he was in possession of the missing key to the chest, then there was only one person he could have got it from. It had belonged to Neville, Julian Horrell's great-uncle. Neville was the brother who had gone off to war, taking his key with him, and never returned; which meant, unless he'd come by the key and its history by some other means, Patrick must be his grandson, which made him Peter's cousin. But as his name was Mulder, not Horrell, he must have inherited the key from his maternal side. To be certain, I

300

needed to know his mother's maiden name and I had no idea how I was going to find it out. If it had been in the information about Mulder that Dean had received from his South African colleagues, then he'd have spotted the name Horrell for himself. Wouldn't he? I decided to give him a call.

'Mulder's mother's maiden name?' he repeated down the phone. 'What the hell do you want that for?'

'It could be important. Have you got it?'

'No,' he said after a minute or so of grumbling and paper rustling.

'Can you find out?' I asked. 'Would his ex-wife know?'

'I am not ringing bloody South Africa to talk to Mulder's ex-wife to find out if she knew what her ex-mother-in-law's maiden name was.'

'But the police in South Africa must have records and you must be in contact with your colleague there by email, surely.'

'Well, maybe I am,' he acknowledged reluctantly, 'but I'm not wasting his time, or mine, unless you tell me why you need to know.'

I hesitated. I wanted the information so I could talk to Amber, but if I told Dean why I wanted it, I would never get to speak to her. The police wouldn't let me. 'I can't, not yet.'

'Suit yourself,' he said, and put the phone down.

'Hell's teeth!' I muttered. Bill was sitting on the arm of the sofa staring at me from his single emerald eye, in case my lap might become available.

'Sorry,' I told him, fending him off as I reached for

301

the laptop. I searched for *county fencing championships, amateur, schools, Devon/Wiltshire* and eventually came up with an article in a local Marlborough paper dating back years. It was about the inter-schools fencing competition. It was a report from the year before Christopher was killed. There was a group photograph and the names of all those young people in the school teams taking part. And among the names I found something else, something that stopped my breath for a moment: something I hadn't been looking for.

CHAPTER TWENTY-SEVEN

It was almost dark when I pulled up at Langworthy Hall. No sign of any police presence. There were lights on downstairs, so Amber must have been at home.

It was quiet. No loud music blaring this time, just a distant chatter of rooks as they settled in the treetops for the night, a sweep of cool breeze whispering through the branches.

The front door was closed and Amber didn't answer to my knock, so I made my way around to the side of the building and into the back garden. The end of the lawn was lost in darkness, the scent of honeysuckle and night-scented stocks stirred by the breeze. French windows in the dining room were flung open to the evening air and I stepped inside, calling Amber's name. There was no reply. Ben whined from behind the kitchen door. I called to him softly and he gave a gentle bark, scratching at the wood on the other side. 'Good dog,' I murmured and carried on down the hall. I knew I wasn't alone in the place. The quiet was like a pent-up breath, as if the house were waiting for something to happen.

I went into the living room. On the iron-bound chest

sat an empty bottle of champagne and two half-drained glasses. I watched the bright bubbles rising through the golden liquid. The keys were sitting in the locks. It was only when I counted all four of them that I realised how completely and utterly I had been fooled. Amber's two keys had been there before, but now there was Patrick Mulder's key. And there was Peter's.

'There's nothing inside.' Amber must have crept down the stairs. I hadn't heard her coming. Her eyes were bright with excitement, her cheeks livid, as if she were suffering from a fever. I guessed she was drunk on something stronger than champagne.

I nodded at the glasses. 'But you've been celebrating.' And with someone else, I added silently. 'Have you found the red diamond?'

'It's not in there.' She gave a little laugh. 'I always knew Granny Horrell was making it up. It was never here.'

'It's not the only thing that was never here, is it?' I said, raising my eyes to hers. 'Tristan was never here either.'

'He's here now,' she answered softly.

Behind me I heard a slither of steel, a metal snake shedding its skin. I tried to ignore the fear that clutched my insides, and fought the impulse to turn around. 'Hello Kirsten,' I said over my shoulder, and I heard the soft whisper of her laugh. 'I've been reading about what a fine swordswoman you used to be. Competing at county level, representing your team in the inter-school fencing championship. Just like your brother, Christopher. But I suppose after you'd got away with his murder, you thought it was wise to give it up.'

She didn't speak, just kept the point of the blade levelled at me as she moved around the chest to stand next to Amber. Her face was the picture of innocence, eyes wide beneath that long, soft fringe.

'No one would be surprised at your decision,' I continued. 'Naturally you'd be upset after Christopher's death. I've been reading about him in the paper. It was strange Amber couldn't remember his surname when it was Blake, same as yours.'

'Tristan confessed to Christopher's murder,' Kirsten said quietly.

'Of course he did. He was just a kid when he was locked up. It would have been easier for him to confess than go on denying it. And after years of psychoanalysis, he probably believed it himself. Maybe he didn't want to believe the real truth, that Christopher's own sister had killed him.'

I waited for her to speak, but she said nothing, just continued to give me her limpid blue gaze. 'You know, I wish I'd read *Syrius Blade and the Twisted Sister* before this afternoon,' I went on. 'I might have guessed then. You killed your brother, Kirsten, after the school fencing match, and it was you who plunged the blade into Patrick Mulder's chest.' My eyes flicked to the four keys in their four locks, and back to Amber's face. 'But I bet it was you who planned it.'

Her mouth twisted in a savage grin. 'That revolting man, Mulder, turning up here. He wanted to open the chest, seemed to think he was entitled to something.'

'Perhaps he was. After all, he was family. But this wasn't the day I came here?'

'No.' She hunched a shoulder dismissively. 'It was days before. He didn't even know my father was dead. When he found out, he wanted to speak to Peter.'

'And you didn't want that to happen.'

She smiled. 'I persuaded him not to approach him, explained how difficult Peter could be. I said he might not welcome the sudden appearance of a stranger claiming to be a long-lost relative. It would be better to let me speak to Peter first, broach the idea to him. Give me a few days, I told him, wait until I contact you. He didn't want to, but he agreed.'

'And then I turned up.'

'Your timing was perfect!' She moved closer to Kirsten and slid an arm around her waist. 'We'd already worked out how we were going to kill Peter, hadn't we? And how to get poor, sad Tristan to take the blame. Then you came here and bought the car and we fitted you into our plan. Getting rid of Cousin Patrick's body was just a bonus.'

'Did he bring you his key?'

'This was never about his key!' Her eyes flashed contempt. 'Or Peter's key either. Yes, I got Kirsten to steal it from his bedroom, but that's not what this was about.'

'Then why kill him?'

'Because my wicked Uncle Peter was robbing my trust fund!' She smiled at Kirsten. 'Killing him wasn't as difficult as we thought.'

'You'd had practice by then,' I kept my eyes on Kirsten, on the blade that never wavered, 'on Cousin Patrick.'

'I phoned him the day after you'd called about the car to tell him Peter would meet him here.' Amber sneered. 'He couldn't get here fast enough. I told him we'd be waiting for him in the garden.'

'Down by the stream, where the Himalayan balsam grows.'

She looked puzzled for a moment. 'Yes, that's right. And Kirsten is such a little mouse, you see.' She reached out to stroke her cheek. 'She was so quiet, creeping up on him. He didn't even know she was behind him until she called his name, and he turned.'

'And having murdered him, between you, you put his body in the boot of Daniel's car. Why?'

'Because no sane person would do such a thing, then drive it to your man friend's door. Only a lunatic, like mad, sad Tristan, and his poor distraught sister, so desperate to protect him. And of course you'd been here the night before, ready to testify to the police that you heard someone in the room above, someone I tried to deny was there.' She laughed. 'Someone you thought was Tristan.'

'When in fact, it was Kirsten.' I focused my attention on her. 'You got into bed with Peter just to gain his trust, to get access to his key.'

'It certainly wasn't because I enjoyed the experience.'

'Was it you who stole the swordstick?'

'Of course.'

'And you made up the story of Tristan arriving at the shop.'

Kirsten smiled her schoolgirl smile. 'And you couldn't wait to come to my rescue.'

'You used me against myself.'

'We used your insatiable curiosity,' Amber replied, 'your inability to mind your own business, your pathetic desire to help others. But most of all,' she said at last, 'we used your ridiculous reputation as a sleuth.'

I felt sick at the thought of it. 'Everything you said to me about Tristan was a lie. And everything you said to the police.'

'But they believed me, though. And do you know why they believed me?' she asked, her eyes dancing in mockery. 'Because they believed *you*!'

I had no answer. I felt as if she'd struck me.

'And you were a witness to the fact Tristan was there in Trinity Church that night,' she carried on remorselessly. 'You didn't see him, you didn't hear him – all you saw and heard was me and Kirsten – but you were convinced he was there, because we told you he was. And you helped to convince the police.'

'Then all it needed was Tristan's glove, which I imagine you stole from his van, and soaked in Peter's blood.'

'Ten out of ten, Detective.'

They had played me from the beginning. Amber selling herself to me as the sister lying to protect her brother, desperately believing in his innocence, when all the time she was lying to set him up. As for Kirsten, she was not at all who she'd pretended to be. Her supposed blunder with Julian's swordstick had been a ruse to send the police on a wild goose chase and to encourage the idea in my mind that she was a dimwit. She'd told me she never even knew Tristan, fed me false information from the start, when in fact, it was she who had killed Christopher. It was difficult to know who was the more accomplished liar, she or Amber.

'Tristan didn't come here before he went to Bristol,' I said. 'He was exactly where Anita said he was, at home with her, in Bath.'

'And what court is going to believe her?' Amber demanded. 'She's his mother. Of course she'll lie.'

'They'll believe Roger Faulkner.'

She gave a triumphant smirk. 'If they can find him.'

I felt cold suddenly. 'Is he dead?'

'He soon will be.' She tapped the corner of the chest with one foot. 'You dead yet?'

I stared at her in horror. Such a beautiful, delicate creature; she was howling insanity behind a porcelain mask. 'And Tristan?' I hardly dared to ask.

'He's upstairs, fast asleep, poor darling. Well, not asleep exactly,' she added with an elegant shrug. 'I swopped his meds for something a little more . . .' she paused, considering, 'hallucinogenic.'

'How can you do it to him? How can you keep torturing him with a guilt that isn't his?'

She laughed. 'All Tris cares about is his drawing. He can draw just as well when he's locked up.'

'*Syrius Blade and the Twisted Sister*,' I quoted. 'Which one of the two of you was he writing about, d'you think? The one who murdered her brother or the one who tried to blame it on him?'

Amber slid a sly glance at Kirsten and then stared back at me. 'What does it matter? When he wakes up later, he won't know who he is or where he is. He suffers from such terrible blackouts, you see. Poor Tris. He doesn't remember killing Peter, and he won't remember killing Roger. He won't even remember killing you.'

I determined to keep my voice steady. 'You can't get away with killing me.'

She raised her eyebrows in amusement. 'And why not?'

'Because of Frazer Bolt.'

She flicked a glance at Kirsten and then back at me, for the first time uncertain. 'Who?'

'Mr Bolt came to see me this afternoon. He told me how he had met your cousin Patrick a few weeks ago when he'd visited the museum, interested in a multi-lock chest that's on display there. They had quite a long chat about it. He told Mr Bolt how he'd been researching his family tree, the connections he'd found with the Horrells . . .'

'You're lying . . .'

'. . . and how he was planning to come to you and claim his share of the family inheritance. And he also told him about the key. And by now, Mr Bolt will have gone to the police with this story, as I told him he should. Straight away. So, at the very least, they will know Patrick Mulder wasn't just an unlucky random stranger turning up here. They'll know he had a reason for coming here and that you had a motive to kill him.'

'Perhaps. But it won't prove Tristan wasn't the one who stabbed him,' she retorted. 'And I really don't see how it's going to help you.'

From the corner of my eye I saw Kirsten tense, ready to make her move. I grabbed the empty champagne bottle by the neck and smashed it against the side of the chest. It shattered into a bouquet of jagged glass and I thrust it out in front of me. 'You think I'll go down without a fight?' I must have cut myself. Blood began to drip steadily between my clenched fingers onto the rug below. Despite the pain I grinned, gripping the neck of the bottle hard. 'Oops! Forensic evidence – sorry about that.'

Kirsten lunged at me. I dived, the point of the blade scraping the wall an inch from where I had stood. Amber was coming at me from the other side and I jabbed the broken bottle in her direction. She shrank back from the ragged glass, her eyes roving the room as she sought out a weapon for herself. Kirsten came at me again, the tip of the blade levelled at my throat. I tried to back away, but I was blocked by the Chinese cabinet in the corner. I couldn't shrink back any further. If she pressed forward an inch, I'd be dead.

'Drop it,' she ordered, almost gently, as if she were telling Ben to drop a ball. 'Drop the bottle.'

I lowered it slowly. Then threw it, high and to the side. It smashed against the mantlepiece, taking a thousand pounds' worth of Delft plate with it and showering Amber with shards of porcelain and glass. She screamed, a hand to her face, and Kirsten, distracted, glanced in her direction, the tip of the blade wavering. It was enough. I grabbed a candlestick in my bleeding fist and used it to swipe the blade sideways, pushing the point away from my face. It knocked her off balance. She danced backward, regaining her stability, raising the blade, ready to come at me again.

'My eye!' Amber was screaming. 'There's glass in my eye.'

Kirsten bit her lip, torn between trying to finish me off or going to help the woman she loved. A sudden confusion of blue lights flashed through mullioned glass. A moment later, the front door crashed in and officers in stab-vests swarmed into the room. A shrill voice was yelling. 'Drop the weapon! Drop it! I have a taser. I will taser you!'

Faced with Cruella armed with a device that could fire ten thousand volts into her backside, Kirsten did what I would have done. She threw down the weapon. Then she flew to Amber's side. 'Let me see,' she begged, her hands going to Amber's bleeding face. 'It's alright! It's alright!' she hushed her. 'Keep still. The glass just missed your eye. Let me brush it away. It's only your lid that's bleeding.'

By now I was on my knees in front of the chest, struggling to turn a key that kept slipping through my bloody fingers. 'Help me!' I cried out. 'We must get it open.'

Someone fell to his knees beside me, turning two locks at once, and I realised it was Dean. Between us we lifted the heavy lid, swung it back, and looked down into the chest. It was empty, nothing in it, a lead-lined void. No body, no nothing. Despite her pain, Amber yelped with laughter. 'Are you going to look in the freezer next?'

'Never mind the freezer,' I cried to Dean. 'Look in the boot of her car.'

In a moment he was gone, two other officers swiftly on his heels. I sat back, eyes closed, drawing in breath, listening to the satisfying clicks of handcuffs and Cruella's voice reading Amber and Kirsten their rights. I was content, for the moment, to do nothing but sit. When I opened my eyes, Inspector Ford was standing over me, looking down and frowning. 'Are you alright, Miss Browne? Do you need a doctor?'

I opened my bloody palm and looked at it and shook my head. As Amber and Kirsten were led away, a police officer came running down the stairs. 'There's a man in one of the bedrooms, sir,' he told the inspector. 'Seems to be heavily sedated.'

'That's Tristan Horrell,' I breathed. 'He's been drugged with God knows what. You'd better get him an ambulance.'

'Better get two,' Dean announced, coming back into the room.

'Roger Faulkner?' the inspector asked.

'Yes, sir. He's had a knock on the head and he wouldn't have lasted much longer in that boot, but he's alive.'

'Thank God,' I breathed.

'Look after Miss Browne, will you, Collins,' the inspector ordered as he followed his officers out of the room.

Dean came to sit next to me. Taking a folded handkerchief from his pocket, he took my bleeding hand in his and pressed it into my palm, gently closing my fingers over it. 'How did you know I was here?' I asked.

'We didn't. But following an interesting conversation with Mr Frazer Bolt, the boss sent Cruella and me here to fetch Amber, take her down to the station for further questioning. That's when we saw your van parked outside. There seemed to be a ruckus going on in here, so we had a peep in the window and decided to call for back-up.'

'You mean, you waited?' I asked, horrified. 'I could have been skewered to death!'

'Yep,' he admitted with a grin. 'Good job you kept her talking.'

'Good job we didn't run out of conversation.'

'Also, I had an email back from my colleague in South Africa.'

I smiled. 'So, you did send one.'

'I did,' he admitted. 'The name was Horrell.' He shook his head at me and sighed. 'Horrell! How did we know you were here? Where else were you going to be?'

CHAPTER TWENTY-EIGHT

'I don't think I quite understand,' Morris said, blinking at me in confusion. 'Why exactly did the police turn up? Just because Mulder's mother's name was Horrell?'

'Not completely.' I watched Ricky reach across the table to refill my empty glass and smiled. A week had passed since Amber and Kirsten had been arrested. I'd spent the day helping to unpack *The Gondoliers* costumes. I'd even begun to stop holding my breath. We were sitting in the shade of the pergola at Druid Lodge, watching another summer evening fading into dusk. 'It seems the pathologist found anomalies in Peter Horrell's post-mortem examination,' I explained. 'There were signs that he hadn't been killed in situ, his body had been moved. Well, this cast suspicion on everything Amber and Kirsten had said about what happened in the church that evening. Inspector Ford wanted them both brought down to the police station for further questioning. That's when Frazer Bolt arrived at the station and told them his story about Patrick Mulder.'

315

'And so that's why Dean and Cruella arrived at Langworthy Hall.' Ricky leant back in his chair.

Morris frowned. 'Then Tristan didn't kill him in the church?'

'Tristan didn't kill him at all,' I told him. 'Tristan has never killed anyone. Forget all that nonsense about Peter and the girls working late at the antique shop and Tristan bursting in on them. It never happened. Kirsten stabbed Peter with the swordstick sometime earlier in the evening.'

'So where was he killed?' Ricky asked, frowning.

'Probably out in the courtyard at *Horrell's Antiques*. It would have been easier for Kirsten and Amber to move his body from there into his car to take him up to the church. He always parked it just outside.'

Ricky frowned. 'They must have carried him through the churchyard, though. Bit of a challenge.'

'They wrapped his body in a tarpaulin and used it to drag him over the ground, the same technique they'd used in the garden with Patrick Mulder. It would have been heavy but it would have slid along quite easily. And the fog was their friend that night. Hardly anyone was about and no one was there to see what they were doing. They had all the time in the world to stage the crime, to set up the scene perfectly. To set me up,' I added bitterly.

'Then Kirsten lured you up there with her phone call.'

'And made a complete fool of me.' I shook my head. 'She made me believe Amber had chased up the steps after Tristan. Whereas at the time, she was driving her

316

murdered cousin's body up to the church in the boot of his own car. Kirsten drove her car up later. After her arrest, police found the tarpaulin folded up in the boot. She and Amber had been planning to burn it.'

Morris shook his head. 'You'd never think such lovely young things could be so wicked.'

'Tristan knew,' I said. 'Maybe not consciously, but on a deeper level. It's why he wrote the tale of the twisted sister, about the young girl who murdered her brother.'

'But why did Kirsten kill Christopher?'

'She claims it was an accident. She was there at St Myrrins that day because Tristan's school was competing against Devon in the junior championships. She and Christopher were on the Devon team.'

'Wasn't Amber there too?' Ricky asked.

I nodded. 'She'd gone there with her parents to support Tristan. A lot of families had come to watch the contest, and there was a lunch for them afterwards. It was always thought it was while the family members were at lunch in the dining hall that Tristan killed Christopher in the gym, then went back to his dormitory where he blacked out. But that isn't what happened. Kirsten confessed that she and Christopher had stayed behind in the gym after the contest to pack up their equipment. Amber was there with them but Tristan had gone back to his dorm complaining of a blinding headache. Apparently, this was often the precursor to one of his blackouts. Kirsten and Christopher were messing about when the button snapped off her foil and he was stabbed. When they realised he was dead, she and Amber panicked, ran off and said nothing.'

'Then Amber knew Tristan didn't do it,' Morris cried. 'But she let him take the blame.'

I took a sip of wine. 'You've got to remember that Amber was obsessed with her brother. Their parents' marriage was breaking up. She desperately wanted Tristan to stay with her and her father. But he wanted to live with Anita. The fact he could love the mother who had walked out on them more than he loved her was a betrayal as far as she was concerned, a rejection.'

'And she decided to punish him and save her friend Kirsten instead.' Ricky lit up a cigarette and inhaled deeply.

'Yes. The difficulty for Tristan was that his mental health problems and his blackouts made him the obvious culprit, while no one had any reason to suspect Christopher's younger sister.'

'All very convenient.'

'That's what Dean thought. Remember, he got hold of the original police file. He thought the investigation at the time didn't go anywhere near deep enough. The police and the school authorities wanted to hush things up as fast as they could. The idea the killer might *not* have been Tristan was never even considered. He'd already started digging into the case himself.' I'd underestimated Dean, and realised to my shame that I was always doing it.

'And don't forget Frazer Bolt,' I went on. 'He went straight to the police station and told them what he'd told me. And if Patrick Mulder was telling the truth, then where was his key? It was Mulder's trump card. With his key the Horrell family could finally open the chest, find the red diamond. And however reluctant they might have been, they would have been forced to accept him into their ranks in order to get their hands on it. But when Amber told the police her story about Tristan murdering Mulder, she never mentioned the key. They knew it wasn't among his possessions at the cottage he rented because they'd searched the place. They didn't find it in the buried rucksack. So where was it? He must have had it on him. That was another thing they wanted to ask Amber about.'

Ricky frowned. 'And is that why you went there?'

'I had to talk to Amber. You see, even if I believed the story she'd told police, that she'd come back home to find Tristan had already stabbed Mulder, there was still the question of the missing key.'

'But did you believe her?'

'I wasn't sure,' I admitted. 'I still believed Tristan had killed Peter Horrell in Trinity Church. I believed it until the moment I saw all four keys in the locks of that chest. Peter would never have let Amber get her hands on his key. There was only one way she could have got it and that was to kill him for it.'

'She was convinced the red diamond was in there?' Morris asked.

'Perhaps she hoped it was. But she had another reason for getting rid of Peter. He was in control of her trust fund. She couldn't get at her money and she wanted it out of his hands. Control would have passed to his solicitors until she reached thirty, as he hadn't named a successor, but for her even that was preferable. She was convinced he was stealing from her.'

319

'Is there any evidence of that?' Ricky asked.

'I don't know. The police will look into it, I suppose.' I felt sorry for Peter Horrell. He might have been a very unpleasant man, but I was beginning to realise he was probably the best of the bunch. He'd known Amber was a nutcase and was just trying to keep a lid on things.

'It sounds as if Amber is as delusional as her brother.'

I shook my head. 'I think she's worse.'

'And Kirsten?'

'She loves Amber, but it's a twisted sort of love that won't stop at murder to prove itself.' I remembered something then that I'd forgotten.

I'd been standing in the fog in the ruins of Trinity Church, waiting for the police to arrive, Kirsten and Amber crouching together in the shadow of the wall, sobbing like children. I remembered sweeping the torchlight around and around, terrified Tristan might appear out of the darkness; and just for a moment, before I heard the police sirens begin to wail, saw the blue lights flash, I swept the light over Kirsten and Amber crouching there, their lips pressed together in a fervent kiss.

Roger Faulkner knew Tristan couldn't have killed Peter Horrell. At the time of his death the two of them had been together, camping in an isolated spot on the moor. The mistake he'd made, when he heard the news of Peter's murder, and that police were hunting for him and Tristan, was to drive to Langworthy Hall to confront Amber. Because, as he told police later, he'd wanted to murder the bitch. She was lying and he was determined to shake the truth out of her. He didn't realise Kirsten was there, or that her prowess with weapons extended to blunt implements, specifically creeping up on him and swiping him across the skull from behind.

I told all this to Daniel on a video call. I told him everything. The truth is, I don't like lying to him. It's not a healthy basis for a relationship. And while I don't lie exactly, I don't always tell him the whole truth either. This time I did.

'Where was Tristan when this happened?' he asked, frowning into the camera on his laptop. 'What did he do?'

'According to Amber, he freaked out completely. He thought Roger was dead. She managed to convince him that this was another murder he would be accused of, and the only way out of it was to do exactly what she told him.'

'Which was?'

'To take the medication she gave him. After that he was out for the count.'

'Lucky for him you turned up.'

'They made a complete fool out of me,' I told him bitterly. 'Used me, my inability to mind my own business, as Amber put it, my pathetic desire to help others, my ridiculous reputation as a sleuth. Those were her words and she was right about all of it.'

'Don't let her get inside your head, Miss B,' Daniel said gently.

That's exactly what Sophie had said; exactly what I'd told her not to let Imogen do. I sighed. 'It's time I gave up all this nonsense.'

He laughed. 'You couldn't if you tried. It's part of you – determination to find the truth, to help other people. Those aren't qualities you should try to change, Miss B. And I love you as you are.'

'I love you too.' I sounded a bit limp because I was trying not to cry.

'That's alright then,' he responded cheerfully. 'Next time I come home I'm coming on the ferry, so I can bring Lottie with me.'

I sniffed. 'That would be lovely.'

'It's Sunday tomorrow. You make sure you get some rest, Miss Browne with an e, have a lie-in.'

'Actually, I can't,' I told him. 'I've got to take a dog for a walk.'

CHAPTER TWENTY-NINE

The streets of Bath are pleasantly familiar to me. I spent my student years in that fair city, although it seems a long time ago now. Throughout the summer it turns into a tourist hell, but on this particular day, we were lucky. Ben and I were able to amble at a pace suited to an elderly spaniel, without having to push and shove our way through crowds. We strolled from Bath Spa station, along elegant Georgian terraces, until we found the address we were seeking in a quiet side street, a little less grand, and I pressed the doorbell.

'This is your new home,' I told him as we waited patiently. He gazed up at me, panting slightly. He'd been bought for Tristan as a puppy and had lived most of his life without him. 'You'll like it here. They've got a garden and there's a lovely big park across the road.'

The front door opened suddenly. Roger Faulkner was a lot less sinister-looking without his bowler hat and truncheon. And his smile made a difference. 'Hello Juno! Come in! It's great to meet you at last.'

He shook my hand in his own strong one, then stood back to let me in. He seemed none the worse for his recent bang over the head, although when he turned to lead me down the hall, I could make out the shadow of a fading bruise in the middle of his bald patch. I followed him to a beautifully proportioned room with a marble fireplace and floor-length windows which opened to a long, walled garden.

The woman who stood to greet me seemed familiar. The long neck, high cheekbones, fair hair and dark eyes she had imprinted on both of her children. But her mouth was softer than Amber's and her voice quieter, the strain of an unhappy marriage sketched in faint lines around her eyes. At the sight of her, Ben whined in his throat, straining at the lead, his tail waving madly. I let the lead drop and Anita knelt to greet her old friend. After a minute or so of patting and cuddling, and Ben trying to lick her face, Roger grabbed the end of his lead. 'I'll take him to David,' he said, and led him into the garden.

It seemed strange, hearing Tristan referred to as David. Anita smiled as if she had read my mind. 'He never liked the name Tristan. David was his middle name, that's what we call him now.'

'I'll try to remember,' I said.

She indicated I should sit on the sofa, and then seated herself on the chair opposite. 'It was always difficult for Amber,' she began after a moment. 'She was the apple of Julian's eye. With her, he was loving and kind. She was too young to understand that her father could be like that with her, and yet with me be controlling and cold. David understood. He had seen his father hit me enough times, and Julian had hit him too. He was a bully, like all the Horrells.' She smiled sadly. 'I expect Amber has told you I ran off with someone.'

'Your yoga instructor.'

She laughed. 'That was a story Julian put about. I think he wanted to believe it himself. He couldn't accept that I could leave him without being led astray by some man, that I would walk out on him simply because I'd had enough.'

'And Amber never knew why?'

'I didn't want to destroy her relationship with her father. She had wanted to stay with him, couldn't forgive me for leaving them both. When she was older I tried to tell her how things were, but she didn't want to hear what I had to say.'

'And Tristan . . . sorry, David . . . did he want to stay with him too?'

She shook her head. 'He wanted to be here with me, as far away from Julian as possible. But the court awarded us shared custody of the children. David was away at school during term-time anyway, so it really only affected him during the holidays.'

'Did Amber ever stay here with you?'

'Once or twice in the early days. But when David came out of that institution she became abusive, aggressive, unbearable. She couldn't accept the fact that he wanted to stay here with me.' She hesitated for a moment, glancing down at her slim hands before looking back at me. 'My son is very vulnerable, fragile you might say. He is easily upset. But she refused to change her behaviour and, in the end, her visits were distressing him so much we begged her to stay away.

She refused and so we had to involve the courts.'

'An injunction.'

She nodded. 'She's not allowed within two hundred yards of David.' She looked thoughtful, sad. 'A terrible thing to have to do to one's own daughter, don't you think? But she was spiteful. She kept testing the limits, hanging around in the park across the road where she knew we could see her from these windows. She'd yell things. Then she started following him around to graphic fiction events, always managing to stay just outside the legal boundary. She became a nightmare. She had always been a talented artist, clever at design. But she started selling her steampunk fashions so she could hang around at these events all day, provoking her brother.'

'Tell me,' I asked tentatively, 'at the time, did you believe that David had killed Christopher Blake?'

She shook her head. 'Not for a moment. He enjoyed fencing but he was never competitive, something his father interpreted as a weakness. And in the place they sent him to, they finally convinced him he had killed Christopher and he'd blotted it out. But I know my son. He's gentle. He suffers from a complex psychosis which makes his life difficult, but he's not a psychopath.' She sighed. 'Whereas Amber, I've never known her to show empathy or remorse. She's a true Horrell in every sense of the word.' She was silent for a few moments. 'Julian's mother understood, Granny Horrell. She'd had fifty years of marriage to Julian's father, so she knew. She encouraged me to escape. She was very generous to me and David. It's because of her that we can afford to live here and I don't have to worry about David's future.'

326

'When did he start writing the Syrius Blade stories?'

She smiled. 'He was always drawing – a talent his father did nothing to encourage. I think it was an escape for him. But despite the treatment he received in the institution, he was encouraged to draw there. They saw it as therapy. And when he came out he had these wonderful drawings, and stories, and well . . . would you like to meet him?'

'Very much,' I said.

'Right. I'll take you to his safe place.'

CHAPTER THIRTY

At the end of the garden was a summerhouse. Through the open doorway I could see the back of Tristan's fair head as he sat at his desk working, his back to the door. As Anita and I walked down the path towards it, Ben padded out to greet us briefly, before turning around to go back in with Tristan and sit at his feet, gazing at him adoringly. Roger was lounging on the lawn and gave us a lazy wave as we passed. 'It's clouding over,' he told us, squinting up at an increasingly overcast sky. 'I'll go and make some tea.'

'I'm so lucky with Roger,' Anita murmured, as he got up and went inside. 'He's brilliant with David, really knows how to handle him.'

We arrived at the summerhouse. Through its windows I could see the walls were papered with sketches of Syrius Blade and his friends. And enemies. Tristan was working on a drawing now, so absorbed in what he was doing that he didn't seem aware of our approach. Anita called his name gently and he twisted around in his seat to look at us. 'It was you who brought Ben,' he said to me. His brown eyes burnt like

Syrius Blade's but his smile was as open as a child's.

I smiled back. 'I'm Juno.'

'I remember you. You asked me to sign your book. You looked wonderful. I drew a picture of you afterwards.' He reached across his desk and handed me a small drawing. It was of a woman looking over her shoulder, a black hat perched on a mass of curling red hair hanging down her back. She wore a tightly laced corset and a military-style coat. She looked remarkably fierce. It was me alright.

'You've made me look . . .' I hunted for the right word. 'Heroic.' I laughed. 'I'm not heroic at all.'

'I call her Lady Destiny,' he went on, as if he were speaking of a character in one of his books. 'You don't mind if I put your face in my book?'

'Do you mind?' Anita asked.

'No. I'd be honoured.'

Tristan smiled. 'This drawing is for you,' he said. 'You can keep it.'

'I'll always treasure it. Thank you, David.'

The sun appeared from behind the clouds and a red glow, about the size of an old penny, was reflected on the white paper on Tristan's desk. I looked up at the window to find the source of the reflection. There was a dreamcatcher hanging there, a glass teardrop, red as blood, dangling on a string from the end of it. For a moment I was dazzled. It flashed and sparkled as the string twisted in a breath of breeze, sparks of red, gold and purple fire glimmering in its blood-red heart.

'Isn't that . . . ?' I began.

'It's glass,' Anita told me, staring at me meaningfully.

'It's just a piece of red glass. Granny Horrell gave it to David before she died, didn't she, David?'

'She said it was mine to keep,' he told me. 'It was to bring me luck. It's my favourite thing.'

He turned back to his drawing and it was clear we were forgotten. Anita tucked her arm into mine as we walked back down the path. 'The worth of a thing lies only in the value we give it, in what it means to us,' she said, looking at me sideways. 'As someone in the antiques trade, wouldn't you agree?'

I turned back for a moment, to see again that blood-red diamond, its light winking as the dreamcatcher twisted in the breeze; then I looked back at her.

'Yes,' I said and smiled. 'Yes, I would.'

I remembered her words again later, on the train, taking me back to Devon, taking me home. I took out the picture Tristan had drawn of me and gazed at it. Lady Destiny. She was going to cause some hilarity back in Ashburton. I didn't care. I was going to get it framed. I put it away in my bag, carefully, so I wouldn't crease it. The worth of a thing lies only in the value we give it, Anita had said, in what it means to us. I sat back and watched the countryside speeding past the train windows, narrowing my eyes against the flashing of the evening sun behind the trees, seeing in my mind the red jewel twisting and turning as the dreamcatcher swung in the breeze. Anita was right. It was only glass.

ACKNOWLEDGEMENTS

I always say that none of the characters in my books are based on real people.

In this case, that isn't true. I have three very real people to thank. First, the wonderful Jenny Donaldson of Gnash! Comics in Ashburton, who has let me use both her shop and herself in this book. I offered to create a fictional persona for Jenny, but her response was that as everyone would assume it was supposed to be her, I might as well use her name. She is immensely supportive of local authors, but it is her passion for graphic fiction which led me to ask her bookshop to promote the books about Syrius Blade in my story. Her colleague, Martin Woollacott, also deserves my thanks for advice about Steampunk literature.

I needed an expert in gemstones and portraiture and in Ashburton we have them both in Reuben Lenkiewicz, whose gorgeous gallery stands at the end of North Street. Actually, Reuben asked to be in the book, either as a murderer or victim. I'm sorry I couldn't bear to murder him as he wished, or make him a murderer, at least not this time.

Finally, Mr Frazer Bolt is a loyal Juno Browne fan who asked to be included and he plays a small but crucial part in the story. I have borrowed his name and his dog.

As always, there are other people to thank: my dear friend Di, fellow author Sue Tingey and all the south Devon crime-writing crowd. Where would I be without those lunches? I have to thank Jolyon Tuck once again, for advice on things legal, and Susie Dunlop and all the team at Allison & Busby for their untiring efforts on my behalf. To the booksellers of Dartmoor and Devon, I love you all.

Teresa Chris, my agent, thank you for believing in me; and putting up with my dreadful phone line. Lastly to Martin for his unfailing support and help, driving me everywhere I need to go, and for putting up with a woman who doesn't always hear what he's saying because she's writing stuff in her head.

STEPHANIE AUSTIN has enjoyed a varied career, working as an artist and an antiques trader, but also for the Devon Schools Library Service. When not writing she is actively involved in amateur theatre as a director and actor, and attempts to be a competent gardener and cook. She lives in Devon.

stephanieaustin.co.uk